ISBN: 979-8-9879071-0-8 (Paperback)
ISBN: 979-8-9879071-2-2 (Hardcover)
ISBN: 979-8-9879071-1-5 Digital)

Miracle From Ukraine

A Forbidden Love, A Dangerous Rival,
and A Journey of Faith

By

James Herbert Harrison

Other Releases by James Herbert Harrison

Andy Moretti's race team was on a high with the lucrative Unibank sponsorship contract until his youngest son and third generation driver has a serious car accident, nearly killing the teenage daughter of the bank's CEO. The Race Girl is a dramatic take of heartbreak, vengeance, and legal jeopardy reaching a climax at the world's greatest motor race.

In the sequel to The Race Girl, Alex Moretti's career in Formula 1 takes off like a rocket until his bride-to-be is kidnapped in Paris. Racer's Fiancée is a suspenseful tale of international intrigue as the exciting jet-set world of Formula 1 intersects with the sleazy and terrifying underworld of the human sex slave trade.

Dedication

Nearly a generation ago, I traveled to pre-war Ukraine twice in search of romance. Maybe it was a midlife crisis (a late one that is), or maybe I just needed the challenge. Maybe I was just getting lonesome. Check All the Above. This venture resulted in my marrying a beautiful gal, ethnic Russian and natively Ukrainian, and I've had the pleasure of fathering yet another son nearly a generation after the first.

So many of the chance circumstances from that whole adventure were so miraculous and bizarre, we always believed divine intervention had to play a part in it all, so much so that I had threatened for years to write about it. A work of fiction, many of the characters and scenes in the story represent actual events, regardless how extraordinary they may appear. I dedicate this novel to my wife, parents, kids, and in-laws, all of whom are represented as fictional characters in the plot.

– James Herbert Harrison

CHAPTER ONE

Angels From Heaven

KIEV, THE UKRAINE

The wind was cold for early spring and the day was cloudy. She wore her finest formal dress, white stockings, and her best overcoat, as well as a *shapka,* the fur winter hat so popular in Russian culture. Women in Eastern European society were habitual in dressing up anytime they left home, seldom to be seen in public wearing sports pants, tee shirts, or no brassieres. Irina Balabanova was a beautiful young woman naturally, not requiring much make-up but having been applied, nonetheless. A native Ukrainian, she was ethnically Russian as her parents were originally from the Moscow *Oblast,* having migrated south to eastern Ukraine as newlyweds in 1977, shortly following her father's release from service in the armed forces.

Boryspil was the largest of the two international airports in Kiev, the Ukrainian capital and city of four million inhabitants. Having accompanied Daryle on the seven-hour ride from home, the two exited the commuter bus in front of the terminal, with Irina planning to escort him all the way to the security check-in as he prepared for the long flight back to the US. The twenty-seven-year-old woman was accustomed to the frigid weather in Ukraine, thus it had little to do with her mood as she became very emotional and unable to hold back her tears.

Daryle Adams was a few years younger, an American graduate student from Boston, working in Ukraine on a twelve-month government-sponsored intern teaching program. Having met through a mutual friend attending one of his classes, the two began dating and engaged in a torrid love affair, eventually sharing her small apartment in Chuguev, her hometown in northeastern Ukraine some fifty kilometers from the large regional Oblast capital city of Kharkov.

Following her graduation from Kharkov University a few years earlier, Irina had endured a period of frustrating relationships, mostly local men predisposed to alcohol abuse and marital infidelity, spawned by the economic despair so prevalent in Ukraine, before and following the collapse of the Soviet Union in the late eighties and throughout the final decade of the twentieth century.

The dream of nearly every young Russian woman was to get married and have a family, challenged by the population disparity between males and females. This phenomenon was extreme in the former Soviet states compared to the Western democracies of the period, due largely to an inordinate number of industrial accidents and a disproportionate rate of alcohol-related deaths. Thus, the Ukraine was generally a male-dominated society, commonly reflected in the often arrogant treatment of the nation's men toward their women.

The collapse of the Soviet Union and the subsequent independence of Ukraine as a nation coincided with a worldwide technology explosion and the breakdown of international barriers regarding travel and communication. Social scenarios that wouldn't have seemed possible just a few years prior were now becoming commonplace, while professional and personal relationships across geopolitical boundaries were occurring worldwide on a massive scale.

Kiev was a modern, bustling European city readily apparent in its international airport. But the upbeat smiling faces from the many nations populating the main terminal failed to lift Irina's spirits, as she had seen in Daryle a dream, a life with a man from America, a future with hope, opportunity, and adventure. As time went on in the relationship, Irina developed an expectation that a plan for future marriage and a growing family was imminent. The fable began to shatter when Daryle's internship approached expiration and it became readily apparent that he had no plans whatsoever to remain in Ukraine nor to include her in any immediate future endeavors.

The long and crowded bus ride was relatively quiet, as small talk between the two could not disguise the overshadowing topic. Once Irina had felt she and Daryle were getting close, she began to do some research regarding the process of acquiring a visa for travel to the United States. She learned of several possibilities that included student exchange programs, temporary work visas, and applying for political asylum, none of which would comfortably fit her situation. The one relatively simple and reasonably quick route was through a K-1 visa, which required a proposal of marriage and strong financial sponsorship from a legal American citizen.

Daryle had never mentioned the word "marriage" in all of their time together and had gone out of his way to avoid the subject. After all, he had plenty of time for that and he was still young, had a career to pursue, places to go, and things to do.

As the bus approached Boryspil, Irina could not keep her thoughts contained. All these months she had kept quiet on the subject of the two getting married and having a family in America, fearing such talk may just scare him away. But now he was just moments from going away, regardless.

What do I have to lose? Irina pondered. *What have our relations this past year meant? If I have not been a future wife to this man, then what have I been?* The likely answer had troubled her greatly for some time. "Daryle, when will we see each other again?"

"Hopefully soon, Irina. I have to get established professionally. You know, pursue my career," he replied, knowing what she wanted to hear, but not a part of his repertoire anytime soon. "We'll keep in close touch."

Keep in close touch? What does that mean? Irina thought, unable to even speak.

As the two embraced in an emotional departure, a promise or even suggestion that Irina would soon follow Daryle to America, and a plan to apply for her to get a K-1 visa, never came.

An empty feeling engrossed Irina as she waited outside at the airport stop for the return commuter bus to arrive, all her hopes and dreams crushed now. *Am I to be relegated to a life of depression here?* She thought as she looked around at the other awaiting commuters, all who seemed to share little conversation while having looks as bleak as the cloudy sky. She boarded the bus and left the airport for the trek back home, a long trip made more difficult with her every tear. A life full of sadness was expected, the dreams of what life could offer outside of Irina's local domain, dreams of seeing the great America, and raising a family there were suddenly gone.

She could hear the sound of a sobbing baby girl behind her, the mother working heartily to calm the child while most of the surrounding commuters looked on without expression. Irina now sat silently in self-doubt while sadly believing she may never have a family of her own. The thought brought her again to tears as she continued to struggle emotionally.

Hours later and sitting across the aisle on the crowded bus was a man somewhat older than her who couldn't avoid noticing the poor girl being so distraught. "Whatever the reason for your sadness, there is always a silver lining in every black cloud."

Irina temporarily took hold of herself, suddenly conscious of the spectacle she must be making in front of the many passengers. She looked over at the stranger and asked, "Are you talking to me?"

"How can a lovely young lady such as yourself be so sad?... I am Forest, by the way," the fellow answered in Irina's native language.

"Forest?" she asked.

"Yes, I am from British Columbia. That is in Canada."

"You speak fluent Russian for a foreigner," she observed, temporarily enlightened as amused by his accent.

"Thank you, young lady. That is very kind of you."

"You look like someone I may have met before," Irina said, further composing herself and slightly relieved at having someone, anyone, to talk to at the moment. "Have you been in Ukraine long?"

4

"No, I just arrived yesterday," he replied gingerly. "First time to visit your country."

Where have I seen this guy before? Irina studied. "Are you heading to Kharkov?"

"Yes, I am."

"Do you have friends or family there, or is it your business?" Irina asked, still misty-eyed and her mascara running down her cheeks from the many tears. She hastily swiped them away as not to appear too stricken.

"No, actually I am traveling there to meet my fiancée," he replied assuredly.

"Your fiancée?" Irina asked, suddenly enduring another quick bout of feeling sorry for herself. "Congratulations, Forest. What is her name? I may know her," Irina asked, still trying to recall his familiar face.

"I do not know her name just yet," he answered strangely.

Irina suddenly froze and looked around, wondering what other passengers were overhearing their conversation, now thinking this gentleman may have some mental problems.

The stranger saw she was rather shocked by his answer and started to chuckle. "What I mean is, I am visiting an international marriage agency in hopes of meeting my new fiancée, you see?"

Irina paused and looked at him with a curious skepticism. "Oh, I see. Well, I do wish you luck, Forest."

"Thank you," he replied. "Oh, I see my stop is coming up," he said while rising from his seat, grabbing his luggage, and preparing to move toward the bus exit doors. "Maybe I'll be fortunate enough to meet a fine young maiden such as yourself... Good day to you, Irina."

"Good day to you, Forest."

She watched with curiosity as the strange man walked off the bus at the third Kharkov bus stop near downtown, knowing the last stop in her hometown of Chuguev was still nearly an hour away. As she gave the exiting foreigner a mild wave, Irina's curiosity peaked. *International marriage agency?... How bizarre?... Best shave that goatee off, Forest... Make you look better...Did I mention to him my name?*

5

The last fifty kilometers seemed to take forever. Irina sat impatiently as the passengers exited with each stop as the bus approached Chuguev, a recurring feeling of loneliness setting in as she had difficulty controlling her sadness, while she thought about Daryle and wondered if she would ever see him again. Her mind drifted back to that guy, Forest, she had met earlier and the strange feeling she had seen him before...

...Located on the Black Sea, the Crimea was the most popular vacation destination in Ukraine, and Irina was off on her annual family vacation that previous summer, her boyfriend taking off and joining them for a few days. She and Daryle shared a hotel room adjacent to her parents, who had made the several-hour drive from Chuguev along with her sister and new husband, Misha.

The weather in Alushta, the very popular resort city near Yalta, was very pleasant as the two strolled hand in hand a few hundred meters down the beach and came upon a small tiki hut-style bar and grill where they decided to grab a late lunch.

"So, honey, did your parents ever finalize their plans to come over and visit?" Irina asked, attempting to table an issue Daryle seemed to want to avoid.

"Uh, no. I got a message they called. I just haven't called them back yet," he replied. "What are you going to have?"

He doesn't want to talk about it, she lamented as she opened and stared hard at the menu. One evening in the apartment near midnight the previous month, she had overheard a call come in, presumably from Boston as the time there would have been late in the afternoon. She didn't understand much English but gathered enough from Daryle's communication that his parents were planning a near future travel to Ukraine to visit him. Despite her subtle attempts to inquire about it, he was very coy about avoiding the subject, and it started to bother her. Feeling the two had reached a seminal moment in their relationship, Irina had become more and more disturbed by it.

Their lunch passed quietly with some casual conversation about the local fare and customs, continuing to place an uncomfortable cloud over the two as Irina worried about Daryle's lack of commitment. Their waiter, a young man of medium height and average looking with cropped brown hair and a goatee, brought their bill which totaled just over five hundred fifty hryvnias, or approximately twenty-one US dollars.

Daryle opened his wallet and retrieved some hryvnia notes. "Here's three hundred," he stated as he looked at Irina. "Do you have any extra cash?"

Irina couldn't even force a smile as she prepared to help pay for lunch, not the first time this sort of thing had happened, and reminded herself that he had not kicked in anything on the apartment for the month yet, either. As she shuffled through her purse for the extra cash, she decided now was the time to press an issue. "Why don't you call your mother and father now, Daryle? Before you get busy," she barked, adding a degree of sarcastic exclamation to the word *busy*.

Having left most of her loose cash with her parents, Irina reluctantly dug out her bank debit card and handed it to the waiter, all the while displaying a show of disappointment toward Daryle. Seeing her mood wasn't going to change and to deflect the subject away from their lunch tab, he retrieved his cell phone from his pocket and dialed the appropriate code and number to make an outbound international call. After hearing a few rings on the other end, he received a voicemail prompt and left a message. "Mother, it's me. Call me when it's convenient. Bye."

Daryle hung up, pleased that he had succeeded in placating Irina, at least for another day. Knowing the hour was pre-dawn on the East Coast and not expecting a return call for a few hours, he would be leaving to catch a bus home by then anyway. His holiday was limited to his few days off while Irina and her family would be staying in the Crimea for another week.

They sat rather silently, Daryle appearing rather distant as he looked out toward the beach. while it seemed to be taking the waiter an eternity to return. Meanwhile, his cell phone, sitting face up on the table between them, began to ring, the obvious incoming number displayed revealing his parents were unexpectedly calling back, despite the early hour in Boston.

Not wanting to answer it, Daryle knew Irina would tune in expecting to hear a dialog regarding their visit and more importantly, listen to hear if he would mention anything about their meeting her in the process. After four rings, he picked up as he strategized in his mind how he would handle this.

"Hello, Mother?... No, no, nothing wrong... I forgot what time it is over there... Sure, everything's going well..."

As expected, Irina had her ear to the conversation when the waiter finally reappeared. "I'm sorry, Miss, but your card has been declined."

Irina was stunned and both she and Daryle stared up at the waiter, who stood and awaited their response expectantly.

"Mom, let me call you back," Daryle said as both looked embarrassed, not knowing what to do about their bill.

"There must be some mistake," Irina stated defensively. "I have way more than five hundred fifty hryvnias in my account!"

"I am sorry, Miss. I ran the card twice."

She shuffled through her purse again, producing nearly two hundred hryvnias. Daryle seemed preoccupied, even as the waiter kept a focused eye on him and after a few uncomfortable moments, Irina broke in. "We're fifty short. We're staying just up the beach. Could I just leave my watch or something while we run and get the rest of the money?"

The waiter then gave her a sympathetic glance. "That's quite all right, Irina. A few hryvnias won't sink us. Please enjoy the rest of your holiday."

"Oh, thank you very much," she replied, still uneasy about Daryle's incoming call that was so conveniently interrupted.

As the waiter gathered up the reduced sum of cash and walked away, she tucked away the card and receipt, still bothered about Daryle and the issue over his parents' visit, noting that he made no effort to call them back in her presence.

How did that waiter know my name was Irina? She wondered as her thoughts cleared. "I'll have to get to a bank close by. I just got paid and know there's nothing wrong with my account."

The two got up from their table and preparing to leave, Irina glanced quickly toward the waiter, who was nearing the entrance to the kitchen and carrying a full tray of dishes, glasses, and refuge. As if he could read her mind, he turned to face her smiling and spoke silently as she could read his lips, "I got it off your card."...

... *Seems like a good guy,* Irina thought, her mind now back to the present regarding the stranger, Forest. *Not my type, but he'll meet some strange woman, fall in love, and no doubt get her a K-1 visa. I wonder if it works the same in Canada as America?... What are you doing wrong, Irina?*

Chuguev finally came into view, the same familiar streets, houses, and shops. She would get to the apartment, hopefully get some badly needed sleep, and then back to the same routine, while adding a bout of loneliness to the mix. As she gathered with the final few passengers to exit the bus, she thought again about the stranger from Canada she had met earlier.

He looks just like that waiter in?... No, this Forest must be twenty years older, she pondered while still mystified as to how this stranger knew her name.

⤜⤜⤜ ⤛⤛⤛

ODESSA, UKRAINE

A few hours to the southwest, the weather was windy but mild as the plane landed and John Masters made his way down the aircraft's dropdown stairway and onto the tarmac. The airport in Odessa was not as large or busy as Boryspil International in Kiev, but fairly modern, easy to get around, and comparably less congested.

Having gathered his luggage, he exited to the curb in front of the terminal where taxicabs were in abundance. John approached the closest one and after a brief introduction the cabbie knew he was a tourist. *Another Westerner* the driver thought. *In effect, has lots of money.*

He handed the driver a note with an address on it and they drove through the city toward the destination, as John noted the city traffic very busy but still flowing freely. His years working in places like Chicago, Atlanta, and LA made commuting through Odessa, Ukraine's third largest city, seem like rolling through a small town.

Having only seen Kiev through the prism of its airport, this became the first large Eastern European city John had ever experienced and first impressions were surprisingly positive. His perspective growing up during the Cold War had painted an image of all cities behind the Iron Curtain as "East Berlins", viewed from the west side of a security wall caked with graffiti and having thick razor wire atop, similar to that surrounding a maximum security prison. The streets and boulevards were all paved, although needing maintenance in places, the automobiles a mix of old and new, and many modern and market appealing businesses scattered everywhere. The overall appearance of the housing, which encompassed mostly apartment complexes, reflected a somewhat lower living standard than that in America, but the city didn't seem to have a "Skid Row" populated with the destitute and homeless, either, although he would come to learn they did exist and were detained wholesale in large mental houses.

The apartment was located on Vulytsia Tulska, a busy avenue near downtown. Stopping in front of the building where he had reserved an apartment, John handed the taxi driver a twenty dollar bill, assuming he may get some change back but accepting it as the total. The cabbie then scribbled something down on a note and then held it up in front of John's face.

40 US Dollars

Thinking it a rip-off reminiscent of New York City, but then not wanting any problems, John begrudgingly handed over another twenty bucks which was readily accepted. "Spasibo, Comrade," the cabbie exclaimed cynically and then sped off. John would learn this was the Russian language word for "thank you", a word he figured to use often, at least hopefully.

Following the collapse of the Soviet Union, all the former republics set up shop as independent nations and part of the process was to consult with the nations of the West, including the Australians, Europeans, Canadians, and Americans, regarding how to establish a constitution. One issue that had to be resolved was real estate, as under the Communist system the central government owned everything. The new government in Ukraine wanted to establish private ownership for nearly all residential properties including individual apartments. Few citizens had any appreciable wealth or cash to purchase tangible property, and as such the government simply mailed its citizens deeds.

As most people in the metropolitan urban centers lived in small apartments, which they now suddenly owned, systems in place to keep up the apartment buildings themselves collapsed. Since most of these dwellings were built by the Communists in the fifties and sixties, many of the structures were falling apart despite efforts by the individual residents themselves to fix up their own places.

Efforts in organizing these new property owners and create apartment building associations to manage maintenance were slow in developing. Still, a few enterprising citizens in the new Ukraine, mostly younger married couples, acquired these properties and a new business opportunity grew from renting out the apartments to Western tourists, many being middle to upper-aged males who now visited in search of romance.

Arriving midafternoon, John was struck by the way things were so run down. A main entrance door, which would have been better described as a gate, had a large security lock, but it was broken and dysfunctional. The stucco on the walls in the hallways and stairwells was chipping off, and chunks would just lie on the concrete floors, appearing to have been there for weeks. The elevators, extremely small anyway, were very hit-and-miss in operation, and mostly miss. Despite all that, he couldn't get over how fancy some of the apartments were, though many seemed to lack any semblance of uniformity and appeared somewhat odd with all the different decors present from door to door, something rarely seen in the West.

The charge of fifty bucks per night was a relative bargain as the standard fare at hotels in Odessa was a hundred fifty and up, again priced at a premium for "Westerners". The couple who owned the place, Vasyli and Sofiya Kobliska, each offered themselves up as interpreters, which over 90 percent of their guests required and were all too happy to pay for.

John took in his surroundings, unpacked his baggage, and decided to grab a few hours of sleep prior to his dinner engagement at seven-thirty. Nadia Kovalenko, an early middle-aged woman whom he had met online, would greet him at the apartment and then accompany him to a popular downtown restaurant where Sofiya would meet them and serve to translate their conversation, a scenario John was very curious about, if not yet totally confident and comfortable with.

Following an afternoon nap to help adjust to the new time zone, John had a problem with the toilet running and called Vasyli, who informed him that someone who resided nearby would stop by in short order and take care of it. Soon thereafter, he heard the doorbell chime, as Nadia had surprisingly shown up a full half an hour early and was not alone. Having just gotten out of the shower, John expected a repairman and opened the door sporting a bathrobe and wearing a face full of shaving cream. A brief moment of laughing embarrassment followed while he and his dinner date both attempted to size each other up, as John invited her and an accompanying young woman in.

Using mostly sign language, some initial communication resulted in the early guests being seated in the front room while John retreated to the bathroom to finish sprucing up. *Nothing like meeting me "in the raw" first,* John thought grinning. *However I present myself in the next segment will be an improvement.*

Finally completing his shave and noting that Nadia had the TV running in the front room, John dialed SOFIYA up on his cell phone. "Sofiya, Nadia showed up with a teenage girl with her. Maybe she's confused and thought she needed to bring her own translator?"

"Hmm, hang on a minute. Let me call her."

While John was on hold, he heard another cell phone ring through the door in the other room and Nadia answered. Following some conversation in that foreign language he heard simply as clucking gibberish, it was assumed that Sofiya had dialed up Nadia's phone to make sure they were all on the same page. Sofiya shortly returned. "Nadia has brought her daughter, Oksana, with her. I hope this doesn't pose a problem with you, Mr. Masters."

"A problem? Well, I suppose not." *Nadia never mentioned in any of her letters about having a daughter. Weird,* John pondered with an air of concern. "Okay, we'll all see you at around seven thirty, then," John replied as he disconnected, starting to get a strange feeling about this budding "relationship" already. *Just try to keep an open mind, ole boy.*

Taking a taxi, the ride to the restaurant was a good twenty minutes through the city and when the three arrived, John got out his wallet and fully expected to dish out another forty to fifty bucks again in cab fare. To her credit, Nadia got in the cabbie's face where a stern tongue-lashing occurred, and then turned to John and took a five-dollar bill from him to pay the fare while even getting a dollar back in change.

Bizarre, John thought. *A two-tier pricing system.*

The restaurant was a popular establishment and John, Nadia, and her daughter were seated, waiting anxiously for Sofiya to show, their discourse practically non-existent and rather uncomfortable due to the language barrier. The mother and daughter did chit-chat a bit together while glancing at John and grinning intermittently, giving him the funny feeling of being at a distinct disadvantage while being scrutinized.

Moments later, Sofiya appeared and sat down, proceeding to translate the conversation. John commented on the cab fare discrepancies and Sofiya explained that so long as he was visiting Odessa and accompanied by Nadia, she should always do the talking, for reasons of both finance and security.

As John had previously come to observe the Kobliskas as having only one vehicle, he inquired about Vasyli's whereabouts, as he couldn't imagine he would just drop Sofiya off, leave, and then make a trip back across town a couple hours later to pick her up. She explained, almost as a matter of routine, that Vasyli was simply waiting outside the restaurant in the car. Whether out of respect or simply wanting to appear generous, John insisted that Vasyli join them immediately. He didn't expect to pay a double fee for having two interpreters there but still picked up the dinner tab for all of them, an act that would come back to bite him later. For his part, Vasyli was gracious enough not to order the most expensive dish on the menu.

The topics of discussion during dinner were relatively interesting as it was John's first experience in closely meeting a "foreign" woman and it was Nadia's first encounter, too, or so he assumed. She seemed to have a number of questions involving his finances, which seemed a bit over the top to him, but he took them in stride and his replies were deemed satisfactory until the issue of the daughter's education came up, particularly in regard to her goal of becoming a doctor.

It was explained to John that doctors in Ukraine had a four-year university requirement, in effect the same as a school teacher or typical engineer. Somewhat stunned, he explained that physicians in American endured an additional four to eight years of medical school over and above four years of college, but they were among the highest paid professionals in the nation, whereas doctors in the Ukraine and all the former Soviet republics earned about the same income as a high school teacher or carpenter. This was something of a fissure that could derail the still-to-be relationship, assuming John had no problem taking on Nadia's daughter and the additional financial commitment that went along with her.

Following dinner, Vasyli and Sofiya provided transportation home, and as Nadia lived in another large apartment building, they pulled up to the curb near the complex entrance where Nadia and her daughter got out of the car. As it was well after dark and the grounds there were not well lit, John insisted on escorting Nadia to her door and half expected to be invited in briefly. This was not to be, however. John had seen more than a few women in his life become guarded about inviting a man into their home to cap off a first date. He understood this, never took offense, and generally respected the protocol. But Nadia didn't seem like the type. There was another reason behind this lack of "openness" and as the two planned to spend more time together, he was determined to find out what it was.

The couple enjoyed two more pleasant evenings together, and in the process John got quite a tour of Odessa, which he came to see as a very historic and touristic city. Still dealing with the language barrier, the two were still in the mixed company of Sofiya, and their time spent enjoyable but still cloaked in mystery. For his final evening in Odessa, John chose to have Nadia over to his apartment for dinner and Sofiya, who lived nearby, would arrive and still provide translation. He was somewhat interested in Nadia's skills as a cook and also curious about the local cuisine generally, as their dining out had been "fully international", including an American-style lunch of cheeseburgers and fries.

She appeared at his door soon after she got off work and the two of them took a taxi to a local food market. John's logic of scaling down his budget by avoiding yet another expensive restaurant quickly faded as he noticed Nadia proceeding to load up the shopping cart with some of the most expensive grocery items available. He attempted to hide his consternation but began to regret his earlier pretense as a very generous guy who no doubt appeared to be carefree with his wallet.

The bountiful dinner would include delicacies, such as caviar and two bottles of imported French wine. John smiled sparingly, as he was by no means a connoisseur of wine and could tell little difference between this expensive dry red and some of the local stuff from wineries in Missouri that sold at Walmart for less than ten bucks per bottle.

When the two returned to the apartment, the voicemail light on the phone was blinking. A message disclosed that Sofiya was not feeling well and Vasyli was also unavailable, but they had arranged for a friend who was fluent in all three languages, English, Russian, and Ukrainian, to serve as a substitute.

The woman appeared shortly thereafter and opening the door, John appeared floored as the woman had a strikingly familiar face, although somewhat younger, different hair, and glasses, that he could recall from,... *somewhere?*

Seeing the woman had a neutral reaction, John smiled sheepishly and spoke. "Let me guess. You've never met me before."

"Excuse me? I am Lana. I am a friend of Sofiya and—"

"Yes, yes, I know," John replied, politely cutting her off while escorting her inside.

Nadia and Lana had some small talk and with little time left and still much to be decided between the two, John plowed forward with questions that continued to bother him, not the least of which was who Nadia actually lived with, who apparently would prohibit him from stepping foot in her place. When Lana translated, Nadia became obviously uncomfortable and replied.

Lana then reversed the translation back to him. "Nadia is divorced but still shares an apartment with her ex-husband, daughter, and nine-year-old son, Alexi."

When John displayed a look of stunned silence, Nadia's expression became blank as she looked away toward the balcony window. *Not really liking the sound of this,* John thought, and Nadia spoke to Lana quickly while studying John's expressions.

"She says Alexi would not be coming to America, just her and her daughter. The boy will be staying with his father."

John saw visions of red flags now, somewhat leery of getting entangled in some sort of long distance international parental dispute. He also had trouble relating to a woman who planned to leave her native country and a young offspring behind, something he didn't believe he could ever do himself. On the other hand, he supposed many sacrifices were made historically by many immigrants who came to America and thus he found himself mentally trying to suppress some instinctive doubts about their whole relationship, or however it should be regarded at that point.

As dinner concluded, John prepared to settle up with Lana and contemplated how he and this Nadia would move forward, feeling a bit awkward as he was heading back home first thing the next morning. While he did find Nadia attractive and thought there may have been potential, he did have lingering concerns about the whole son and daughter issue and wasn't prepared to overly commit to much just yet. To the contrary, he wasn't totally convinced that Nadia was sold on him, either.

Feeling he needed to take advantage of Lana's bilingual services one last time, John stated frankly, as he threw a glance toward Nadia, "Lana, I think I should plan a return visit to see where the future takes us. I was probably somewhat naïve in thinking I could just fly over here for a few days and expect a serious relationship to take hold."

Knowing Nadia didn't understand what he was saying and trusting Lana to relay the right words, John continued. "Honestly, Lana, I think Nadia likes me, but I'm not sure how much."

Before speaking in the native language, Lana replied with an observation and question for him. "I believe she likes you, John. How much? I'm not sure. The question is, do you like her?"

John thought carefully about his answer, thinking it strange the way this interpreter asked, as if she really meant, *Are you sure you really like her?* "I don't know. That's why I think I may have to return sometime. How soon? I'm not sure of that either."

The dinner conversation lasted into a late hour, largely because compared to Sofiya, Lana seemed to provide much more than straight translation, as she would add a lengthy perspective on everything. While John found this to seem much more informative, the entire affair took on more of a two-way personal conversation between Lana and himself, while Nadia did very little talking, a setting much to her disliking. As it was another work night for Nadia, John assumed she would just catch a ride home with Lana, but she declined the offer and the stand-in interpreter prepared to depart.

"John, I am available in the future should you and Nadia need me, or if you should wish to meet someone else in Ukraine. Bye now," Lana said while shooting him a rather cunning smile, a look not lost on Nadia.

Sounds like Lana assumes I would want to return, and for the purpose of meeting someone else. John thought, somewhat confused, if not more or less intrigued by it.

Their translator having departed, John studied on how to end the evening and the Odessa holiday in general, when Nadia took explicit action, threw off her dress, displayed a seductive see-through corset-type garment, and then ran and jumped up on John, wrapping her arms and legs around him while pressing her lips on him rather forcefully. Had a third-party observer been present, they would have witnessed an extraordinary expression on John's face, wide-eyed and amusingly shell-shocked.

Just as Nadia backed off and began to unbutton John's shirt, the two heard a hard knock on the door. Looking at each other for a moment, the two decompressed and Nadia ran to the bathroom, and quickly donning John's bathrobe, paced toward the door. Opening it, her eyes shot daggers at Lana, who boldly strolled in past her and approached John, who was still stunned by Nadia's behavior and became suddenly entertained by Lana's, who in a strange way seemed to know exactly what she had just interrupted.

"I am so sorry. I must have left my phone," Lana claimed. Looking around carefree and checking the various rooms, she added, "Could one of you call me? Here is the number," she stated, hesitating before writing it down on a magazine cover while acting oblivious to Nadia's temper, which was now tantamount to a time bomb.

Matters got worse when Nadia dialed Lana's number and it began to ring, the sound coming from inside Lana's own purse!

"Oh, silly me," Lana declared, laughing and displaying little sign of embarrassment. "Well, thank you two again and I hope I didn't interrupt anything. I'll use your bathroom before I leave, if that's all right?"

John looked at the two with a neutral, if somewhat embarrassed, expression. *You most definitely interrupted something, Lana,* he was thinking. *But why am I not upset with you over it?*

Nadia was ready to boil over when Lana just walked past them and into John's bathroom, almost as if she owned the place. John was now seeing a side of Nadia he'd yet known existed. For her part, Nadia began to show displeasure toward John, if only because his level of vitriol over this most untimely incursion failed to match her own.

The momentum of spontaneous intimacy seemed to be irrecoverable as Nadia couldn't shake her sour mood and realizing the late hour, she began to gather herself up and prepared to leave, barely saying another word. John felt very strange, as if in unchartered waters, unsure of what to do or say next.

Meanwhile, Lana heard the apartment door open and close before reappearing from the bathroom, herself headed for the exit while taking a parting glance toward John on the way out, all the while displaying that same mischievous smile.

Sitting in the aftermath of quite an evening, John tried to pick up the mental pieces of a trip that began as "Looking for Love" and seemed to end as "Flirting with Disaster". He kind of regretted the way things worked out with Nadia, but mostly couldn't stop thinking about this Lana,... not in a romantic sense, but... *Who is this woman?*

John returned home while he and Nadia never shared another word, written or otherwise. As a few days passed, what was expected to be a bout of depression began to settle in as relief. The visions of an attractive foreign woman, and the intrigue surrounding the out-of-the-box chase, were replaced by a welcome dose of reality, and all the things that gave John some degree of apprehension were now gone.

A man of great personal pride, he had to admit that his melancholy was more from his looking rather foolish in the eyes of friends and family, as opposed to the realization that his overseas encounter with this woman, Nadia Kovalenko, didn't work out. He couldn't shake the inexplicable feeling that he would somehow see or hear from this woman, Lana, again.

CHAPTER TWO

Unwanted Advance

CHUGUEV, UKRAINE

In most cultures, weddings are large social gatherings and for ethnic Russians it was no different. All the aunts, uncles, and cousins, many of whom that lived on the same street, were there along with dozens of other guests from as far away as Moscow. Irina's first cousin, Vera, whom she resembled immensely, had exchanged vows with a coworker, a young man she had known since early childhood. The music, food, and beverages were abound, and the entire Balabanove family was immersed in the celebration.

Being one of the gathering's most eligible bachelorettes, Irina entertained offers to dance throughout the evening, and being an excellent dancer, she found it most exhilarating. One overzealous young man began to cling to her at the point of being annoying as his breath reeked with a rancid combination of tobacco and vodka. Having kicked the habit of smoking two years earlier, Irina found the aroma of cigarette smoke to be quite offensive. Kolya Stasevich was an ex-army comrade of her sister Alika's husband who lived in Rossoshi, a small village an hour to the northwest, thirty kilometers from Kharkov. Both he and Irina were in Alika and Misha's wedding party, but Irina had shown little interest in him.

The reception began to wind down near midnight, and Irina, whose family had since departed, reluctantly agreed to allow Kolya to drive her home. The aged Lada sedan was filthy with cigarette butts all over the seats and old carpet while Irina held her seat with both hands as the two rambled through the streets of Chuguev, her praying they wouldn't get in an accident or get pulled over by the police. The intoxicated young man began to salivate at the site of his female passenger, anticipating his reward for playing chauffer. He cavalierly placed his hand on her thigh when she froze and screamed.

"Watch your driving! You want to get us both killed?"

She began to lighten up when they pulled in front of her apartment building, but things got disagreeable when Kolya reached around her neck to try and force a kiss. She resisted and he kept on, getting more and more aggressive.

"I think you should invite me in. We could warm each other up," he spoke in slurred Russkie.

"No Kolya! You're drunk! Go home!"

"What is the matter? Your American boyfriend left you months ago! You know you want it!"

Now extremely angry, Irina swung her purse rapidly upside his head, causing him to take his hands off her and quickly hold a palm to his battered cheek, checking for a wound. She then quickly opened the door and shot out to the curb, slamming the door while running toward the apartment security entrance. She quickly punched in the numbered code to get in, fearing he would chase after her, but he simply sat in the car idling a few moments, and then drove off.

Irina entered the apartment and headed straight for her bedroom. Undressing and collapsing on her bedspread, some strong mixed emotions set in, happiness for her cousin, Vera, and an ongoing sadness she felt in her own life. *When will my prayers be answered?*

SAINT LOUIS, MISSOURI USA

The crowd cheered as the Cardinals' star first basement rocketed a three-run homer, giving the home team a lead in the fifth inning. Johnny came shuffling down the aisle, toting a cardboard tray populated with hot dogs, nachos, and two drinks. The seats were sixteen rows behind the opposing team's dugout in the old dual purpose Busch Stadium, the new ballpark having already broken ground on the adjacent property to the south. This was the first professional baseball game John and his son had attended together since the move back from California, the weather perfect, and the crowd massive, as this was appearing to be the best all-around Cardinal team in nearly twenty years.

John Senior and Junior had been in Missouri for nearly two years now, residing in Cape Girardeau, a city of forty thousand just over a hundred miles south of St. Louis and best known as the boyhood home of Rush Limbaugh, the Godfather of AM talk radio for nearly a generation.

"Dad, are you really going back to Russia and look for a wife?" Johnny asked, half jokingly.

"Hey, I am. Actually, it's Ukraine," John stated flatly as he chomped down on the tasty hot dog. "You know what I've been through, son. I may be no spring chicken, but I've still got a little gas left in the tank. This pop culture movement,...the way the conventional family is now being run down,... I can't deal with it."

"Come on, Dad. That woman from Dupo, Illinois, was pretty cool... And Becky was nice."

"Yeah, right. But they just didn't work out. And I'm getting tired of playing games," John replied as he continued stuffing himself.

"Do you really think it will be different over there this time, Dad?"

John had never forgotten his insurance agent in Lake Arrowhead, a man who had married a Russian gal ten years before. John had been quite impressed with her, to the point of believing her look-alike had reappeared during his previous overseas visit, and had always been intrigued by his friend's story on how they had met. John had been doing quite a lot of homework on the subject of international travel and the web-based mail-order bride business, which since the collapse of the Soviet Union had become a booming cottage industry.

"The women over there have the same values I grew up with, son. They actually dream of having a husband and their own family. I miss the time when men were men and women were glad. We've lost that here."

"Well, Dad, I know you've been through a lot. I'm surprised you'd even want to get married again. You do know Grandma and Grandpa both think you've completely lost your mind."

John chuckled. "And so does everybody else I know... And I've been through a lot? What about you, son?"

Johnny's mother was the victim of a brutal rape twelve years earlier while John was out-of-town on business. Her post trauma depression gradually turned into a serious prescription drug addiction, a condition that had torn the marriage, as well as the whole family, apart.

"Just don't get over there and get yourself in trouble, Dad," Johnny said, after a big play on the field and the crowd applause had died down.

"I won't get into trouble. You know me," John replied as the two shared a laugh.

"Like I said, Dad..."

John took yet another huge bite out of his hot dog, thinking back on all he and his son had been through. *Have I lost my mind?... Well, maybe.*

⋙⟩ ⟨⋘

CHUGUEV, UKRAINE

The small three-room house sat on an acre of ground and was quite private and cozy by local standards, as most of the working class lived in the aged apartments built by the Communist government and often occupied by two and sometimes three family generations. Irina's father, Mikhail, had located to the eastern part of Ukraine following a stint in the Red Army in the late seventies, gaining employment as an engineer at a petrol refinery.

Although Mikhail's salary, meager by Western standards, was completely regulated by the government, his superiors had taken a liking to him over time and bonuses were awarded by providing some free buckets of petrol disbursed after hours, extra income to be earned selling the fuel on the black market. As such, the Balabanove family enjoyed a slightly higher living standard than average, having moved from their two-room endured apartment of fourteen years to the three-room cottage on the river.

Mikhail had suffered a recent series of minor strokes, partially paralyzing his left arm muscles and forcing an early retirement. He had acquired quite a skill as an auto body repairman and turned the small garage on the property into a shop where many locals brought him their well-worn Ladas and Skodas for repair.

The family prepared for the evening dinner featuring the common Russian cuisine, borscht, kholodets, an array of garden veggies, and hot tea, along with an intermittent toast of vodka. Nadine Balabanova was always content in having her family around her, husband Mikhail, daughters Irina and Alika, and Alika's recently wed husband, Misha.

The table conversation included the usual topics regarding the corrupt government, shortages at the market, gossip around the neighborhood, and small talk about Mikhail's auto repair business which included Misha, who worked for him.

"Where is Dimitri?" Mikhail asked robustly, after he and Misha downed a couple large shot glasses of vodka.

"I'm not ready to have him here, Papa," Irina replied while half rolling her eyes. Dimitri was a young man she worked with at the security supply company and close friend of Misha's, who had recently rented a room in her small apartment, a temporary arrangement made purely out of economic expediency, at least from her vantage point.

"You know he's always welcome, daughter."

I don't want Dimitri to get the feeling he and I are anything more than roommates, she thought, knowing that having a new acquaintance over to meet the parents would be taken as a sign the two were connected romantically, the last thing Irina wanted to convey upon this guy, one she had simply taken on as a tenant.

Following dinner, the men stepped outside on the guise of checking on their German Shepherd, the family "junk yard" dog that scared away unwanted visitors, but mostly a thinly veiled excuse to consume more vodka. The women took to the habit of cleaning up after dinner and washing dishes while enjoying the usual female gossip, more and more often subject to the highs and lows of Irina's love life.

"Your father thinks it's odd that you seem to never bring your new boyfriend around, Irina."

"He's not my boyfriend, Momma!"

"You're living together. Doesn't look right."

"I know, Momma, I know, but I just can't afford it alone," she replied as she gave Alika a look to imply the subject needed to change.

"Momma, Dimitri is not the right man for her," Alika broke in, lowering her voice in case the men could hear them outside. "She can do better."

After a brief pause, Nadine replied, "She'll have a hard time finding a good husband when she lives with another man!"

"Things are different than they used to be, Momma," Irina interjected. "He's just my roommate. It's not like we're sleeping together."

"You need a husband, not a roommate!"

"Calm down, Momma," Alika spoke again in Irina's defense. "She's working on it."

Nadine paused and appeared confused. "Working on it? Is there something going on that your father and I don't know about?"

The two siblings shared a brief grin and the conversation ended as Mikhail and Misha returned from outside. Nadine smiled to herself as she switched the small talk to the men, now knowing something was up with her still-unmarried daughter.

⤜⤜⤜ ⤛⤛⤛

Colonel Pavel Kuznetsov was the senior officer for the State Security of Ukraine Kharkov Oblast Region. The colonel entered the company's outer office and

Irina stiffened uncomfortably as he approached her desk, gesturing as always that he formally greet her with a kiss of her hand. He seemed to be stopping by the office more frequently as of late for menial tasks that could easily have been handled by phone or by other low-level staffers.

"*Privet*, hello, Irina, You are looking lovely today, as always. I am on the run but need a quick word with Arkady."

Why not just barge into his office as if you owned the place, Colonel? You were never shy about such intrusions before, Irina thought, quietly intimidated as the arrogant SSU officer attempted to indulge in small talk with her, something she had little appetite for.

Arkady Petrov, the owner of the company, heard the exchange through his open door and quickly entered the outer foyer, greeting Kuznetsov with a handshake prior to the two men moving their meeting to his executive office.

"I wasn't expecting you to stop by, Comrade," Petrov stated, using the old Red Army prefix as a form of flattery to a man who held sway over the future viability of his small but growing company. "I must congratulate you on your recent promotion."

"Spasibo, Arkady," Kuznetsov replied rather insincerely, a man who believed his recent promotion to lieutenant colonel was long overdue. The advancement, which followed the retirement of his former SSU superior officer, gave Kuznetsov new responsibilities which included the handling of most Oblast security related business dealings with contractors and suppliers.

"I was passing by and just wanted to clear up some details before I submit your proposal to the Council Budget Committee. I have some questions but unfortunately don't have a lot of time today," Kuznetsov grunted while making a display of looking at his watch.

"If you could have someone on your staff send us whatever questions that remain, in an email perhaps, I will see to it your outstanding issues are taken care of," Petrov replied anxiously. The large contract for security phone and camera systems at all the Oblast's SSU facilities would supersede anything his growing firm had previously concluded and double his annual revenues. Following a lengthy bidding process, the countless back and forth, paperwork, and phone calls, it appeared the lucrative contract would finally come to fruition.

"I appreciate your efforts to serve us, Arkady. We have put so much work in putting this deal together."

Petrov looked on as the former KGB captain seemed to suspend his statement as the businessman thought, *I do not recall your doing much of anything, Colonel, other than disrupt the process. And here it comes, some sort of under the table payback.* He wished the corrupt and arrogant officer would just spit out a sum upfront instead of playing these games after all this time. He despised the very idea of having to pay money under the table to sell products and services he worked so hard to provide and detested the very fact that he could ill afford not to pay for this shakedown.

Kuznetsov rose from his chair and made his way around Petrov's desk, perching himself directly on one corner and surprising the businessman, who was not sure what he was up to. "Arkady, I propose we have an exquisite dinner to finalize and celebrate this deal. I have made reservations at Nika's on Universytetska in Kharkov. Be there tomorrow evening by seven thirty sharp. Bring your girl, Irina, along also. I know she has put much work into this."

Petrov was surprised the demand for cash had not come, at least yet, and knew Kuznetsov had eyes on his young office manager. He also knew that her feelings regarding the brazen SSU colonel were not in any way mutual. "I'll make it a point to be there, Comrade. I'll check with Irina and see if she is free to join us, but if not, I'm sure you and I can conclude our business."

Kuznetsov was not pleased. "I am pressed for time on this, Arkady. We do have another bid the committee has to consider and this must all be completed by the end of the year. I wouldn't want your bid to be held up over some petty details, such as Kiev demanding updated security clearances on you and your entire staff," the SSU colonel stated with a disingenuous look of concern. "Irina seems to be very smart on details... You will have her attend, correct?"

Petrov felt an immense and uncomfortable pressure to call Irina into his office as the arrogant Kuznetsov sat impatiently awaiting his response. He knew no other Ukrainian firm existed that could provide the security system upgrades the Oblast needed. But the threat of personnel security background checks, the worst nightmare for any small company, was an old trick he recalled from the former Soviet days, used by the KGB to get whatever they wanted, usually kickbacks in cash or other "personal" favors. Knowing he could ill-afford to lose faith with the high ranking and overbearing SSU officer, he pressed a button on his phone and instructed his office manager to join the two of them in his office.

Irina entered a minute later, facing Arkady and standing at a comfortable distance from Kuznetsov. "Yes, Sir?"

"Colonel Kuznetsov says we are nearing the end of finalizing the equipment and support contract we've proposed to the Oblast SSU and wanted to have dinner with us tomorrow evening, to clear up any lingering details."

Kuznetsov interrupted as he addressed the young woman directly. "Irina, you have put so much work into this and I know you need to be involved in resolving any minor issues we have. As a reward and to reach a conclusion, the SSU wishes to include you in a celebratory dinner at Nika's in Kharkov."

Irina held a blank look as her boss displayed a shameful expression before adding, "We'll leave here at six thirty, Irina, and I will personally drive you back home."

"What should I bring?" She asked after a brief thought gathering, wanting to somehow object but the words couldn't seem to come to her.

"I think a copy of the master document should suffice, don't you agree, Comrade Colonel?" Petrov replied as he awaited approval from the expecting government strongman.

Kuznetsov paid little attention to Petrov as he stood and gave Irina a final quick visual inspection. "Splendid, then," he exclaimed and then turned to vacate the building, looking forward to doing *business* the next evening with Petrov's lovely young office manager.

As she and her boss watched the overzealous SSU officer leave the office, Irina couldn't keep from thinking back to the first time she had come to know Colonel Pavel Kuznetsov, less than a year earlier...

... More Security Supply was celebrating its fifth business anniversary, and indeed the previous year had been its best thus far. The small but growing company specialized in providing security equipment systems for other free enterprise companies and also did a volume of business with the State Security of Ukraine, the national agency modeled after the American FBI and European Interpol, but in many ways was a spin-off of the former KGB. Irina's boss and company owner, Arkady Petrov, was a former SSU officer himself, although his relationship with the local Oblast regional office was at times tenuous.

In concert with Christmas and the Old Russian New Year, Petrov had thrown a dinner party that cold January evening for all his employees and their immediate families, as well as inviting some key customers. The most important of these for both prior and future business were state and local government officials, and due to proximity, most of the officers from the local SSU Oblast office in Kharkov were there. The large, rented ballroom was loud with music, and the attendees were in high spirits following the robust dinner, which included generous amounts of beverages.

At the head of the guest table sat a rather boisterous SSU officer accompanied by his very attractive mistress, a younger woman who struggled to feign happiness while tolerating the behavior of her overly intoxicated man.

Irina sat at the head table, assuming the role of party hostess as she was office manager for Petrov's company and by coincidence the only female employee. Throughout the evening, she would become uncomfortably conscious of the uniformed SSU man staring at her, attempting to flirt while becoming blatantly insensitive to the needs of the young female companion at his side.

The former Soviet commissar and KGB captain had recently been transferred from Donetsk and placed in charge of security for the Kharkov Oblast. Tall and fit for a man forty two, his head was clean shaven, and the man was ruggedly handsome, although always seemed to wear a devious expression.

Approaching Petrov as he spied the party host making the social rounds, Major Kuznetsov placed a hand on his shoulder and spoke into his ear, or more accurately spat as the uniformed officer reeked with the smell of cheap cologne, cigars, and liquor.

"Arkady, you have done well for yourself. She is beautiful," he told Petrov while nodding toward Irina, who now sat alone at the head table chatting with other company employees and their spouses.

"Oh no, Major. It is not what you think. She is only my office manager," Petrov replied sheepishly. "And don't get any ideas, she is taken."

Major Kuznetsov chuckled lightly. "Too late for old fools like us, huh?... But I must have missed something. Where is her husband?"

"She is not married, but does have a boyfriend, an American who has left for the holidays."

"An American, you say?" The SSU officer tensed up as if needing to control a hidden vitriol. "A pity to leave such a vivacious beauty so unattended. She looks as though she needs a good Russian man to service her, wouldn't you say, Arkady?" Kuznetsov bellowed as he slapped Petrov on the back.

"Do you have such a man in mind, Major?" Petrov answered jokingly, knowing the officer's reputation as a man who believed himself to be God's gift to women.

"I may indeed. You say she is your office manager?"

Petrov sensed the intoxicated major had an implied insistence on meeting his lone female employee, and as such an introduction couldn't be avoided, he escorted the unrelenting officer toward the head table.

"Irina Balabanova, this is Major Pavel Kuznetsov, in charge of security now at the Oblast facilities," Petrov stated smiling.

"Happy to meet you, Sir," Irina said politely, offering to shake the SSU officer's hand and blushing when he held her hand up for a light kiss, an overture unexpected and making her somewhat uncomfortable.

"I will be involved more with Arkady's entire staff now, Irina," Kuznetsov stated, a bit too direct as she wished to avoid his piercing stare. "I look so forward to our getting better acquainted."

Irina forced a smile, desperately needing an excuse to separate herself from this encounter and looked toward her boss for some sort of extraction. As Petrov seemed unsettled and failed to take the hint, Irina interjected, "Excuse me gentlemen, but I must visit the ladies' room."

Breaking away, she began to head for the ballroom exit, sighting across the room Kuznetsov's mistress, a girl perhaps her own age, sitting alone and staring in her direction. *An angry stare?... No, a sad and tearful one....*

.... She picked up the office phone with the standard greeting, smiling until the commandeering voice on the other end responded.

"Good morning, Colonel Kuznetsov."

"Oh Irina, call me Pavel. And kindly connect me with Arkady."

She pressed a button and awaited a reply. "Sir, Colonel Kuznetsov is on line two." *Please pick up!* She thought, *I do not wish to talk with this man any more than I have to.*

She saw the line two light go out moments later, followed almost immediately by a beep of her speaker phone. Petrov called for her to come into his office and as she entered, she faced a man who appeared somewhat shaken.

"Irina, something has come up and I cannot attend the dinner tonight. I need you to handle the meeting with Colonel Kuznetsov personally."

Her intuition told her this was a very bad idea, something she had not signed on for. She could tell her boss was ordering, not requesting. "I am not comfortable with this, Sir."

"I will increase your salary if this deal gets closed this month," Petrov claimed sheepishly. "Here are some hryvnias to cover a taxi back and forth."

Irina gave her boss a blank stare. "But that Nika's is an expensive place, Arkady," she replied, addressing the boss by his first name, feeling it to be more than appropriate at the moment. "And I know it will be assumed that we would pay for such a dinner."

Petrov doubted that Kuznetsov would have her pay, unlike the case if he himself were there. But not wanting to make too much a point of it, he reached into his wallet and extracted several thousand more hryvnias and handed them to her. "That should more than adequately take care of the final bill at Nika's."

Irina collected the stack of currency and left Petrov's office without a sign of gratitude, both sharing the uneasy acknowledgment that the money, which accounted for triple the amount of her monthly salary, was to be her compensation for any "services rendered" necessary to placate the client. The thought of it created a nauseating feeling in her stomach and threatened to forever change what had always been a cordial relationship between her and her employer. *I'll treat with Colonel Kuznetsov on my own terms,* Irina spoke silently to herself, *and if it costs Arkady Petrov the SSU contract, so be it. He can fire me.*

⤜⟩⟩⟩ ⟨⟨⟨⤛

She arrived at Nika's restaurant in Kharkov at just past seven and was escorted to a backroom corner table where Kuznetsov stood with his usual forward act of charm by kissing her hand in greeting and followed by the gentlemanly move to seat her. She sat down and attempted to deflect some discomfort by propping up her briefcase on an adjacent chair and fumble through it as though working with documents.

"Business before pleasure, Irina?" Kuznetsov blabbered, his breath already smelling of vodka shots consumed earlier.

What pleasure? The man is a pig, Irina thought. "I have the master copy of the contract here, Colonel."

"Oh please, Irina. No need for formalities here. Just call me Pavel."

The two chattered with small talk as he choked down more vodka and some hors d'oeuvres while Irina sipped on a single glass of white wine and became annoyed when Kuznetsov ordered entrees for the both of them, even as she still reviewed the menu.

Following dinner, she asked the former commissar what questions he still had on the contract proposal, irritated that he seemed to express no interest in the documents at all. His embarrassing efforts to flirt with her had grown all the more annoying with every minute and reached a breaking point when Kuznetsov reached under the table, placing his meaty hand on her left thigh. Irina froze, not knowing whether to yell, cry, or just get up and leave. Keeping her head, she reached down and pushed his hand away while backing her chair away from the table slightly.

The drunken colonel was about to reach over the table and attempt to force a kiss after he had stated rather arrogantly that he could get her a job as his private secretary and arrange for her own prepaid apartment in Kharkov, as though he still thought he was in the old USSR.

The restaurant staff seemed to overlook the indecent behavior as they feared the SSU colonel, when all the sudden the maître d' approached the table to inform the colonel that he had an important phone call that was on hold for him in their back office. Agitated, he got up stumbling while instructing a nearby waiter to provide his "guest" with another glass of wine. Irina sat there, desperately wanting to leave despite knowing her job may depend on this meeting culminating in success, success being defined as quite more than her administrative skills regarding company contracts.

Barging rudely forward and into the restaurant office, Kuznetsov, who had carelessly turned his cell phone ringer off, picked up the phone yelling, "What are you doing calling me!?"

His expression changed rapidly when he was surprised and quickly sobered by the caller.

"When did this happen, Comrade General?... I see... Yes, Comrade... Of course, Comrade... I will get on it and call you right back."

Kuznetsov quickly hung up the phone, stunned by this sudden crisis, strong reprimand, and call to action delivered by his SSU commander in Kiev. Thinking briefly about returning to his table to stall his "prey", the embattled officer thought better of it, picked up the phone again and dialed. He listened to the repeated ringtone impatiently, hung up, and then rang again...and again, no answer. He then redialed his commanding officer, Lieutenant General Nikolai Morozov, who was now in charge of operations for the entire SSU, Ukraine's renaming of the local KGB.

"General, I don't know what is happening. There is no answer at the base office."

"What do you mean, there is no answer? There is no one on duty at your station? You sound as though you have had too much to drink, Colonel!"

Even in his intoxicated state, the SSU colonel knew the implications of a separatist attack on the Oblast Division Headquarters happening on his watch and Morozov having to inform him about it. About to become completely unhinged, he inadvertently hung up on the general and in a panicked motion redialed. Line busy. "Ohhh!" he yelled and then redialed base headquarters...and again no answer!

The maître d' stood just outside the office door, worried the colonel's eyes were going to pop out of his head or he was going to have a stroke. Kuznetsov, shaking his head violently, noticed the restaurant employee, slammed down the phone and barked, "Don't just stand there you imbecile! Yell for my driver to pull out in front... Now!"

As the now fear-ridden and enraged colonel thundered out the door, he passed by a mild-mannered cab driver who calmly walked through the restaurant and approached Irina, still a bit shaken while sitting at her table, and escorted her outside to his awaiting taxicab to transport her the forty-five kilometers back home.

It was a bit dark and the driver, a man with his cabbie hat pulled low and wearing a trimmed goatee, nodded to Irina through the front mirror.

"I live at 16 Kozheduba"....

"Yes, I have that information, thank you," the cabbie stated, quickly. The half-hour drive was pleasantly uneventful as she worked to calm her nerves, hoping against hope she would have no more business with Colonel Pavel Kuznetsov again, ever.

Meanwhile, the besieged colonel's staff car entered the well-lit division office parking lot, the driver not even coming to a full stop when the fuming base commandant stormed out of the car and into the building, ready to extract a pound of flesh from the first officer he could find.

The shift officers and staff, unaccustomed to the intoxicated Kuznetsov appearing this late in the evening, all stood and saluted while confused at the reason for all the excitement. The phone system was in perfect working order and the whole evening throughout the entire Oblast had been relatively quiet.

Stopping in front of her apartment in Chuguev, the taxi driver got out and moved rapidly to the right side of the vehicle to open his passenger's door. "Good evening, Irina," he expressed, standing by to make certain things on the dark street were safely quiet. "My fare has been taken care of."

She exited to the curb, nodding briefly as she moved passed him and walked toward her apartment building. She paused at the front entrance, looking around as a thought suddenly entered her mind. "Say, how do you know my?"...

Before she could complete the question, the taxicab was gone.

CHAPTER THREE

Unpleasant Memories

After many weeks of anticipation, the day had finally arrived. The holiday was planned for late November as John's business would be shut down over the Thanksgiving weekend and thus it worked out that he'd only miss about five working days total during the eleven-day trip.

He was most excited about his meeting a woman from Kharkov, thirty-eight years of age, very attractive, and having one small child. Her name was Anna, and they had been writing each other back and forth for nearly four months. She had never asked for money before their meeting, which would have been a tell-tale sign of a con, and her letters all seemed most reassuring.

Deciding he would hedge his bets, John also planned a return to Odessa to meet a doctor named Larisa, a woman in her mid-thirties with apparently no baggage as she had never been married, although that in itself had stirred a level of skepticism on his part. But this woman was quite pretty in her own right, at least according to her posted pictures, and he figured he'd split the time with both her and this Anna in Kharkov. *Hopefully, I'll get lucky.*

The other consideration was that Odessa, a city he was already familiar with, was a much nicer place to visit in late November, while Kharkov was located in the far northeastern part of Ukraine with an average monthly temperature colder than Chicago. Few ever went there to visit in late November, and literally no one as a tourist. However, John felt this Anna had struck his fancy, and he was most optimistic about meeting her.

In both cities, he'd chosen this trip to work through local agencies that not only generated revenue by charging to translate email letters and deliver them by regular mail, but also provided interpreters and arranged apartment rentals, needs that John had chosen to handle himself back in April, when he had been to Odessa the first time.

The firm in Kharkov was called the Belanov Marriage Agency, owned by an early middle-aged woman, Natalyia Belanov, someone who seemed extraordinarily helpful and encouraging over the phone, despite never having met him personally. John dealt mostly with her assistant, a young man named Sergei who spoke fluent English as well as both local languages, Russian and Ukrainian. John couldn't tell the difference when hearing the two or even glancing at their written words, but the natives spoke both dialects, and with Belanov he figured the bases were covered. Prior to his traveling there previously, John hadn't even known there was a Ukrainian language as he assumed the entire former USSR spoke Russian.

In 2005, online communication technology, such as Viber, had not been widely introduced yet and thus communication by phone between the United States and the Ukraine was quite expensive. The cell phone companies and international carriers had mutual trade agreements and mobile communication providers in the Ukraine charged outrageous per minute roaming fees. Those were billed through John's cell phone account, exorbitant amounts and subject to no recourse accountability. As such, John had conversed mostly with Sergei through emails.

The plan was set for John to fly out of Lambert International Airport in St. Louis on Northwest early the morning of Wednesday, November 16th, make connection in Minneapolis, fly KLM Dutch Airlines to Amsterdam, and finally catch a Ukrainian International flight to Kiev. From there, he would take a small shuttle commuter-type plane to Kharkov, spend four days, then shuttle back to Kiev and on to Odessa the following Monday for a stay through Friday.

Trusting everything would go to plan, he would arrive in Kharkov late on Thursday around 9:30 PM local time. Sergei had arranged an apartment not too far from their office and John requested that he have Anna meet him at the airport.

John's mother and father drove him the two hours to St. Louis and dropped him off at the airport at 5:30 AM. With the eight-hour time difference, John chose to call Belanov by phone as he cleared security and headed toward his gate. The early morning call in Missouri would be received in Kharkov at around 2:00 PM.

The young agent answered, and John instructed, "Sergei, I should be flying into Kharkov at 9:30 PM tomorrow. Make certain that Anna will be there to meet me."

"Good morning, John," Sergei replied, by now on a first-name basis and conscious of the time difference. "I haven't spoken to Anna in about a week and have to contact her to confirm she'll be there. As soon as I get this confirmed, I'll call you back."

"You won't be able to call me, Sergei, as I'm about to get on the plane now. But just send me an email and I'll stop to check it when I connect in Minneapolis during my forty-five-minute layover."

"I sure will, John. Have a good trip and I look forward to meeting you," the agency assistant replied sincerely and the two disconnected.

As luck would have it, John's plane was thirty minutes late taking off due to some foul weather delays in Minneapolis. His forty five minute layover scheduled there would be reduced to fifteen minutes, just long enough to deplane at the Northwest domestic concourse and scurry through the airport to catch his KLM flight to Amsterdam. As the Boeing 737 began to descend, signaling the final approach, John stared out the window at the forests and farm fields of southern Minnesota while his mind drifted back in time to events that began to trigger this unforeseen overseas quest for happiness....

.... The traffic was atrocious as was usually the case in the Los Angeles area during midafternoon on a weekday, six years prior. Following a productive meeting with a lease broker in Westwood, John headed east on Wilshire Boulevard to rendezvous for a late lunch with one of his sales reps, prior to an afternoon follow-up visit planned with the local chairman of the Korean Auto Service Association, an ethnic membership club in Los Angeles that had made a large purchase of equipment as a group.

His company-provided sedan, a four-door Pontiac Grand Am, featured a floor-mounted, hard-wired cellular phone, a trendy luxury in the pre-wireless period when battery-operated pagers were still the norm.

The loud ringer sounded as John turned down the radio knob before picking up and answering.

"Is this Mr. John Masters?"

"Yes, this is John," he answered cautiously as the voice sounded uncharacteristic from most incoming calls he received.

"Mr. Masters, this is Deputy Sheriff Mark Ortiz of the Orange County Sheriff Department. Do you have a spouse, Teresa Diane Masters, residing at 17619 Joshua Circle, Huntington Beach, California?"

Oh my lord, what in the world has she done now? "Yes, Deputy, what can I do for you?"

"Mr. Masters, you have a serious problem. Your wife has been contacting nearly every pharmacy in Orange County, representing herself as a nurse from Orange County Medical Center and attempting to call in a prescription for OxyContin," the deputy explained seriously. "This is a violation of California Health and Safety Code 11173, punishable by fines of up to ten thousand dollars per incident and up to ten years imprisonment."

John was speechless, searching for the right words.

"Mr. Masters, your wife has no previous criminal record. As such, we're going to give you a rare opportunity to handle this personally."

Oh my god! "I appreciate that, Deputy," John answered as his heartbeat was lowered, just slightly. "I'm over an hour away up in LA."

"I'll wait for you at your residence, Sir. You know your young son is here and your spouse appears to be rather unstable. I suggest you drive safely but get here as soon as possible."

John arrived just over an hour later. The deputy sheriff's car in the driveway attracted several curious neighbors who hung out on the street in front of the house. John walked in through the garage door and met Deputy Ortiz and another officer standing in the kitchen, Teresa Masters sitting at the table in front of them, obviously distraught and eyes stressed red from the dried tears. Their ten-year-old son, Johnny, sat nervously at the kitchen table beside his mother, afraid and knowing something bad was happening.

The stress of John's job and Teresa's addiction had taken its toll on a once happy marriage, John committing to stick it out until Johnny became of legal age, fourteen, where state circuit court judges generally awarded parental custody according to the expressed desire of the child, extenuating circumstances notwithstanding.

After thanking the deputies, John and his young son shared a solemn look as he glanced toward the ceiling and slowly shook his head. Teresa, just a few years past a lovely vibrant woman, began to beg John to take her to a hospital emergency room for a Demerol shot, an excruciating visit that was all too often for the Masters and nearly as routine as stopping to fill the gas tank in one of their vehicles, only the gas station didn't have sixty to eighty "patients" ahead of you in the emergency room, many being uninsured parents whose kid had a slight fever.

⤞⤝

Nearly three years later, the snowplows were out in the higher elevation communities working overtime as a weather front had blanketed the mountains around Lake Arrowhead with snow overnight. John awoke early and prodded Johnny to get out of bed and help him shovel off the driveway. The two labored furiously as at least twelve inches had fallen, and to add insult to injury, the plows had shoved a huge berm of snow in front of their entire driveway, over three feet tall and blocking access to the street.

"Come on, son. As soon as we're done, we'll go into town and grab some breakfast."

It had been two months since Johnny's mother, Teresa, had left for a lengthy visit with her daughter and son-in-law in southern Illinois, as the marriage of fourteen years had come to loggerheads over her prescription drug addiction.

She had been treated by an older neurologist at UCI Medical Center in Orange named Van Der Slitt. Following months of experimentation spirited on by a steady stream of pain symptoms, the doc prescribed OxyContin. In short order, a month's supply would be gone in a week, always accompanied by an excuse of an accidental spilling of the bottle down the toilet or garbage disposal. Ever sympathetic, Van Der Slitt continued to crank out the prescription slips without question.

Having gone through a period of exhausting ER visits, rehab assignments, and Teresa's other drug-related incidents, John decided to relocate the family from Huntington Beach to Lake Arrowhead, having been captivated with the place following a weekend getaway a couple months before. Purchasing the home in the mountains above San Bernardino had been an effort on John's part to help clear the air and stabilize the family. The commute to the office for John would be two to three hours depending on rush hour traffic, but he felt the sacrifice would be worth it just to get his spouse away from Van Der Slitt. Things initially began to look up, at least superficially, when Teresa was hired as an assistant manager at a local fast-food restaurant.

Lake Arrowhead is a mountain resort town with a population of just under ten thousand and many "chalets" serving as weekend getaways for the wealthy from LA. Most permanent residents were either retired couples or married family households who were actively involved in the community. They all knew each other well, including those in the medical profession.

As there were no neurologists on the mountain, Teresa began to visit the few various local family physicians and that wasn't going well. Within a period of a few months, she had fallen out with every one of them over their unwillingness to openly prescribe her narcotics. Word among their professional community traveled quickly to include the nearby mountain villages of Crestline and Big Bear. She had become well-known in the mountains and not in a good way.

Having missed too much time with calling in sick, Teresa was let go by the restaurant owner and one weekday while John was at work and Johnny in school, she drove down the mountain and all the way to UCI in Orange County to see Van Der Slitt. The endless cycle of OxyContin prescriptions reconstituted, Teresa began to quickly go downhill again and John started to become angry to the point of no return. Things at home couldn't seem to get much worse when Van Der Slitt called and asked the both of them to visit his office to disclose his diagnosis of Teresa having an advanced case of multiple sclerosis.

Suddenly, John felt a bout of severe remorse as he had become very distant toward her over time and had been strongly contemplating how to get out of the marriage. Upon hearing such news, he decided to suck it up, treat her with as much kindness as he could muster, and to support her and the marriage through the remainder of her years, however many that may be.

By this time, Teresa did virtually nothing with the rest of the family, even when her older children, whom John had welcomed as his own, came to visit.

He and Johnny took their Blazer through the snow-covered streets and entered Bill's Villager, a very popular local café in Lake Arrowhead Village, the popular lakefront area shopping and entertainment district. The café was small and had a service counter with individual stools occupied by the many patrons as well as a long row of booths along the front windows, offering a great view of the lake. In the rear of the building was an array of arcade games, and John accompanied his son in playing them the twenty or so minutes while they waited for a booth.

Their name called, the two headed back up front to a center booth, passing by a few locals whom he knew, if not by name by facial recognition. Johnny wolfed down his kid's portion breakfast quickly and as his dad enjoyed his ample plate, asked if he could be excused to return to the arcade room. John delivered his familiar parental lecture about cleaning his plate and then handed the boy a couple bucks to get some quarters from the cashier, smiling to himself as his son excitedly scurried away.

A gentleman looked on from a couple booths down and got up as his family was about to leave and approached. "Excuse me. You're Mr. Masters, aren't you?"

John looked up, not certain he knew the man, and offered his hand. "Yes, I'm John."

"I'm Doctor Hutchins. My wife was Johnny's teacher last year. Your wife is Teresa, I believe?"

"Yes," John replied.

"How is she doing?" The doctor asked, expressing concern.

"Well, not so good. With that MS, she's had to quit working, Doc."

"She's still on OxyContin, huh?"

John started to get slightly embarrassed, never comfortable with so much of the local community knowing much of his personal business. "Yeah, sad but true," he replied slowly as he seemed to sigh.

Doctor Hutchins looked around briefly and took the liberty of sitting down in the booth across from John. "Can I tell you something, off the record?" He asked quietly while again checking their surroundings.

John paused, momentarily at a loss for words. "Sure Doc."

"Teresa no more has multiple sclerosis than the man in the moon. That Van Der Slitt down at UCI just came up with that to get your insurance company to keep paying her medical bills."

John just sat in shock, staring forward at Hutchins and unable to even respond.

"I'm sorry to burden you with such news, John."

"How certain are you about this, Doc?" John asked, still obviously completely stunned.

"She came to see me about a year ago, wanting pain medication. I ordered a workup of blood tests, not sure if she ever got them, and she never came back. She then sought similar treatment from all the other clinics up here. Van Der Slitt has a reputation for that kind of thing; He should be run out of the profession. John, here's my card if I can help you in any way," the doctor expressed as he got up, shaking John's hand while departing.

43

John stood up, his face now full of emotion. "Thank you, Doc," he said as he watched the good doctor and his family walk out the door... *What a nightmare.*

Fighting off his malaise, he gathered Johnny, proceeded to the cashier's counter, and encountered another familiar face, his insurance agent, Steve Hollister. Both men shared greetings as Steve introduced him to his wife.

"John, this is my wife, Kathy. I'm sure you have spoken to her by phone before."

"Yes, of course. Pleased to meet you," John replied as he softly held her hand, taken off guard by the lovely woman. She had sparkling brown eyes, full lips covering a beautiful smile, and in fantastic shape for a woman he took to be nearly his age.

"I am so happy to meet you, John Masters," Ekaterina replied gracefully.

"Where does that accent come from?"

"She's Russian," her husband answered. "From St. Petersburg."

"Russian?" John replied a bit quickly. *I wonder how...*

As if reading his mind, Steve injected, "Stop by the office sometime this week. I have some more information on that life policy we talked about and it's time to go over your annual homeowner's and auto insurance. I'll share with you how Kathy and I met, over a cup of coffee."

"Sure, I'll stop by, maybe around Wednesday first thing."

"Very good. Look forward to it," Steve said as he handed the cashier his credit card.

John nodded and smiled as he grabbed his own card.

"Good luck to you, John," Ekaterina exclaimed smiling, as she and her husband walked away.

John watched them briefly, strangely confused by the woman's comment. *Good luck?... Good luck about what?*

>>>>> <<<<<

Three weeks later the third heavy storm of the season had fallen, the drifts so high that all the mountain residents would be snowbound indoors for at least two days. John found Teresa's prescription bottle and counting the remaining OxyContin pills, calculated that fully half of the allotted month's supply had been consumed in four days. By this time, John and his son were sleeping in the master bedroom together while Teresa occupied the guest room.

"Dad, Mom's not going to react well to this," Johnny stated, seeing John stowing the meds in the master bathroom.

"It's for her own good, son," John replied, deeply saddened at having his boy having to grow up and constantly see his mother in such a state.

The family saga was now six years running, nearly half of young Johnny's life. A dozen rehab centers, at least a hundred doctor visits, more late night ER stops for Demerol shots than father or son could even count, and no light at the end of the tunnel. John had cancelled a whole week's business travel, handling as much by phone as he could, but his position as national sales manager for the small California test equipment manufacturer was critical and the owner was getting anxious.

John himself had taken to prescription Ambien as the stress had robbed him of what little semblance of sleep that remained. He often attempted to read something to Johnny in an attempt to get both their minds off the family crisis, but Johnny was a very astute child and spent an equal amount of time thinking he needed to console his dad. On this night, John took the additional step of locking their door, and at just past 11:00 PM, the two fell off to sleep.

In a scene right out of a horror movie, the two were awakened at 2:00 AM by an extreme hammering noise. At first, John thought an intruder had broken into the house and started to think about retrieving his nine-millimeter pistol hidden away, but upon flipping on the small bedside lamp, he stared in shock toward the sound's direction as the pointed end of a hatchet was tearing a hole completely through the center of their bedroom door, accompanied by Teresa on the other side screaming for her pill bottle.

Johnny was terrified as John jumped up out of the bed, quickly unlocked the door, and rushing to open it, quickly grabbed the hatchet out of Teresa's hands, the two struggling together briefly before sinking down to the carpet. John held his wife securely as she cried out while Johnny ran toward them, taking the dangerous tool away. As Teresa tired and morphed from a scream to a whimper, John and his son just looked at each other exhausted and speechless, momentarily unsure of what would come next....

.... John was awakened from his unpleasant memories by an elderly passenger who needed access to the aisle, as he noticed on the "breadcrumb" display they would soon be flying over the continent of Europe. He was full of anticipation although somewhat in suspense about still not getting a confirmation back from Sergei regarding Anna greeting him upon arrival in Kharkov. Following the small complimentary coffee served by the KLM stewardesses and a cursory browsing through the airline's monthly magazine, he chose to go ahead and spend the money and login to the web through the flight's online service to check his Yahoo email, disappointed at the result:

ERROR—UNABLE TO ACCESS SERVER

What is this? John thought, it being his first experience in using the internet on an airplane. By chance, as he had the Belanov website tab saved in his favorites, he clicked on it. *Voila! It works! But why did Yahoo give me problems?*

John opened the Belanov featured pages for Anna, again reviewing her posted information and admiring her photos... *Indeed a beautiful gal! I hope she looks as good as her pictures,* John thought, as he was struck by how much this Anna looked so much like another woman he'd met, an internet connection "match" that totally bombed, just over a year ago....

....He drove east on Interstate 64 with the reserved optimism he always felt when approaching another of these web-induced "hook-ups". *Bad word,* he thought. *That's the new slang that the younger generation used to describe a meeting for casual sex with a "friend".*

John was getting tired and somewhat fed up with trying to meet someone over the internet. He perceived the problem as working as a salesman in the automotive service industry, a trade which was male-dominated. He had attended church on occasion, but most fellow churchgoers were the elderly with a few families mixed in, but not many early to middle-aged single women there. His profession had taught him the key to success was in the numbers, as one had to make a lot of calls to strike gold. You had to experience a lot of rejection as in "no" to get a "yes", a concept he convinced himself would work eventually in this world of web-based matchmaking.

This latest female "prospect" was different than the rest and rather bold. Instead of insisting on the common practice of a brief meeting at a public restaurant or lounge, and often over lunch, this woman wanted John to stop by her place of residence and take her out to dinner, a place that turned out to be quite upscale and formal for a such a small community of just a few thousand residents.

He found her address quite easily as the street grid of the small town of three thousand was laid out around a square featuring an old county courthouse, as were many rural communities in the Midwest. Her place was quite intriguing, an old three-story Victorian era looking mansion, John convinced it must have been listed on the National Registry of Historic Places. He parked out on the street and entered through a wrought iron gate, part of an ornate black fence protecting a well-manicured lawn that featured two huge magnolia trees. The house appeared rather dark with a yellow light on out front, a single ceiling-mounted fixture in the center of the large veranda that nearly surrounded the entire structure.

Knocking on the door, John waited anxiously while already anticipating an evening that could be interesting, if not altogether fruitful. The large oak door opened and a woman greeted him, one dressed to kill. Perhaps forty but appearing much younger, Lisa was tall, nearly six feet, trim, and beautiful. *Wow!*

The interior was outfitted with expensive, ornate-looking furniture and oil paintings on wallpaper that seemed to match the home itself. John wondered if there were any other family members or "hired personnel" he would be introduced to, but there were none, adding to the mystique of this woman and how bold she was, inviting a total stranger in her home after dark while being all alone.

After brief introductions were made, John somewhat expected some sort of tour of the house would be in order, or hoping as he had always enjoyed museums. But an exploration was not to be as Lisa raised her arm in an obvious gesture that he escort her out for the evening. John felt a tinge of embarrassment as he opened the passenger door of his five-year-old Chevy Blazer, thinking this woman was no doubt accustomed to limousines. But this Lisa got in smiling and took it all in stride.

The restaurant was not large but quite fancy and crowded. The staff and waiters were all uniformed to match the ambiance of the establishment, even "offering" John a tie, which was required. After having been seated at a white cloth covered table near the center of the main dining room - John would have preferred a corner booth - the two ordered a bottle of wine and some hors d'oeuvres. Four course dinners followed as John worried slightly about the limit on his credit cards. He wasn't accustomed to or prepared for such a "hit" but didn't mind too much because that "thing" he had always expected and required, that something that needed to "click". It was there!

The two talked and laughed and shared stories over dinner for nearly three hours. Lisa's husband was a doctor and had been killed in a small plane accident four years prior. She was fairly set financially as her husband had a generous life insurance policy to add to the couples' acquired wealth over the years. She was employed as an office manager at nearby Scott Air Force Base, mostly just needing something to do.

John listened with genuine interest, while in the back of his mind feeling this woman was revealing a bit much of her personal business to a total stranger. *Does this mean she actually likes and trusts me?... Or is she just haphazardly bold?*

She could never have children physically, she disclosed, hoping that wouldn't be a deal breaker for John, a man she apparently liked as evidenced by her insistence to dance with a few other couples on the small dance floor, a soft piano providing music.

John had pride in his reputation for good tastes in women and this gal Lisa fit the bill with beauty and class to spare. Her infertility is no problem... *Don't need any more kids, been there, done that, no need to do that again.* Believing this first "date" was going extremely well, John half wondered if he'd be invited to spend the night. He was a bit old-fashioned in that way and thought a bit of courtin' was normally in order first. But if the invite was there, he wasn't going to say no.

Lisa reached her hand across the small table and grabbed John's hand. *This is going to be good,* he thought... *Almost too good.*

She looked serious and right at John for a moment as they touched. "There is something about me that you need to know. I'll tell you what it is and you tell me if you have a problem with it or not."

John's optimism took a sudden dive. This Lisa "Classy and Too Good to be True" gal was bent on tabling something serious. *Oh, oh, what's this? She's already in a relationship... Perhaps she has some terminal disease... She's bi-sexual... She's trans-sexual... She won't have my son living with her?... What?*

"I have this gift," She stated solemnly, a moment of silence ensuing as she expected John to respond somehow.

Following a few more awkward seconds, John asked, "A gift? What kind of gift?" *Maybe this babe is a world-class tennis player... A professional singer?... What?*

"I can talk to the dead," Lisa replied seriously.

John listened in shock. *Was this some sort of joke?* She didn't seem the humorous type. He froze for a moment, not knowing what to say.

"Well, say something," she added, a bit too loudly.

"What do you mean, you talk to dead people?" he responded, as though now thinking this must be a joke,... And not too funny.

"Sincerely, I have a side business where I have people over to my home. In the basement is a room where we have séances."

"Séances?"

"Yes, séances. People pay me good money to talk to their dead relatives, through me."

John was speechless, just kind of lowering his head, staring at her while struggling not to appear worried or dismissive, and unsure what the proper reaction should be at that moment.

"Are you going to say something?" Lisa asked, still clutching John's hand and looking worried.

John began to look around a bit, trying to think of the right words. "I don't know about this, Lisa. Somehow or another, I could just see myself spending the night at your place a few weeks later and having nightmares thinking the place was haunted." He was kind of joking, but kind of not.

He looked at his watch and as if on cue, Lisa began to break down. The woman was balling,...and balling badly. The other patrons began to stare at the two, wondering what terrible thing this man did or said to this poor lovely woman. The waiter quickly approached, asking if he could help.

Embarrassed, John just ask him to quickly bring out their check.

Lisa looked up, still in tears but trying to compose herself. "You are no different from all the others. You'll never be back."

When John couldn't seem to reply, she began to cry again, and by now the entire restaurant was looking on and John felt about two inches tall. A few minutes passed and the waiter brought the check. The whole bill was just under one hundred twenty dollars, and John, not wanting to take time fooling with a credit card, threw down a hundred and fifty in cash, got up out of his chair and walked around to Lisa, grabbing her by the shoulders and escorted her through the crowd, past the bar, out through the lobby, and to the parking lot.

Following a quiet trip back, John pulled in front of her mansion with the engine running, no longer hoping or expecting an invite inside. He did reach over the console to offer Lisa a slight embrace, but she didn't move.

"You're never going to call me again, are you?"

John wavered at first. "I don't know, Lisa. I just don't know."

"You'll never be back."

John started to open his door, planning to escort her in, but Lisa reached over and grabbed his arm, stopping him. "I'll see my own way in," she spoke, starting to exit on her own. "I'm sorry," she said lowly while turning away.

"Lisa, I'm sorry. I wish you would have told me all this on the phone."

She turned toward him, just prior to closing the door. "I was just hoping the physical attraction, which I felt, and our chemistry would have made it work."

The ninety-minute drive home seemed long, and John paid little mind to the country music on his car stereo, somewhat shaken after a "date" that seemed to have so much promise earlier.

I'm just toast, he thought....

....The vibration brought John back to the present as the sounds of extending landing gear indicated arrival was near. The flight being uneventful, a positive when considering air travel, the large Airbus plane landed in Amsterdam at approximately 7:00 AM local time, the schedule being somewhat inconvenient to accommodate the least expensive fare that included a long layover, as the connecting flight on Ukraine International Airlines would not depart until just after 1:00 PM. As the passengers moved forward in single file to exit the aircraft, a stewardess stood by the door, as was customary, to express appreciation for flying on behalf of the airline.

As John passed by near the door, there appeared a new stewardess. "Thanks for flying with KLM, Sir. Enjoy your stay in the Ukraine."

Taken aback momentarily as it hit him that this stewardess looked strangely familiar, John wanted to stop and give her a second look, but the herd of passengers soon motioned him forward and onto the gangway. Once exiting into the terminal building, he paused again with a puzzled look and glanced back over his shoulder.

How did she know I was connecting to Ukraine?

CHAPTER FOUR

Blind Date Bust

The two headed northwest early Thursday on Moskovsky Prospekt, the main expressway that ran between their hometown village of Chuguev and Kharkov, Ukraine's second largest city. Irina's two-door Fiat coupe was over twelve years old, a car fixed up by her father in the home garage.

She was in a hurry as she was to meet a suitor from Reno, Nevada, an American man who had traveled to Kharkov in hopes of meeting his new bride to emigrate to America. The small agency staff expected her by 11:00 AM.

A longtime friend and college classmate had convinced Irina to take out an ad with the local agency after she herself had done so in the spring, the result in meeting her future Dutch husband within a few weeks.

Irina was excited to finally meet someone after the many weeks of having her ad online, not only at the agency but on several associated international marriage arrangement websites. She felt perhaps the long period of anticipation was finally bearing fruit.

"Why can't I just go with you to the agency?" her sister asked zestfully.

"No! Come on, Alika. That would be a little too weird, you know. I'll just have you drop me off and you can kill some time shopping or something. Sergei says we'll probably have lunch some place close. I'll call you and I'm sure they won't mind if you join us, but I want to meet him first."

"Oh! I can't wait! You think maybe he's rich?" Alika asked, rather bubbly.

"He's from some place called Lake Tahoe, in the mountains, I think. He has some kind of construction business. I do not care if he is so rich. Money is power,...and I have seen what power does to some men."

Alika giggled. "When are you going to tell Momma and Papa?"

"Alika! Promise me you won't say a word... Not a word! Let's see how this goes, first. And please tell me Misha doesn't know anything about this."

Alika sighed in obvious disappointment. "I promise. Misha would think you're crazy for doing this anyway."

Both sisters knew Alika's husband was openly opposed to his sister-in-law having an American boyfriend and the whole idea of these now popular international marriage agencies, as were most Russian and Ukrainian men. They also knew he wouldn't hesitate to tell their father about Irina's dealing with the agency, a topic which would cause some unpleasant conversation at the family dinner table.

"I'll tell Momma and Papa when the time is right," Irina stated.

⟫⟫⟫ ⟪⟪⟪

Fortunately, at least, the Amsterdam Schiphol International Airport was fairly new and modern with ample shops, exhibits, and restaurants, including three internet cafes, which were becoming very popular for travelers in an age prior to the widespread distribution of smartphones.

John walked into one of the cafes, purchased a coffee which was grossly overpriced, and sat down in front of one of the unoccupied PCs, operated by inserting a credit card which started charging the account by the minute. Anxious to retrieve his emails and particularly the one expected from Sergei, he typed in the website URL for Yahoo and was yet again frustrated when the screen kept displaying an error message:

ERROR—UNABLE TO ACCESS SERVER

He tried it again a couple times, and thinking perhaps the problem was caused by the café's system, John repeatedly entered a couple other websites he often used, including his main business software page, both of which pulled up immediately. *An ongoing problem with Yahoo email! How lucky can I be?*

Exasperated at sitting there staring at a computer screen while the meter was running, John logged out, pulled his card from the small device, and grabbed the printed receipt for seven euros and change, the equivalent of about ten US dollars.

Choosing to stroll around the concourse in order to shake off some jet lag, he killed some time by stopping in a small restaurant which served a decent breakfast along with another two cups of over-priced coffee. As he consumed the pleasantly tasty eggs benedict, he glanced around the busy terminal and spied two thirty something women who appeared to be sisters, reminding him of an incident over a year before....

.....He sat at the bar and ordered some appetizers and a drink, arriving twenty minutes early. The National League Division Playoffs were on the corner flat screen and he looked on as his team, the St. Louis Cardinals, were participating. It was a popular neighborhood pub in old St. Charles that his "date" had suggested as a first-time meeting place. He had told her on the phone that he would be wearing a Cardinal baseball cap and dark blue windbreaker jacket.

The woman approached and recognized John immediately from his posted photographs, smiling as the two exchanged a brief social introduction, just prior to her grabbing the adjacent empty bar stool. Her name was Carol, and she appeared somewhat older and heavier than her "match" ad had presented.

They chatted over a few drinks, sharing the typical life stories so common with blind dates. As with all such internet connection type greetings, John felt that something needed to "click". It wasn't there. Trying to be a gentleman by nature, he feigned interest but realized within minutes this "meet and greet" was a colossal waste of time.

The whole "internet" dating thing was anything but an exact science. The first thing John realized was these match dot com and similar websites were just personal infomercials, a place where virtual and reality were rarely mutual. The personal resumes often painted a very rosy picture of a perfect mating prospect with loads of positives and never anything negative. It was understandable. After all, one never applied for a job and bragged about punching the former boss in the nose. And the photographs,...only the very best of a person and often a cropped image from a group picture were posted. John could hardly criticize the women, he did the same thing himself, but at least his images were relatively current and to his credit, he was relatively fit for a man his age, having dropped over twenty pounds and spending some time in the gym since the divorce. And everyone past forty had to have some personal baggage, *didn't they?*

This gal had way too much make-up and John began to joke to himself how scary she would look getting out of bed in the morning. She had a propensity for using the F-word in every other sentence, a habit that snow-balled with every drink. Though not believing himself a "holier-than-thou" person, John became embarrassed over it and felt his skin crawl under his collar as he consciously wanted to look around and see if anyone else was staring at them or worse, may know him!

Sometimes fate does intercede, as Carol suddenly turned beet red as another woman tapped her on the shoulder and started to make some small talk, the two obviously well acquainted. When the woman smiled and looked over at John, he saw a resemblance in the two but the new gal obviously being younger and better looking.

"I'm Sherri, Carol's sister," the standing woman stated, following an awkward moment waiting for her sister to introduce her.

"John. A pleasure to meet you," he replied, smiling uncomfortably while throwing Carol a questioning glance.

You're the one in the pictures!... Give me a break!...

The rest of the introductory meeting became somewhat of a mockery as John had more of a conversation with the sister, even making a comment that Carol's picture looked more like Sheri, giving Carol the dubious look that the gig was up. The ball game ended which gave John a smooth way to say *Adios....*

....Watching as the two "sisters" entered one of the airport's restrooms, John was anxious to return to checking his emails. Venturing to an adjacent concourse to attempt another access to Yahoo, he found another internet café which appeared to be owned and operated by the same outfit, *so much for competitive pricing,* and repeated the previous exercise of entering his credit card and logging in, only to get the same exasperating result:

ERROR—UNABLE TO ACCESS SERVER

Looking at his watch for what seemed to be the thousandth time, John noticed it was now late morning. *Two and half more hours to kill before boarding my connecting flight.*

〜≫⟩⟩ ⟨⟨⟨〜

Alika dropped her sister off and Irina nervously walked into the building entrance, making her way to the second floor office. Sergei had not arrived yet with the gentleman, whom he had traveled through town to "collect". Irina's expectation was quite high for this "special occasion" and she had prepared herself and dressed accordingly.

Being a bit early, Natalyia Belanov invited Irina into her office for some coffee. An emotional pressure was in the air as even Natalyia herself appeared surprised that such an attractive young woman like Irina had not received much interest, especially since she had no children, which was a virtue in itself that generally served to attract more suitors. For the past four months, she had pushed her small staff to literally flood the system with "love" letters from Irina to nearly every male in the system between the ages of thirty and sixty-five years of age. Receiving, translating, and delivering the replies were indeed a main source of income for the "trade" and emailing out mass form letters were common, but for some strange reason Irina had received far less responses than average.

"Did this Robert travel all the way here just to see me?" Irina asked, with a mix of genuine curiosity and hope.

"Well, you are one of the main girls he's here for," the marriage agent replied, disguising the truth. Robert Smith had actually contacted Belanov directly and arranged to travel to Ukraine, planning to visit several such agencies in various cities in hopes of just meeting a woman on site. Few agents bought off on his last name as truly being *Smith,* as it seemed like over half the men from Europe, Canada, and America were either Smith or Jones. But they weren't in the business of questioning names, so long as these foreigners had money to spend. Of course, if and when a serious connection would occur, the name issue would surface, but agents would simply blame the men themselves and let them work to resolve it. "But if you do not see him as a fit for you, do not lose faith. When one door closes, another door always opens."

Irina's heart began to sink a little. *Oh no, all these months and finally a real live man and I have competition. And why would Natalyia tell me that before I even met this guy?*

Sergei and the gentleman soon arrived and the assistant agent introduced him to Irina, an exchange that seemed somewhat awkward when it was obvious the man didn't even recognize her by name, as if he hadn't specifically known in advance who he was meeting.

Despite this, his face brightened as he was quite smitten with this lovely girl, whose smile presented a maiden who could have easily passed for being even much younger than her twenty-seven years. His mood became somewhat bubbly at the prospect that a man like himself, hardly a poster boy for GQ magazine, could have an opportunity like this.

To his misfortune, Irina didn't feel the same "spark" for Robert. The man was relatively short, perhaps five foot eight, bald-headed, and had a beard that made him appear older than his age of forty-two years, augmented by much more gray hair than what appeared in his ad.

Irina was looking for the man who would literally change her life. After all the disappointments Irina had suffered through, she had placed high hopes on this working and a feeling of letdown set in. She feigned a smile while not avoiding a sideways glance toward Sergei's boss Natalyia, who forced an embarrassed smile herself, knowing immediately this was not going to become a match made in heaven.

Following an awkward silence, Sergei suggested the three of them break for an early lunch. Smith had done some research in advance and suggested they take a taxi to an upscale place in the northern part of the city. Irina was struggling to hide her disappointment and thoughts raced through her mind about what to do about her sister as she didn't really want Alika to meet this guy, nor did she want Smith to get the wrong idea that having the sister show up signaled any more interest on her part than was readily present.

Parking just up the crowded street, the French-style bistro was right next door to a popular night spot, one that Irina remembered all too well...

... Irina was fuming as she had been home from work two hours and put her weekend house cleaning into overdrive, a habit she seemed to always have at home when not in the best mood. Daryle had been away for five days visiting his parents who had flown into Kiev. It being mid-week and knowing that Irina worked, he hadn't offered to invite her to make the trip, a seven-hour drive, or had made any mention of his folks arranging travel to Kharkov, which all told implied he didn't want them meeting her. She angrily held back her tears as she wondered what this all meant. *Has he ever even mentioned me to his parents?*

She decided to call her friend, Olga, an old college roommate who lived in Kharkov that she hadn't seen in months, and the two decided to go out on the town. Irina showered and got dressed, about to head out when she heard the front door lock mechanism turn and a sheepish-looking Daryle walked in, his small roll-on baggage in tow.

Momentarily stunned, he approached and embraced Irina, all the while having the mixed emotion of seeing her look so stunning and yet wondering why she was obviously preparing to go out without him or even inquiring about his own whereabouts.

"Hey baby! Are you going out on a date?" He asked, attempting to lighten the mood.

"Well, hello Daryle. No, I didn't know you were back in town, so one of my best friends from college and I are going out... You're welcome to go with us."

Oh, oh. She's calling me "Daryle", not "honey"... Not good, Daryle observed. "Sure. Could I grab a quick shower first?"

The Galaktika Club, located on Augusta Street just a few kilometers north of downtown, was one of Kharkov's most popular night spots, catering mostly to the college-aged crowd. The place was packed as was typical for a Friday night in January, the first weekend following the Christmas and New Year holiday break.

The three paid the token cover charge, Irina reminded with mild disgust that she and Daryle seemed to always go "Dutch". Both Irina and Olga caught their share of stares and catcalls as they moved through the throng of party animals, an observation not lost on Daryle. Following nearly half an hour of standing in the crowd and waiting for a table or booth, the three shared mixed drinks while taking in the extreme sound system.

Spying a corner booth vacated by some other patrons, the three sat down, continuing to take in the rambunctious party ambience and spent quite a bit of time on the crowded dance floor. For her part, Irina had seemed to lose most of her temperamental vitriol toward Daryle, as the celebratory atmosphere took effect. The three offered toasts, laughed, and partied along with the crowd, running well past midnight.

As Olga got up to go and relieve herself, Daryle and Irina repeatedly hit the dance floor. She was an exceptional dancer and the two enjoyed one tune after another, the beat of the music loud among the thick mass and flashing strobe lights. She was here with her guy back, she had renewed her friendship with Olga, and the place just rocked. Life at the moment was good.

Following at least twenty minutes of shaking to the loud music, they shuffled back through the packed house to their booth and sat down, stealing a brief kiss together after commenting that Olga had been gone for quite a while. The attractive young woman, seductively clad in a tight-fitting and very short dress, returned several moments later complaining about the long wait in line to get into the women's room.

Irina had spent the evening holding off going to the restroom, knowing how long the line would be and not wanting to deal with it. Mother Nature, however, does eventually take its course and she finally succumbed to the pressure, left their booth, and headed through the crowd.

Arriving in the hallway near the front entrance that led to the restrooms, she saw how many girls were waiting in line, extending clear out into the crowd. After standing in the queue several minutes with seemingly no movement, she felt the bladder pressure was too great and worried she couldn't hold it. About that time, a guy who appeared to be with the club approached and whispered low that she was over an hour from the restroom door but if she wanted to go out in the parking lot behind the building, he would meet her at the front door and let her back in. She took advantage and stepped out into the cold, found a private spot to relieve herself, and then made her way back to the club's front entrance. The guy was there, standing in the doorway as if assigned as her personal bodyguard, a short, bearded man wearing sharp pressed slacks and matching coat. As he escorted Irina back in with little fanfare, she thought she recognized him, but in the dark, smoky place, who could be sure?

Re-entering the club and shaking off the cold but satisfied at how much time she'd saved, Irina made her way back through the crowd and approached their booth, freezing in shock. There before her sat her boyfriend and old college roommate all over each other while lip-locked together as if they were long-lost lovers, both who seemed fully oblivious to her presence. After screaming some out-of-character expletives, Irina's anger quickly became tears as she turned away and started for the exit.

"Irina, wait!" Daryle yelled as he caught her backside moving away through the crowd. It would all be dealt with in the following days with gifts and apologies. As Irina struggled on the drive home, her optimism about a future of life in America with the guy she thought as faithful suddenly seemed non-existent. Irina and Olga would never speak again. The damage had been done....

....A waiter appeared shortly after the three were seated, catching Irina's attention. After each ordered lunch entries, Sergei translated the back and forth.

Irina felt strange as she again looked up at the waiter and spoke to him in Russkie. "Do you have a brother?"

"Yes," the waiter replied. "But I am sorry to say he passed away many years ago."

"I am sorry. I just thought you look like someone—"

"Could I offer you drinks from the bar?" he asked, smoothly cutting her off.

The waiter, having gathered their drinks order, walked away with Irina still giving the man a curious look. *He's younger, but I swear he's the same...*

Smith, as it was learned, had never been married and gave the appearance of having a substantial degree of wealth, a point that he made certain was known to everyone present. Consuming a couple strong mixed drinks a bit too quickly, which was not lost on both Sergei and Irina, the tourist became a bit boisterous.

"So, Irina, how do you support yourself? I understand you people don't get paid very much."

Following Sergei's translation, she replied, "I'm a manager at a security company. I get paid okay. I know not as much as in America."

"Well, that would be no problem. You'll have a credit card with a budget, and you can go shopping and get you some nice clothes," he said, almost as a boast while awkwardly implying that her attire didn't meet with his specifications.

Irina took in Sergei's translation and ground her teeth. *This haughty ass thinks he's better than me!* She responded by instructing Sergei to answer with a stern, "I understand." She then sent Alika a text regarding where they were and to call her when she got close.

The lunch meeting continued to go downhill, notwithstanding Sergei's attempts to smooth things over with small talk. While the two locals each ordered hot tea, their waiter kept Smith indulged with more mixed drinks, causing him to become more and more flirty to the point of becoming an embarrassment.

For her part, Irina worked to remain polite but became quite uncomfortable and found herself looking around the café and hoping she wouldn't see anyone she knew there. The low point came when Sergei took it upon himself to bring up the topic of having children. Although still young by Western standards, a woman in her late twenties and still without a husband and children was looked upon questionably in Russian culture. Like many younger women who took out advertisements seeking marriage abroad, having children in the marriage would be an important condition to be discussed and agreed on.

"Irina wants to have a child with her husband, Robert. Is that something you would approve of?" Sergei asked innocently, then noticing Irina's blank look and knowing the question was overly presumptive and adding immeasurably to the discomfort of the visit.

"Oh yes!" Smith replied, answering with an awkwardly forward gesture of reaching out to hold Irina's hand. "We would look forward and would enjoy that part of the process, wouldn't we, Irina?"

Sergei turned beet red with embarrassment, knowing he had totally blown this event and feeling really bad for Irina being so subjected. He by now had a personal contempt himself for Smith and wished he and Irina could just leave the drunk and head out.

Irina didn't know how to react and feeling a hard lump in her throat, she quickly looked down at her watch, wondering where Alika was. Unwilling to endure any more of the disgusting slob, Irina tugged at Sergei's sleeve. "Oh my, I have to get going. My sister will be waiting for me."

Watching the young girl abruptly get up from their table and walk out on her own, Smith was temporarily speechless and then bellowed at Sergei, "What? Did I say something wrong?"

Meanwhile, John went through a few terminal shops and being an avid reader, browsed through the many hardcover books for sale, most in a foreign language, and various magazines which were mostly oriented toward European travelers. Focusing on nothing in particular, John purchased some mints and began the long hike back to his assigned concourse, stopping one last time at the first internet café to check his emails. Yet again, John was confronted with the same network error message that fed the mixed anxiety he would feel on that last three-hour flight, final arrival in Ukraine and wanting, no hoping, that the email from Sergei would be awaiting to access.

In anticipation of meeting Anna, John had done some yeoman research on her city, wanting to see and do some interesting things while he was there. What he learned was that Kharkov was mostly a regional industrial and distribution city, and while it did have a large university there, there were no well-known museums or landmarks that he could see. John was prone to have interest in historical sites and Kharkov did have a long past militarily, particularly during the Great Patriotic War, but visiting old battlefields wouldn't serve to promote any romance. And the place was cold! The average temperature there in late November was below freezing. *I hope Anna is worth this,* he thought... *Well, there's always Odessa.*

Due to poor quality cell phone service, Alika had not received the text message and thus remained stranded, wandering what had happened, not-to-mention being annoyed and worried about her sister. Irina had stepped outside in the weather and called Alika, who took a full twenty minutes to motor through the city and picked her up around the corner from the bistro.

"Well? Tell me about it, Irina!" Alika asked anxiously.

Having all kinds of emotions right then, Irina's disappointment abound foretold that the dream man she drove to meet was more like a nightmare. She felt anger toward the agency that they couldn't produce a better man for her and having a hard time understanding why she had received such limited interest from these foreign men, she began to wither in self-doubt. The agency had thought from day one that a lovely young single woman with no children would attract an extreme amount of attention. At the security company where she was office manager, all the guys who worked there would hit on her constantly.

But she was not going to settle for any of their type, a life of misery with men who were alcoholics, and she wasn't going to become a trophy for a rich criminal who cheated on his wife. She was trying not to lose hope, but it was becoming difficult...very difficult.

"The entire lunch meeting was awful! The guy was a pig! Sergei was asking very personal questions! I couldn't wait to leave. I'm so sorry you didn't get my text. The only bright spot was the waiter, who made sure that fool got drunk and gave me an easy excuse to get out... Almost as though he knew me... What a nightmare!"

The two sisters rode back southeast toward Chuguev, both now well-worn for the experience. The two talked more at length about Irina's huge letdown and Alika knew that her sister was devastated.

"Look at the bright side, Irina. At least now you will not have to shock Momma and Papa," Alika said, in a futile effort to cheer her sister up.

Irina just rode on in silence. *Sure, Alika. Little comfort that is, though.*

"Misha says Kolya is still asking about you."

"No," Irina replied simply, not wanting to imply that anyone like her brother-in-law was undesirable. Kolya was kind of handsome, for certain, but what kind of life would she have to look forward to? A crowded apartment, living from paycheck to paycheck, never seeing beyond the borders of the Oblast, and an average Ukrainian man who drank too much and cheated on his wife? *I'll pass.*

Still disappointed her relationship with Daryle hadn't worked out and indeed seeing his departure as a betrayal, the young American had opened her eyes to new possibilities, opportunities of a whole world out there, one that beckoned beyond the borders of the Kharkov Oblast. She had seen the Belanov

Agency as a possible gateway to that world, a gateway that now seemed abundantly distasteful. *There has to be something better for me... Somewhere.*

CHAPTER FIVE

Poor Internet Connections

T he three-hour flight aboard the Ukrainian International Airlines Boeing 737 was smooth and uneventful with John passing the time reading the newest Vince Flynn novel. He noticed the passengers having a much less "Yankee" feel compared to the flight from the states to Amsterdam, and strangely found himself looking astutely at the onboard stewardesses, subconsciously thinking the mysterious woman whom he'd seen before was destined to reappear. He recalled Boryspil, a large and busy facility as was typical for European capital cities. After nearly an hour spent retrieving his luggage from baggage claim, John lumbered through the immigration customs line.

Having grown up and being educated to fear and guard against the Soviet Union, KGB, etc., John's anxiety from the entry here back in the spring was somewhat calmed this trip because of having no issues before.

John had no mobile phone as his own wouldn't work here unless he was willing to pay an arm and a leg in roaming and access charges to use it. There were various resources, including outlets at the airport to acquire throw away phones but, again, the cost of using such phones to call home was astronomical and he couldn't use them to communicate with the locals because of the language barrier, regardless.

Spying the internet café, John sat down and repeated his well-rehearsed exercise of logging in to these rent-a-computers and attempting to access his emails. *Bad luck! Again!*

ERROR—UNABLE TO ACCESS SERVER

Now John was nearly beside himself, wishing he had a different or alternate email address. His final leg flight tickets were not purchased yet as UIA offered shuttle flights to and from Kiev and Ukraine's other larger cities two or three times per day, with ample availability pretty much on the spot, something which he recalled from his earlier trip.

He found himself wandering around the airport terminal, somehow willing his Yahoo emails to magically appear and all the while in a panic as to what he should do next. *Perhaps this is an omen...that I shouldn't even go to Kharkov.*

⟫⟫ ⟪⟪

Irina got home that evening, blowing off an invite from her parents to have dinner. Never one to hide her emotions for very long, she didn't feel like sitting in front of the family and having to explain anything. She strolled into the apartment, went straight for her bedroom, shut the door, laid down, and began to sob. *How could this all happen to me? I feel so used.*

Moments later, she heard a knock on the door. "Irina, is everything okay?"

Dimitri...please go away!

"Irina? It's Dimitri. Are you all right?"

Who else could it be? "Yes Dimitri, good night!"

⟫⟫ ⟪⟪

The weather outside was cold and wet. Having still no confirmation of any kind that everything with Sergei and Anna was a go, John was torn on what to do. Kharkov was Ukraine's second largest city, indeed about the size of metropolitan St Louis, but it's location in the northeastern part of the country didn't render the place as much of a touristic paradise, at least not in late November. Odessa, on the other hand, was on the Black Sea, and having been there before, John was generally more comfortable going there, especially having known real people, Sofiya, her husband Vasyli, and their friend Lana.

He worked his way up to the UIA ticket counter, thinking he would just fly to Odessa, grab a hotel room for the night, contact the agency there, arrange an apartment earlier than planned, and meet with this Larisa, the pretty doctor. The whole ordeal about not being able to access his Yahoo emails just felt bad and John was disgruntled with getting himself into such an indecisive spot when twenty-four hours earlier he had left home with such high hopes.

The ticket agent spoke broken English and John understood she was punching in the information off his passport and seemed stymied that her system wouldn't take it for the next flight he wanted.

John initially felt disgust toward the system these Ukrainians no doubt had, probably DOS based, but then thought better of it. *Yahoo is an American company and look at them!*

Becoming impatient, the agent apologized. "I am sorry Mr. Masters, but there seems to be a problem with the shuttle flights to Odessa."

Now Odessa?... Please. John thought, not knowing what to say.

"If you would kindly stand by, I will get my supervisor."

John stood looking around, his immediate thoughts concerned they were having a problem with his passport. After a brief wait, an authoritative but attractive woman approached the counter with her subordinate. Not just authoritative...but strangely familiar.

You?... No... Yes, you!... I must be losing it. He then subconsciously turned, making a gesture with his thumb to point backward and made a quiet statement. "You were just"...

The supervisor interrupted John, who seemed to have his mind somewhere else. "Excuse me, sir?"

Briefly coming out of his malaise, John replied, "Yes."

"Sir, I'm afraid there has been some sort of chemical gas leak at the airport in Odessa. All flights into Odessa have been cancelled until further notice."

"Cancelled until further notice? What does that mean?" he asked, rolling his eyes and wondering what else could go wrong.

"I'm afraid that's all I can tell you, Sir. May I help you with anything else?"

John wasn't sure how to respond, mesmerized that this woman kept appearing. *I must be going crazy... All these foreign women are looking alike now.* John looked at his watch, again. He could try to check into a hotel, but with his luck, the disaster that was causing all the problems in Odessa would still be there tomorrow. Meanwhile, other travelers were waiting impatiently in line behind him.

"Sir?"

"Okay, what about a flight to Kharkov?"

The supervisor took control of the screen herself and replied, "Yes, sir. There is availability on the next shuttle to Kharkov, departing at 7:30 PM and arriving at 9:40 PM. The fare one-way is nineteen hundred seventy-two hryvnias... That is eighty US dollars," she stated with a slight grin as if knowing he wouldn't be familiar with the local currency.

"All right, sell me a ticket to Kharkov," John told the two.

The supervisor pointed to something on the screen and then turned the process over to the original agent, moving away to the adjacent counter to assist another agent. Completing the transaction and retrieving his documents, John prepared to depart as he and the supervisor shared a very brief and final glance.

Did she just wink at me?

⟫⟫ ⟪⟪

It struck John like a bolt of lightning. Unlike the modern, sleek commuter jet he had flown on in April between Kiev and Odessa, this plane appeared to be an old dual-engine prop plane that appeared on the tarmac as "shaky" at best, while John and the few other passengers jogged through the falling rain to board it.

The plane had a narrow fuselage with an aisle in the center and two really cramped and uncomfortable rows of seats on each side. One of the first things that struck him was the back of the seats in front of him were constructed out of plywood. A fellow passenger sat across the aisle, a gentleman who appeared as either another American, or perhaps a Canadian or Western European.

"State-of-the-art, huh?" John asked the fellow, sarcastically while feigning a glance around the plane's interior.

"Yes, it is," the stranger replied, shaking hands with John and introducing himself as Nigel, while a young man appearing to be right out of high school and sporting the uniform of a pilot, squeezed up the aisle between the two passengers, carrying some sort of notebook. "I think that's the flight instruction manual."

The two shared a brief chuckle prior to hearing the twin engines come to life as the single stewardess paraded down the aisle to check the seat belt status for each passenger. They felt the craft shutter as it taxied down the tarmac before roaring to life, turning and running hard down the runway.

John found himself reaching down and grabbing the edges of his seat in an imagined effort to secure himself as the Yakovlev "Yak", an early 1980s-built plane, seemed to vibrate heavily before finally smoothing out as it became airborne, beginning the two-hour flight to Kharkov.

Unlike the three previous flights that were all smooth to the point of being relaxing, this shuttle flight was anything but, to the point of being frightening. The hard rain had turned into a thunderous storm causing the small plane, which vibrated in fair weather, to shake rather violently. John, who was quite a study of history militarily, found himself glancing out the window of the old plane and fantasizing about German Messerschmitt fighters coming at them. Not a fearful person by nature, he closed his eyes and began to pray, thinking he'd best make peace with his maker.

As if the shuttle flight itself wasn't enough of a shock, the arrival at the airport in Kharkov did little to lower John's anxiety, although there was the temporary sensation of feeling the plane touch down. The weather had changed from a cold rain to a mixture of sleet and light snow. As Kharkov had a population of nearly two million, he expected a relatively large and modern airport. What he encountered was an airport reminiscent of the small regional airport in his hometown of Cape Girardeau, as the plane came to a stop several hundred meters from the terminal. With no baggage transport system or baggage claim, he and the other passengers had to wait outside the aircraft in the elements to retrieve their stowed luggage and then scurry afoot through the freezing rain to the terminal entrance.

Once inside, all the passengers had to undergo a check-in through security, as though he was entering yet another country. John was confronted by a very grim and suspicious-looking woman, middle-aged, stocky, and with short cut hair that he saw as a maroon color, made all the more homely with her three front gold teeth and wearing an official uniform that appeared to be a couple sizes too small. John saw her as a mental image of the "KGB woman", the result of the many cold war motion pictures produced by Hollywood over the years. *Surely my dream woman won't look so intimidating when she gets…my age?*

Glaring at John's passport for what felt like an eternity, she looked up at him in a suspicious tone and asked, "What is your business here in Kharkov, Mr. Masters?"

"I am here as a tourist on personal business."

"I see. Do you have any cash or narcotics in your baggage?"

"No, none of that," he replied. "I have a few dollars in my wallet."

"Open please so I may examine," she demanded.

John quickly complied, wondering why she asked about the contents when she planned to rummage through his belongings anyway. The stern woman pulled out every item, piece by piece, all the while watching for John's reaction as if he worried about something. Following the ransacking of his luggage, the "KGB woman" registered the weight of the bag, stamped his passport, and then handed it back while the both shared a speechless stare.

After passing through the checkpoint, John made his way to the main lobby of the terminal and looked around for Anna, or anyone else holding up any type of welcome sign with his name on it. Much to his chagrin, no one in the crowded terminal looked familiar or seemed whatsoever to be on the lookout for a guy like him. Adding to his consternation, unlike the airport in Kiev which was much more "international", there was no signage in English or any other foreign language and no one within ear-sight spoke a word he could comprehend, as John now wondered how he would even communicate with a taxi driver.

After thirty to forty minutes of wandering around and getting more and more desperate with the airport obviously near closing time, John spied a young woman with her back to him talking on a cell phone. Walking up to her and tapping her on the shoulder, John again thought he was seeing things when she turned around.

Oh my god! "You again?"

The woman was younger, blond-headed, wearing a scarf, and heavy coat with little or no makeup or lipstick, although facially appeared strikingly familiar. She smiled in mild confusion and threw up her hands. "English, no. Only Russkie or Ukrainian."

John could swear he knew her, but she reacted as though she had never seen him before, thus he reached into his shirt pocket and pulled out a note with Sergei's name and local phone number, as well as a twenty-dollar bill. After some initial confusion and a few minutes of rather theatrical sign language, the young woman figured out what John was attempting to communicate, took the twenty, and dialed Sergei's number.

Hoping Sergei would answer and not get a voicemail, John was relieved when he heard her speaking to someone and after a moment handed John her phone.

"Hello," John stated while sharing a look of gratitude toward the young woman whose cell phone he was temporarily *renting*.

"Hello John," Sergei answered, assuming his guest client had arrived safely by the local number that appeared on his cell. "Welcome to Kharkov. Did you get my message?"

"No Sergei. There was a problem with my Yahoo email and I haven't been able to retrieve any emails since I left home. Where is Anna?"

"Oh, John. I sent you an email just after we talked yesterday. Anna is very busy, and she will not be available to meet you until Saturday afternoon."

John felt as though he was stabbed right in the back. "What? This woman knew I was traveling halfway around the world to meet her, and she's busy! I'm here at the airport and don't know a soul!"

Sergei could tell by the tone that John was not a happy camper. "John, would you like me to come pick you up or would you prefer to take a taxi to your apartment?"

Looking at his watch and seeing it was now past ten thirty, the extremely distraught American replied, "I guess I can take a taxi, Sergei." He really didn't want to see Sergei in his current state, blatantly upset and suspecting the agency was partially to blame.

"There's a security kiosk at the apartment that has your key to get in, John. I will give the address to Yana. That is her name. Call me if you have any problems. Otherwise, I'll call you in the morning when I get to the office."

John gave the young woman her phone back. She and Sergei spoke briefly and he asked that she assist John in arranging a cab for the ride into the city, and then closed by thanking her. Yana ended up playing cab driver herself and chauffeured the American to the apartment near downtown.

The trip from the airport took nearly thirty minutes. A still angry John was feeling both foolish and somewhat vulnerable as the small vehicle stopped in front of what appeared to be an alley. He prepared to get out of her car and reached for his wallet to pay. To his surprise, Yana looked at him shaking her head and held up her hands, telling him she would not accept any more compensation. As he exited the car, she smiled and waved as she quickly drove off.

Feigning a smile himself, John strolled down the narrow, dimly lit lane several meters before finally approaching a rather tired looking young man in a security kiosk, who asked for identification prior to handing over a key and note with an apartment number to John, who thanked him sincerely, receiving a simple nod in return.

He then strode to the entrance of the building and assumed the elevator wouldn't operate, thus chose the stairway instead and made his way up to the second floor to his apartment. Unlocking the door and entering, the three-room dwelling appeared somewhat dingy compared to the apartment he rented in Odessa seven months before and was extremely cold as the thermostat was set at seven degrees Celsius, which was forty-five degrees Fahrenheit.

The entire episode of the flight, no one to meet him at the airport, and now this cold apartment began to give John pause about his decision to come to Kharkov, and he started to think he might just pack up first thing in the morning and head back to Kiev, still hoping to salvage something out of the trip in Odessa.

It was a typical Soviet era apartment starting with a hallway and closet, which had coat hangers, shoe racks, and a mirror. There was a bathroom accessible from the corridor which served the entire residence, one bedroom furnished with a double bed, a parlor or front room (although it wasn't located near the front), and a small kitchen. The parlor had some rudimentary furniture, including a couch with a fold-out bed which served as a second bedroom when serving multiple occupants.

Adjusting the heat up to twenty-one degrees Celsius, John waited a few moments and worried the heat wouldn't kick in. To his relief, the old blower motor finally began to whine and the floor vents began to put out a musty smelling but warm draft while John began to unpack. The place did have a land line phone and internet, but it was of the old phone jack variety and thoughts subsided over sending a message home to Johnny that he'd made it over safely. A very tired John now looked forward to some sleep.

Waking up early, John searched the near empty apartment for anything that resembled breakfast. The weather outside was cold and cloudy and without any means of transportation or knowledge of the neighborhood, he wasn't all that anxious to take off on foot in search of something.

He did find a small jar of instant coffee in the cupboard and a hot water kettle with that funny looking plug-in attached to it. He searched the refrigerator, an old rounded unit that he recalled as a child, commonly referred to as an ice box, for some bottled water and creamer but found nothing but some sort of homemade-looking cheese. He quickly grabbed it and after a brief examination and with a sour look on his face, discarded it in the small waste basket in the cabinet under the sink.

Turning on the faucet, he eyed the water suspiciously, trying to decide if this city water was pure enough to drink or not. *Come on, John boy. This isn't Mexico.* Assuming the electric kettle would heat to a boil, he filled it and plugged it in when he heard a dull pop and the lights in the kitchen and the parlor all went dark. Looking around for some semblance of a circuit breaker or fuse box, he couldn't find one and hoped against hope he still had hot water.

At just past 8:00 AM local time, the land line phone in the parlor rang and he rushed to pick it up, hearing Sergei's welcome voice on the other end.

"Good morning, John. Does the apartment meet with your expectations?"

"It's okay, Sergei, except I need to know where the circuit breaker box is." John replied, a man by nature as having seldom spent money for upscale lodging when traveling, needing only a clean, warm bed and a hot shower.

"Oh, John! I forgot to warn you about not turning on too many lights and appliances at once. The apartment shares a master fuse box with three others."

About that time, the apartment lights came back on, and in short order, a very hard knock was heard coming from the front door. John started to move toward answering it when he realized he had a cord attached to the phone and its length wasn't going to cooperate with him. Meanwhile, the pounding on the door persisted.

"Hang on a minute, Sergei. Someone at the door."

Hope this isn't the KGB, planning to drag my rear end out of here and send me to the gulags... No, that would have happened in the middle of the night.

John opened the door and was confronted by a very old woman, dressed rather shabbily and screaming at him in Russian while holding up an ancient-looking darkened glass fuse. Unable to communicate but assuming it must have something to do with the kettle blow up, John first held up a finger to indicate a pause and pointed to himself.

"American...uh, only speak English. No Russian. No Ukrainian." Sensing his remarks had garnered no sympathy from the obviously outraged babushka,

John waved her in and motioned for her to follow him into the parlor before picking up the phone.

"Sergei, this woman here is mad as can be about something and I think it's the fuse box thing. Talk to her, please!"

John handed the phone to the woman, who then proceeded to engage in a heated conversation with Sergei for a few moments. Finally calming down a slight bit, she handed the phone back over.

"John, this is one of your neighbors there. Whatever you did that caused that fuse to blow affected her apartment, also. She has already replaced the blown fuse but is demanding you either replace it or pay her for it."

Wow, the electricians who built this place had too much vodka. "I can do that. How much is it?"

"It would be about twenty hryvnias," Sergei answered quickly, having obviously a history of dealing with this fuse issue in John's apartment before.

"How much is that in US dollars?"

"It is about one US dollar, John."

"Okay, hang on a minute."

John put the phone down on the couch, gave a hand signal to the stern looking woman, and ran into the bedroom. Retrieving his wallet, he saw that he didn't have anything less than a five-dollar bill, thinking it would be too complicated to get change. The five was worth it just to get her to shut up. He moved quickly back to the parlor where the cantankerous old woman stood, held the Lincoln note up in front of her, and then handed it over before ushering her toward the door.

Like giving a pacifier to a baby, the woman quickly lowered her tone, and while walking out, John could hear her mumble something as she turned to look back at him, understanding none of her gibberish except picking out the word *Amerikans*, the context not sounding full of gratitude but her level of vitriol diminished nevertheless.

"Okay Sergei. Now, where were we?"

"John, since Anna won't be available until tomorrow afternoon, what are your plans for today?" Sergei was such a congenial young man, John had difficulty blaming him for what was, thus far, a less than stellar impression of Kharkov.

"Sergei, first of all, I am not having any meeting with this Anna. This woman knew I was traveling halfway around the globe to meet her and she's too busy! Screw that! I'm not meeting her tomorrow or any day for that matter. If you wouldn't mind giving me a ride to the airport, I'd just like to pack up and head back home," John stated, not disclosing his plan to just head across country to Odessa a few days earlier than planned. "Question now is, how could I get a refund on the rest of the rent for this apartment?"

Sergei could tell John was still quite upset and attempted to lower the temperature with some polite diplomacy. "John, I'm sorry for the mix up with Anna. How about I come by to collect you and bring you to our office? While you're here, perhaps we could introduce you to someone else."

John paused to think about it, feeling a bit guilty if he came across as rude to this young man, one who wasn't responsible for Yahoo's email server and likely not responsible for this Anna's footloose attitude. "I guess I could do that, Sergei." *What would I have to lose?*

"Great, John. Could you be ready by ten o'clock?"

"I'll be waiting."

Sergei showed up at ten sharp and the two departed in his mid-nineties model Chevy Malibu while John noticed an infant safety seat in the back. *A young family to feed.* He indicated the need for some breakfast and was happy when Sergei took him to visit a nearby McDonald's restaurant where he enjoyed a meal distinctly American, although the coffee was extremely stronger and cups smaller than he was used to.

The morning weather was chilly but clear as they drove through downtown Kharkov and John's attitude toward the eastern Ukrainian city began to thaw as he saw streets and business establishments relatively clean without an excess of rubbish and vagrants, readily too visible in the larger cities back home. Located just off Kooperatyvna, a main east-west boulevard, the Belanov Agency was a small one room office on the second floor of a five-story building, above a clothing storefront.

Sergei introduced John to his boss, Natalyia, and John became wide-eyed and nearly froze. *You're the same woman!... My old insurance agent's wife, the stewardess on KLM, the ticket agent's supervisor, the girl with the phone at the airport, and now...The folks are right. I really have lost my mind!*

John held his tongue, not familiar with the local customs on committing those to a mental institution. They discussed the situation with Anna, and Natalyia admitted the woman was kind of a flake and not a serious woman.

After speaking briefly about what John was looking for, Natalyia instructed Sergei to hand him their catalog. Now before the foreigner was a thick three-ring binder, one with many pages having transparent sleeves to insert photographs, letters, etc. Each ad presentation encompassed two pages and included a half-page summary that spelled out most pertinent "specifications" about each woman, or as the agency liked to refer to them as "girls".

He glanced through the pages briefly before commenting. *There must be two hundred women here!* John thought to himself. "These gals are all available?"

Sergei and his boss chuckled at John's referring to the women as *gals. An American guy definitely from the American South or Midwest.* "Just start on page one and note the ones you would like to meet," Sergei declared.

"All of them?" John yelled.

"You can meet anyone you want, John. But you can only take one home," Sergei replied jokingly.

John slowly began to venture through the pages of the catalog, all two-page ads featuring two or three photographs and an outline form of basic information on each woman indicating their age, height and weight, city of residence, children if any, and short paragraph regarding their desires, John noting that nearly all of those were pretty much identical, a dream to meet and marry a *Western* man and raise a family. He also noted that all of them promoted their culinary skills in cooking "tasty dishes".

John browsed past a goodly half the pages before hesitating and stopping abruptly at one. *Wow... Looks like Cindy Crawford!* "I think I would like to meet this one," he declared excitedly as he sat viewing the open two-page ad featuring an extremely beautiful tall brunette. *At thirty, probably too young, but WOW!*

Sergei glanced over to Natalyia as if unable to advise on his own and his boss got up from behind her desk and walked over to the leather couch, sitting down next to this potential suitor, one whom she appeared to have a very good impression of.

"John, let me ask you a question. Are you a rich man?"

John appeared puzzled for a moment, unsure of the purpose of such a question. "Well, no. I do very well in my profession in America, but I wouldn't be one who would be considered rich."

"John, this girl is one you Americans would refer to as high maintenance."

John grinned as he tried to hide his disappointment. "Oh, no!... Well, I guess we can't have that."

Natalyia continued to sit next to him, causing a little bit of a distraction because he felt as if he knew her, or thought she was mysteriously familiar. He examined a few more ads and stopped at a second one, a lovely looking woman, thirty-four years of age, her featured photographs jumping out at him as she was nearly nude! *Looks wild,* he thought, reminding himself of a girlfriend he had back in his twenties, her lifelong goal to become a centerfold for Playboy magazine.

Sergei observed his reaction and commented. "She is a really nice person."

Somehow your tone doesn't support that, John observed slowly shaking his head. "No, a bit bold for my tastes."

Still disappointed that *Cindy Crawford* was off the table and not wanting a girl from the local gentleman's club, he browsed through and past most of the remaining ads quickly as Natalyia took note. *My, this American is picky!*

When John quickly by-passed one particular girl, Natalyia interrupted him and backtracked to reopen the two-page ad she thought he should have interest in but passed over a bit too soon. "Say, what about this girl?"

John studied the ad for a moment. "I remember this gal. I think she sent me a letter back in August, or around then. I didn't reply to it."

Not letting go, Natalyia asked, "Why not?"

John looked over the ad again briefly, remembering he had pulled up this one on the web, after he received her letter. "Well, she's too young for one thing. I'd like a woman somewhat younger than me, eight to twelve years maybe, but she's only twenty-seven! That's too much difference and besides that, she weighs as much as I do!"

Sergei began to chuckle as he and his boss shared a look. "John, she was in here yesterday and she's not much overweight." Sergie realized his boss had typed in Irina's weight incorrectly when setting up her ad. The 97 kilograms should have been 57 kilograms. *Now we know why Irina's responses have been so few.*

"Well, it says here she weighs ninety-seven kilograms," he replied. "I remember calculating the conversion when I first saw this." He then retrieved his flip cell phone from his pocket, not active overseas but still functioning as a calculator, among other things. "Oh! That's two hundred thirteen pounds!"

Natalyia reached over and pointed to the photos displayed in the ad. "Does that look like a big woman to you?"

"Hey," John replied, "I have a little experience with these online pictures being, should I say, outdated. It doesn't matter, she's still too young for me anyway."

Natalyia backed off and headed back to her desk as a call had come in, all the while grinning at him as though poking fun. John got completely to the end of the catalog, and with the exception of the *Cindy Crawford* look-alike, he wasn't all that drawn to any of them. He then began to review the ads again, spending a bit more time on each one. *How stupid am I? Why should I assume half these women in here would think I'm such a bargain either?*

John seemed to settle on a woman named Tonya, thirty-eight years of age, fairly attractive, and had a fourteen-year-old daughter. "I guess I could meet this gal," John claimed as he turned the catalog around to show Sergei the ad.

"Oh yes, Tonya. Very nice person. She works at an office just down the street. How about I call her?" Sergie offered.

"Okay."

Sergei dialed the phone, got an answer, and then proceeded to have a conversation, none of which John could understand, of course. After a few minutes, Sergei held his hand over the phone's mic. "Tonya says she can meet you for lunch, if you'd like."

Wow, that was easy. "Sure. I assume you would be joining us. The language thing." John wished he could just meet and talk to one of these women one-on-one, but not practical yet, unless he wanted to try all sign language.

Sergei concluded the call and informed John they would be meeting Tonya at a restaurant down the street at noon, about an hour away. Natalyia could tell John wasn't all that excited about it and pushed for something to be revisited. She again got up from behind her desk and walked over to where he was sitting, grabbed the catalog that he was obviously finished with, and proceeded to open it to a predetermined page.

"John Masters, you should meet this girl. She's perfect for you!"

John didn't argue and refocused on the ad that this woman, the one with different colored hair, lipstick, and glasses but still all too familiar, was so insistent upon. *Irina Balabanova. She is kind of pretty. No kids. If I was just a few years younger...*

"I'm just not looking for a woman that much younger than me," John stated, although a bit more reserved.

Natalyia persisted, "If she doesn't have a problem with your age, why would you have a problem with hers?"

John paused and looked at Natalyia a brief moment before answering, glancing at this Irina's ad again. *Actually, she really is quite pretty.* "I guess that's a good question," John replied. "Is she paying you an extra commission or something? Why are you so adamant about promoting this girl?" he added, now himself referring to the young woman as a "girl".

"I'm telling you, John Masters! Irina Balabanova is perfect for you! Why not just agree to meet her? What harm would that do?"

"Oh, I'm all right with meeting her." *Waste of time, though.* "Let's make it this evening, perhaps."

Natalyia grinned and scurried back to her desk. "I'll call her myself."

❧❧❧❧

Irina sat at her desk struggling to work on a new contract, wishing she had just called in sick again. She was still upset at the way the meeting had gone in Kharkov with this Robert character and she was just put out with Sergei, his boss Natalyia, and the whole internet marriage ad routine.

One of the techs, Alexa, came into her office to drop off his report and like most of the rest of the crew, couldn't resist the chance to hit on their attractive office manager, as the whole company all knew she didn't seem to have a man in her life now, and hadn't had for months. "Irina? You look so down today. Maybe I could cheer you up by taking you out to lunch?"

"Thanks Alexa, but I'm in no mood and have to run some errands at lunch, anyway," she countered. *Yes, I could use some cheering up. But it wouldn't come from someone like you,...or any of the other grunts in this company,...or anyone in this whole town either.*

Alexa walked out, dejected. Irina didn't like to hurt his feelings but the company frowned heavily on fraternization anyway, and he should have known better. She had spent months waiting and waiting and finally the agency had called, as a real live man from America was coming to their office to meet her. She had spent hours spinning in her mind a vision of what this man would be like. How would he look? How would he dress? How would he treat her? How many days would he be here? Would he like her?

She had taken a sick day off the day before and got up early, fixing her hair, applying the perfect makeup, and adorning her best holiday dress. Even her roommate, Dimitri, noticed something was up. He had always desired her and noticed how fine she always appeared, even just to go to work at the security company. But today? She was different and he worried, always thinking in the back of his mind that if her loneliness became great enough and he lived there?... *Well, maybe.*

"Will you be in late tonight, Irina?" he had asked her that previous morning, just before leaving for work himself.

Taken aback, she had paused while adding the perfect touch of lipstick. *What business is that of yours?* she had thought and decided not to answer.

With all the excitement building up to the previous day's event, Irina had talked her sister into tagging along, and Alika was all too willing, as the intrigue of her sister meeting some stranger through an international marriage agency excited her also. But the entire day had been a total flop, a complete letdown,...an emotional disaster.

Irina kept glancing up at the clock and willing the day to move quickly,...And for what? To sit and sulk in her apartment while Dimitri kept playing his little unwelcome come-ons all weekend? *Oh god, spare me.*

She left the building for lunch and grabbed a quick to-go sandwich before walking down to the post office and then to a nearby market to shop for some personal items. She returned to the office just under an hour later and spied a bouquet of flowers on her desk. Picking up the large attached envelope, she opened it and read the handwritten note:

Cheer up, my lovely. Tomorrow will be a brighter day!
– A secret friend and admirer

Slightly blushing, she looked around the office, at first thinking it must have been one of the staff techs, as more than one had a crush on her, but discounted it and now thinking maybe it could possibly be that Robert who had met her yesterday. *But how would he know where I worked? And if it was him, he surely wouldn't sign it as "A Secret Admirer".* She thought momentarily about calling Belanov and asking them about it, but then thought better of it. *I hope this isn't some trick to give this Robert a second chance... No way.*

Hanging on the desk phone multiple times that afternoon, Irina droned on with a very old and boring woman who worked for one of the company's customers, a typical complaint about their bill, when she heard the familiar ring and vibration of her cell phone chattering away in her purse. Switching the land line to her left hand and reaching down to her purse with the other, she opened it and retrieved her cell, seeing the caller ID pop up on the small screen.

Belanov Agency? I'll let it go to voicemail.

Irina concluded her conversation with the client, strolling over to a file cabinet where she would pull the file pertaining to the billing discrepancy she was quite certain the customer was misguided about, when her cell phone rang again.

Belanov again... Probably want to apologize. Irina paused while letting it ring four times and then decided to answer as a two-way conversation ensued. "This is Irina."

"Irina! This is Natalyia Belanov! I have a man from America here that you have to meet!"

Get real, please! "Natalyia, I think I'm through with this internet match-making stuff. It's just not working out for me," Irina replied.

"Irina, wait! I know that guy yesterday was a disappointment. I know you're not happy about it. But there is a guy named John Masters, right here in my office, and he's just perfect for you!"

Leaning back in her chair and rolling her eyes in resignation, Irina prepared to listen, at least briefly. "All right. What can you tell me about him?"

"Irina, he's tall, he has blond hair, a mustache, good shape... Irina, he is so handsome. He's perfect for you!"

Sounds too good to be true. "Where is he from?"

"He is from Missouri, near St. Louis. That is in the center of America. Irina, he is just the right guy for you!"

"Natalyia, how old is he?"

"He's fifty. Irina, you have to meet him!"

Irina was shocked. "Fifty! Fifty?... No."

Natalyia was not deterred. "Irina, I know you and I know this man. You would be perfect together!"

"You know him? How?"

"Irina, you just have to trust me on this. I know what I'm doing."

Yeah, sure. Like that pig, Robert, you had me meet yesterday. "He's too old for me! I don't want to go to Kharkov again and waste my time, Natalyia."

"Irina, if he doesn't have a problem with your age, why would you have a problem with his?"

Fair question. But why is she so pushy about this? "I will meet him, but I know it's a waste of time."

"How soon can you get here?"

"I'm working today, Natalyia, and because I took off yesterday, I'm behind and will have to work late. Maybe tomorrow?"

"Hang on a moment," Natalyia said quickly and covered the microphone with her hand. "John, how about tomorrow over lunch?"

John looked up, somewhat encouraged by these women all being so cooperative. "Lunch tomorrow? Sure."

Natalyia returned to her conversation with Irina. "It's on. Be here in the office by eleven. Irina, you're going to like this guy."

"We'll see, Natalyia. Bye," she answered before disconnecting, much less enthusiastic than she was the last time they called.

At the Belanov office, Natalyia hung up her phone and twisted around in her chair, smiling. "It's set for tomorrow at lunch, John. Irina Balabanova cannot wait to meet you!"

❯❯❯❯ ❮❮❮❮

Irina got back to work, always having a habit to complete all open projects on Friday as not to begin the next week with a full desk. She couldn't help thinking about the next day's lunch meeting, dubious as she felt after yesterday's disaster. *What makes Natalyia think this John is so perfect for me? She doesn't know me that well. At least she should know a bit about what I'm NOT looking for now.*

Twenty minutes later, Arkady Petrov, the owner of the company, walked in and the two had some casual routine conversation about the business, scheduling, pending contracts, etc. The two had shared a less than cordial relationship since the fiasco with Colonel Kuznetsov, who had not returned to their facility since. As he left to walk back in his office, he paused and turned. "Oh, I forgot to tell you, Irina. A gentleman walked in while you were gone to lunch and dropped off those flowers."

"Yes, I saw them. Would you happen to know who it was?"

"No, never saw him before," her boss replied, his tone indicating a curiosity that she didn't know and a general observation that the courier didn't exactly look her type.

"If you don't mind me asking, Sir, what did he look like?"

"Oh, the man was perhaps forty, had short brown hair and wore a beard. I never saw him before but he acted as though he knew you... Strangely, he kind of acted like he knew me, too. He addressed me as 'Arkady' and simply said, be sure Irina gets these."

"He knew you and me, but you don't know him?" she asked, genuinely curious now.

"Irina, every peddler in the Oblast comes in here and calls me by name. They see it on all those business permits. You know that," Petrov replied as he pointed toward the various framed licenses that hung in the foyer. "But that is strange, now that I think about it. The man was not trying to sell me anything."

A puzzled Irina took in the beauty and aroma of the flowers while rereading the card. *Beard, huh?*

CHAPTER SIX

Love at First Sight

Sergei and John departed the agency office a few minutes before noon and chose to walk the few blocks to a local downtown café the agent had chosen, waiting up front for Tonya to arrive prior to being seated. The establishment was busy with the noon lunch crowd that started to pile in.

Tonya walked in a few minutes later and Sergei proceeded with introductions. She and John shared a warm handshake and the three were escorted to their table. He was a bit impressed at her attire and pleasantly recalled the fact that most of the women in Ukraine presented themselves well when in public.

The three ordered the lunch special, which included borscht, a common and favorite Russian soup, and chicken sandwich on rye bread. John noted that Tonya was dressed as though ready for a formal dinner engagement, and he became suddenly a bit self-conscience sporting his jeans and cowboy boots.

The interview was rather structured, and John had trouble gauging whether this woman had much interest in him, a mental challenge he had seldom faced regarding those in the opposite sex. Not all that anxious about it, he wasn't sure about his own level of interest either. While Tonya was an attractive woman, she seemed very reserved as someone who John wasn't sure he could get close to.

Perhaps she's just nervous, he thought. *But maybe she doesn't like me and is just trying to be nice. Been there, done that.*

As all of their communication went through Sergei's interpretation, the two had trouble with eye contact with one another, and near the end of their lunch, John was certain Tonya had to get back to work. It struck him as odd that over the course of an hour-long lunch, this "meet and greet" hadn't accomplished much. It was disclosed that she had a fourteen-year-old daughter, John hoping the girl didn't have professional aspirations of being a doctor or would object to the idea of the education commitment required to practice certain professions in America. He also learned that Tonya's daughter spoke English, as she had studied it in school.

This "courting" through an interpreter wasn't easy, and John felt they were at a crossroads, needing more time to figure out which path to take. As such, he instructed Sergei to inform Tonya that if she didn't have plans for the evening, he would be happy to take her and her daughter out to dinner. He also informed Sergei, who he knew had a wife and small child at home, that since Tonya's daughter spoke English, he figured the three of them could get along without him and give him the night off.

Sergei and Tonya conversed briefly, she accepted the invite, and the three decided on a restaurant, a log cabin-style place fairly close to John's apartment that specialized in American-style barbeque, something he thought he'd never get in Kharkov.

Once John and Sergei returned to the agency office, John chose to go back through their catalog again, thinking perhaps he may have missed on something, a tell-tale indication he wasn't bought and sold on the woman whom he had just met. After revisiting every ad cover to cover, the same five ads continued to grab his attention; "no show" Anna, Cindy Crawford's clone, the budding Playboy bunny, Tonya, and Irina Balabanova, the young woman Sergei's boss seemed so bent on his meeting.

As Sergei couldn't leave the office for another few hours, John agreed to take a stroll around the area and return about quitting time, as Sergei would drive him back to the apartment. Following a hike around several blocks, John passed by many different shops, offices, and eateries, eyeing a couple restaurants that looked interesting and that he may wish to check out, that is if he remained in Kharkov for any extended period.

Returning to the agency, John asked to use one of their PCs to see if his email was back online, as Sergei still had work to clear up and calls to make before he could leave. John accessed his Yahoo account, and lo and behold, it popped right up. After scrolling through the various emails, some personal, some business, and some junk, there it was, that email from Sergei from Wednesday afternoon stating that Anna was busy and couldn't meet him until Saturday.

He did take the time to send Yahoo's support site a snide message about him not being able to access their site, due to a server error, for over forty-eight hours, noting specifically the time and dates as well as his locations. Five o'clock came finally as Sergei wrapped things up, allowing him to give John a lift and even arrange a cab to the restaurant later at normal fare. Following a hot shower, John had over an hour before meeting Tonya and her daughter at the restaurant, thus he decided to get on his own laptop to again access his Yahoo account, which was now working here in the apartment as well. He had a new message from Yahoo's Customer Service that claimed they had suffered no known server outage issues at any time during the previous entire week.

Odd? So you're telling me I'm just unlucky?

Irina made a visit to the folks for dinner that evening, desperate to hide her disappointment and embarrassment of the previous day while hoping Alika wouldn't let on either. She was also tightlipped about her meeting another "agency" guy the next day, a meeting she had little faith in, anyway.

Much of the early conversation around the table regarded the tense dispute with Russia on the eastern border, a situation that threatened to become a full-blown civil war. Since the fall of the USSR, the Russian president had made eyes on regaining the part of Ukraine that was predominantly ethnic Russians, an area that had strong geopolitical implications. The Crimea, Ukraine's popular tourist destination, had been home to the Soviet Black Sea Fleet, while in addition, a huge energy pipeline passed through eastern Ukraine, control of which would give the Russian government near total leverage over natural gas supplies to much of Europe. The Balabanove property in Chuguev was ominously close to ground zero.

"Before long, this house will be worthless," Mikhail exclaimed. "We cannot assume it will be safe here either."

Irina's father was generally pro-Russian, long accepting the leadership in Moscow to be ruthless and corrupt, but also feeling the fledgling government in Kiev to be equally corrupt while also weak. The girls thought of themselves as ethnic Russian but considered themselves Ukrainians, as did most of the country's younger generation. Alika's husband, Misha, was Ukrainian and had served in their army recently alongside US forces in Iraq. Nadine, for her part, was neutral on politics, only wanting safety and security for her family.

The family matriarch chimed in, "Let's not have talk about war. There must be more pleasant things around us, surely."

"How are you feeling, Irina?" Misha asked with an air of sarcasm. "I assume Alika took you to Kharkov to see a doctor, as you took a sick day, right Alika?"

"I invited Alika to go visit some old college classmates," Irina answered quickly, as not to put her sister on the spot. *Dimitri told Misha I took off yesterday and also told him about my dressing up to go out. Having that blabber mouth move in is the biggest mistake I ever made.*

"Kolya was asking about you today," Misha added.

"I don't think she's interested, Misha," Alika answered, noticing both parents tuned in intently to her answer. "Besides, Kolya has never asked her out or anything. You would think he would if he was really serious."

Irina sat and continued with her dinner, silently wishing the family conversation would take another turn.

"He thinks she has something going on with Pavel Kuznetsov," Alika's husband replied, immediately regretting it after thinking he had to defend his pal, Kolya. Misha avoided Irina's angered stare as well as an uneasy silence from the rest of the family, all of whom knew the SSU officer's reputation was somewhat known as an abusive womanizer. The implication was that Misha's friend feared Colonel Kuznetsov, who had his eyes on his young sister-in-law.

"Irina, is there any truth to this?" Mikhail asked as more of a demand.

"No Papa, none!" She replied, angry that her father would even question her about it. "That pig colonel tried to hit on me over a dinner that was supposed to be all business. That was it."

An uneasy silence engulfed the family dinner table as Irina stared downward, angry at both her father and brother-in-law.

"Please Mikhail. Enough of this talk," Nadine stated finally. "Why don't you and Misha go out and check on the dog?"

⋙ ⋘

Tonya and her daughter were already present when John's cab dropped him off at the Pioneer Grill, a theme restaurant that sat on a lot next to a small amusement park, located some ten blocks from John's apartment.

Tonya was dressed as if going to a ball and her daughter, Svetlana, appeared more as a typical teenager. John wore a pair of dress slacks, nice button-down shirt, and a blue sport coat, an attire not to Tonya's level but as good as he had packed. The menu featured entrees normally seen at a Famous Dave's BBQ in the States. John ordered a full plate of ribs, BBQ beans, and mashed potatoes, while Tonya and her daughter ordered some grilled chicken, a salad, and dessert. John and Tonya had some house wine while Svetlana settled for a Coca-Cola.

Much to John's dismay, there was an issue with communication as the daughter's English lacked much to be understandable. John could decipher few of her words, and thus the same challenge that occurred over lunch remained, as John wasn't sure to what degree this Tonya even liked him and his feeling toward her was mutual. It was a very odd and he thought uncomfortable setting with two people supposedly there to entertain a serious relationship having such a mundane conversation. Dinner lasted until just past ten o'clock and as the weather had gotten worse, John asked Svetlana about calling a cab. Tonya broke in and insisted that she and her daughter would walk John back home, the distance being of no concern. Having only his light sport coat on and John dreading the cold wind, the three left the restaurant and trudged off through the snow, John seeing this as common place for people here as many didn't have cars and couldn't afford the cabs.

Arriving at the apartment, John invited both in briefly, apologizing that he hadn't expected company and had nothing to offer them except a cup of black instant coffee, and even then would have to recruit Tonya to help heat up the water in a pot as the hot water kettle had electrical problems. Both declined but thanked him nonetheless.

It was getting a bit awkward now as both John and Tonya needed to set up another date or something if they planned to move the relationship forward. He was concerned his plan for the two to get better acquainted over dinner had mostly failed, and sensing they were at an impasse, Tonya and her daughter spoke together in their native language for a few minutes. Then Svetlana turned toward John and said, "Mom knows you plan to be in town a few days and that she is willing to take off work and stay with you here the whole time, if you would like."

Taken aback by this totally unexpected response from Tonya, and especially it coming from her daughter, John told Svetlana that he had to meet with Sergei in the morning, as he had to visit the airline office to get some tickets changed, and after that they would call her. The mother and daughter then chatted as Svetlana relayed the message. The teen then stepped away to use the bathroom while Tonya approached John and embraced him heartily, following up by pressing her lips strongly against his.

Taken completely off guard by this, John now saw Tonya as being totally unpredictable in going from one extreme to another. She backed away and smiled in a way as if looking for some sort of acknowledgment, but John felt suddenly strange and unable to present the desired response, having instead to force a return smile. Tonya left him with mixed feelings, the two seeming unsure of how sold they were on each other, but the picture had certainly changed in the past few minutes and the decision to advance this romantic relationship, if it could be referred to as such, certainly appeared to be John's to make.

I wonder how she would have reacted if her daughter wasn't along... Over thirty years of relations with women, and I still haven't figured them out!

As if on cue, Sergei rang the apartment phone a few minutes later, although John was not expecting to hear from him at the late hour. "Hello John, just checking in. How did your dinner go with Tonya and her daughter?"

"It went fine, Sergei," he replied in a measured tone.

"So John, do you like her?" the agent's interpreter asked sincerely.

"I kind of like her," John replied back, sounding somewhat unconvinced. "She offered to miss work and stay with me a few days."

"Well, Tonya must definitely like you, then. Do you want me to cancel the lunch meeting tomorrow with Irina Balabanova?"

John didn't hesitate. "No, don't do that, Sergei. Honestly, I'm kind of intrigued by this girl, particularly since your boss has been so militant in wanting me to meet her."

"Very well, John," the young man replied somewhat enthused. "She is to be at the office by eleven. What about Tonya?"

John was unsure how to reply. "I don't know."

"We could revisit about it after your meeting tomorrow, I suppose."

"Yes, I guess that would work," John answered as a decisive thought just entered his mind.

"Sergei, how about you bring her here from your office and pick me up. Then we can all go have lunch somewhere afterward," John instructed, having a gut feeling that this Irina spending a few minutes in front of Sergei's boss, just prior to meeting him, may be a good thing.

The two concluded their call and John went to the bedroom, preparing for a good night's sleep, something very hit-and-miss for him. His plan was to leave Kharkov Monday morning and head to Odessa. Should his meet and greet tomorrow with this twenty-seven year old Irina happen to bomb, a consideration he knew possible, if not likely, any thoughts of pursuing something with Tonya would mean cancelling Odessa altogether, as there just wouldn't be enough time. He now began to feel extremely conflicted. Was he prepared to dedicate his entire trip to this woman, Tonya? *There had to be a spark, a feeling to go all in, right?... It wasn't there... Hope for magic tomorrow, though.*

John logged into his Yahoo email and blasted off an update to Johnny, just prior to crashing.

⇥⇥ ⇤⇤

Irina chose to take the commuter bus to Kharkov this time and didn't tell anyone, including her sister, what she was up to. Still down and somewhat embarrassed by what had happened on Thursday, she got all the way to the bus stop and nearly decided to just blow it off. Only the mystery behind why Natalyia Belanov had kept on and on, not taking no for an answer, seemed to draw her into the bus at the last moment, the bus driver seeming to hold on a few extra seconds on her behalf. She entered through the sliding side door and found a seat on the right side toward the rear. She glanced forward and spied the driver looking at her through the large mirror up front as he gave her a slight nod, a small man wearing his uniform hat, thick glasses, and...*a small goatee.*

She exited the bus at the first downtown stop and walked the several blocks toward the Belanov office, the day cold and damp with rain threatening to pour down any minute. Irina chose not to wear a dress as she did on Thursday, a subliminal message to Belanov that perhaps she didn't regard this meeting seriously. She entered with a level of shyness at meeting yet another strange foreign man and was curiously relieved when no one was there except Natalyia and Sergei. Greetings were shared and Sergei explained the plan for meeting this guy, John Masters, for lunch.

Natalyia looked at Irina's attire and makeup with a slight air of disappointment, expecting the same girl who had shown up two days before. Seeing her wearing a cynical look of reservation, the owner tried to comfort the apprehensive girl prior to Sergei escorting her out the door. "Irina, let me assure you, this is nothing like the other day. You are going to really like this man."

How do you know? Irina thought. "Okay. I hope this works out." She glanced at Sergei, looking for some sign of agreement in the young man but he was just smiling as always, revealing very little.

He called John to let him know they were on their way as the two left in Sergei's car and he could tell his passenger was still nervous. "Things will be fine, Irina. This man is nothing like Robert," he stated, now knowing she didn't care for Robert Smith at all and feeling a bit guilty about it.

"Different? How?" She asked, staring forward through the windshield, her expression mostly blank.

"You saw his photos, right?"

"Yes, last night. But those were old. No way those photos were of a man fifty years old. Robert looked good in his photos too," she came back, a little snippier than she wanted to be. "When he touched me, my skin crawled."

"Actually, John really looks like his photos. He is the most particular man we've had in the office since I started and he did choose to meet you." Sergei chose not to disclose the fact that John had planned on meeting another of their clients, which didn't work out, and that he had met and had a dinner date with a second client.

Irina tried to suppress her pessimism. *Okay, Sergei. I'm just glad you're with me.*

⟫⟫ ⟪⟪

John paced nervously around the apartment as he anticipated the upcoming meeting. He dressed in a pair of khaki dress slacks, a dress shirt, and his blue sport coat, similar to the attire worn at dinner the previous evening, deciding his jeans, matching denim jacket, and cowboy boots may play better another day, perhaps.

The knock on the door finally came, and John opened it, inviting in Sergei and Irina, both sharing initial smiles. Accustomed to the women here sprucing up to meet him, a first thought hit him that Sergei must have just grabbed the girl next door and brought her around. Wearing jeans, a dark blouse, and what he would describe as Russian boots and a hat, John was yet taken by this lovely girl and moved to embrace her following their introduction.

For her part, Irina was quite pleasantly surprised with him as well. He was tall, fit, and rather handsome as advertised, and she was quite impressed with his seemingly genuine character, not blusterous compared to Smith.

Sharing some small talk through Sergei, John suggested they take some photographs in the apartment prior to leaving for lunch, mostly wanting to gauge her reaction. They all knew that part of the process in applying for any fiancée visa would require photographs to prove actual acquaintance.

Irina was all too happy to oblige and saw John's wanting photographs as a sign herself. Following Sergei's acting as photographer, she excused herself to use the restroom. In front of the mirror, she applied an update of lipstick and smiled to herself. *Sergei was right. This guy is different.*

The men waited patiently in the parlor, John and Sergei briefly discussing a good place to have lunch. Sergei could tell John wanted a nicer restaurant than the lunch café yesterday which prompted an early question, which he asked quietly. "Well, John, do you like her?"

John stood proudly as Irina quickly reappeared in the foyer. Assuming she wouldn't comprehend his answer anyway, he smiled at Sergei. "So far, so good."

The three chose an upscale place called Pushka, which was within easy walking distance of the apartment. The two shared some cordial conversation that gradually became what both John and Irina felt as rather serious for a first meeting. Unlike the earlier meetings Sergei moderated involving Robert and Tonya, the dialog was going quite smoothly, with both John and Irina comfortably asking and answering their various inquiries.

One of the most important items to be checked off by Irina was her desire to have a child and she left little doubt about her level of interest in John Masters when she asked the question herself.

She and Sergei were both impressed and amused by his answer. "I'm okay with that. I've been there, done that already, don't have to do it again. But I'm good with it. How would I prevent it, anyway?"

The remainder of their lunch proceeded very well, extending well past lunch hour and into mid-afternoon. The couple each gave a brief litany of their personal histories with John feeling this girl was intelligent and mature beyond her years, and Irina felt him to be very much a gentleman and looked very good for his age. The next day being Sunday, Irina offered to return and spend the day with John, an offer readily accepted. Believing Sergei should be home with his family, the two agreed they could sacrifice and communicate with each other using translation software on John's laptop.

Irina would need to catch the last bus pickup for Chuguev, which was 4:15 PM. The stop, by coincidence, was right across from the McDonald's that Sergei had taken John to the day before and reasonably close to John's apartment. As such, he suggested they meet there as he was inclined to hoof it over there on Sunday morning anyway for coffee. The three left the Pushka restaurant as John and Sergei escorted Irina to the fast food restaurant and the two shared a brief kiss prior to her departing.

John and Sergei walked back to the apartment, by now having developed a degree of comradery.

"She's likes you, John. I can tell," Sergei stated confidently. "May I assume you don't want to call Tonya back?"

"No," John replied. "I hate to hurt her feelings, but she and I just didn't click."

"Click?" Sergei spoke very good English but was not always familiar with the American slang part of it.

John saw this and was amused. "Connect. We just didn't connect. I thought it was mostly the language barrier,...that we could overcome it. Now I know better."

"So you and Irina,...clicked?"

"I think so, Sergei."

Irina's thoughts raced at a thousand miles per hour as the bus ride back to Chuguev seemed so much shorter. This man, John. Was he for real? Is this all really possible? They were half a world apart from each other. They didn't speak the same language, indeed were from two totally different cultures. They were from two totally different generations. Nothing made sense. Yet, there was something there, a spark.

How would I break the news to Momma and Papa? Momma wouldn't be a problem. She would be saddened by my leaving for America, but she had already resigned herself to that happening with Daryle, although I know now that was never going to happen. But Papa? Oooh! When he finds out I'm not only moving halfway around the world but it's also with a man his age... My god, he'll hit the roof! Best not a whisper about John yet... I may be too presumptive anyway. We've spent a lunch together with an interpreter and I'm already fantasizing about marrying the guy and moving to America... Silly girl. We're a long way from his asking and my accepting, and I'm not ready to accept yet, am I? But we did talk about having a baby. I can't believe I asked him about that already!

She had been so disappointed before, crushed emotionally and almost to the point of no longer dreaming. But now she felt driven by some emotional momentum, sufficient to have her get back on that bus tomorrow, head back to Kharkov, and spend more time with this American guy.

John returned to his apartment with a new burst of optimism. This woman, this girl, Irina, seemed too good to be true. How is this possible? Sure, a man his age would have little trouble being attracted to a gal twenty-three years younger, but nothing other than her appearance reminded him of the younger women back home. She appeared to share the same family values that he grew up with.

She didn't have any kids but wanted some, at least one. Being a father of a seventeen-year-old and two older step kids, undocumented but close to him nevertheless, John certainly didn't have need to be a daddy anymore but wasn't close to retiring and couldn't think of any good reason to oppose it.

Absorbing a very light dinner as having only the to-go box from the restaurant, John was buzzed as if knowing he was about to have a sudden change of fortune. In recent years he had experienced problems with insomnia, with even the Ambien having little effect. Now he was up and down most of the night, feeling wired for two twenty and hoping he didn't short out.

What if she gets second thoughts and chooses not to show up in the morning? What if she does show up and we can't communicate? What if she has me meet her folks? They must be around my age.

John finally fell off to sleep at 3:00 AM, waking up at just past eight. Getting up and about, he decided to just head on down to the McDonald's early and catch some breakfast. The staff there recalled him from his coming in on Friday and he had little difficulty ordering, as he simply pointed to the images on the menu board behind the counter and pronounced the local language Egg McMuffin as best he could. As the coffee was served in small cups, John ordered three which tickled the staff, who were all generally quite helpful.

These people must think us Americans drink a tremendous amount of coffee. How do I tell them I have a new romantic interest and don't want to fall asleep on her.

Leaving the restaurant and still having a couple hours to kill, John decided with the light traffic and few people wandering around on a Sunday morning, he would just take a walk around downtown and check out a few more places. The weather was chilly but sunny, and he began to warm up to Kharkov a bit, appreciating the cleanliness and architecture as the main part of town appeared on par with Odessa and even safer than many American cities. Keeping a close eye on his watch, John made his way back toward the McDonalds and arrived there thirty minutes early where he ordered, of course, more coffee.

Irina passed the kilometers between Chuguev and Kharkov staring out the window at the small farms, finding herself anxious about being with John again. She had been at the folks' dinner table last night and struggled to keep

99

things secret as the entire family sat in total amazement at her change in mood, a change that had come over her since they had last seen her Friday evening.

She kept looking at her phone, checking the time. The bus ran late today by a few minutes and she somehow worried he wouldn't be there. *No. It's Sunday morning and he's here in a strange city, eight thousand miles from home. He'll be there. Stop worrying.*

John sat at McDonalds and started to panic himself a bit when his watch told him it was quarter after, but he quickly lightened up when Irina walked in. He stood up and the two embraced briefly before they approached the counter to get Irina some coffee. She was satisfied with a single small cup, which John made light of.

Having his laptop with him and connecting through the restaurant's wi-fi, the two attempted communication with bilingual software, actually having a bit of fun in the process. Because the English and Russian languages structure their sentences and paragraphs so differently, the word-for-word translations would often make little sense and were even outright comical, giving a whole new meaning to "reading between the lines".

Being close to lunchtime, the two strolled back to the Pushka, a place they both knew by now and one that John considered a good omen. The time was limited on communication as John's laptop battery would last less than an hour, the restaurant had no plug-in power access near any of the dining tables or booths, and the 220-volt European-style outlets wouldn't accommodate his power cord anyway, as John hadn't considered packing along his purchased adapter kit.

Their waiter introduced himself as Andrei, who luckily spoke decent English, and as Sunday was not a busy lunch day for the eatery, he served as the quasi-part-time interpreter by default. The arrangement made ordering lunch seamless for both as they enjoyed a light seafood dish and tea. Irina acquired a strange expression when the waiter came around and John asked her what she was thinking about, the translation communicated through the waiter.

She waved it off as if nothing but couldn't shake some strange thoughts. *This waiter, Andrei? He looks like the same guy on the bus? In the Crimea? At the*

Galaktika Club?... But he's clean shaven? "Did you used to work at a beach bar and grill in The Crimea?"

"I have worked many places. Do you visit the Crimea?" the waiter asked with a confident smile.

"Oh yes. My family has spent their vacation there every year since I was a little girl."

"Well then. You may have seen me there at some time in the past," he answered nonchalantly. "Sir, may I get you something else?"

John, who sat curiously as he witnessed the interaction between the two, responded, "No, I think we're ready to settle up."

"Settle up, sir?" Andrei asked curiously.

"Yes. Pay you."

"Oh, I see," Andrei replied smiling. "I will bring your check right away."

Andrei brought the lunch check back quickly and John added a fifteen percent tip, something not customary or expected in Ukraine or any former states of the USSR. He handed John his credit card and took the restaurant receipt slip while smiling at Irina, commented in their native Russian, "Very generous man you have, Irina."

"Da, spasibo." *That smile... That look... I know I've seen it before,* Irina thought as the two departed, noting that her name had not been mentioned earlier but by now having little wonder about this waiter knowing it.

John and Irina ventured around the corner to a local market, where she observed him randomly pulling things off shelves and out of coolers, often pausing to point and question by expression, sometimes affecting some humor between the two and some curious looks from other shoppers. Irina held up a bottle of red wine and asked by gesture if it was all right with him to purchase it, and John replied smiling by grabbing a second bottle as they rolled forward.

He was struck by how unfriendly nearly all the other patrons were toward him and Irina, or toward each other for that matter. When the two had finally worked their way to the checkout counter, the older female cashier punched in their items slowly as they didn't have the scanning equipment so prevalent in the States for years. He paid with hryvnias and they left, John struck by the fact that the cashier simply handed him his change with a blank stare and no pleasantries were exchanged.

The two entered the apartment mid-afternoon and following the unpacking of the various food and drink items, John plugged his laptop in, which had died at the restaurant. Irina had brought a small photo album to share, and the two reviewed many images on the computer screen, mostly related to places in both native countries, Irina being very inquisitive about life in America.

It was curious, if not surprising, that much of her vision of his country involved New York, Florida, Las Vegas, and LA. John came to realize how many foreigners had an impression of America and Americans dramatically different from his native state of Missouri and his own culture personally, hoping and trusting the surprises she felt were mostly positive.

Nearing 4:00 PM, the time Irina indicated was the last bus stop on Sunday, she grabbed John's laptop and typed in a sentence as John looked on anxiously for the software to translate.

"Could you meet for lunch tomorrow with me and my sister?"

She watched curiously as John read the request, his head backing away from the screen before giving her a questioning glance, getting somewhat caught off guard. *Her sister? I may expect her to want the parents to meet me, or if she had kids… But her sister?* He typed a reply.

"Sure. Why not? What is your sister's name?"

Irina replied that her sister's name was Alika, and they agreed to meet again the next day, eleven thirty at where else? Their favorite restaurant, Pushka.

As John escorted Irina back toward the bus stop near the McDonald's, he was now gaining confidence in this relationship, one that on its face was still hard to grasp. *Why would she have me meet her sister, who also lives several miles away, if she wasn't serious about me? I suppose I am to pass some sort of litmus test. But why the sister? Why not the parents?*

By this time, John had decided to put all his effort toward this courtship with Irina and likely blow off his visit to Odessa. He decided that, following the lunch meeting tomorrow, he would send a kindly worded email to Larisa that circumstances had come up and his trip to Odessa just didn't work out. He could see he had one shot at getting this right, and after all, the lady doctor could have turned out to be another Anna, or chances are they just wouldn't click like he felt he and Irina had. Another consideration hit John, almost as an afterthought, was the additional education and internships the medical industry in the States required to just start up as a licensed physician may not appeal to an existing doctor in the Ukraine. *Hey, a bird in hand is worth two in the bush.*

As John and Irina strolled arm in arm to her bus stop, the two began to feel very close to each other, close in a way unforeseen for having just met a day before. The two embraced as they saw the bus coming and she smiled passionately at him through the window as it pulled away.

CHAPTER SEVEN

Bilingual Proposal

I rina had a warm heart full of optimism all the way home. *This man, John, is almost too good to be true. He wasn't sophisticated, extremely educated, or even that stylish. Those cowboy boots are funny. But he was ruggedly handsome, warm, and seemed to be easy to get close to.*

She had pondered whether to tell her mom and dad but thought better of it, still knowing they would have a fit learning how old John was. Her father had suffered the two strokes and even though he appeared to have recovered well, the family still worried and she didn't want to shake him up unnecessarily.

I have had so many disappointments in my life and this could still all fall apart. Even if we would agree to be married, there were still so many steps, and I'm not there mentally yet, anyway. There would be months and months of applications, letters, waiting, and she had a nagging feeling that with her luck something could just crash the whole process. *Why worry about any of it? There are a thousand things that could cause John to lose faith once back home and I would never see him again... But I can hope and pray.*

As the highway landmarks passed by and dusk was near, Irina fantasized about what life would be like in America. *What were the houses like? What was the shopping like? The food, the cars? What would John's family be like? Would they accept me?* All she had gotten out of him through their translations so far was that his family thought he was ready for the mental house for even daring to come over to Ukraine.

⋙ ⋘

John returned to the apartment, slightly amused after he passed by the old woman in the hallway that had confronted him over the blown fuse, her giving him a slight nod as if not knowing whether to frown or smile at him. It had been an eventful day, full of promise and excitement over the new girl in his life. He struggled to think of her as a woman just yet, and thinking she had to be serious about him. *After all, meeting her sister?*

He opened his email and fired off a message to Johnny, not knowing if or when he would read it, but knowing his mother and father didn't even have a computer as of yet, much less an email account. He wondered how the folks would all take the news about his new love being so much younger than him, probably adding to their opinion that he had lost his mind. *Best to keep this news close to the vest, at least for now. This isn't a done deal yet, ole boy.*

⋙ ⋘

Dimitri didn't notice anything unusual about Monday morning as Irina exited the bathroom, made up and dressed for work as always, until she pulled her travel bag out of the closet, taking her time packing up some clothing and other items as if leaving on a trip. "Irina, I will be stopping by the market on the way home from work. Would you like me to bring you anything?"

He never volunteers anything like that. He's just being nosy. "No," she replied, not wanting to disclose any more information to her roommate, one who would blab news about her to anyone.

"I thought we might have a nice dinner together," he added as he wormed his way down the hall and stood in her bedroom doorway.

105

Dinner? Get real! Should have listened and never let a co-worker move in. "No, Dmitri. I'll be away visiting friends for a few days."

Going away? Visiting friends? What's with the makeup? He thought. "Well, if anyone calls, when should I tell them you'll be back?"

Anyone calls? He thinks he's my secretary now. "If the office calls, tell them I'm at the doctor," Irina replied, annoyed and now regretting she didn't wait until Dimitri left before packing. She didn't believe her roommate would tell on her to the boss, but also knew that given to the effects of some after work drinking, he couldn't be trusted to keep quiet, either. "If anyone important calls, they have my cell phone number."

Irina and her sister, Alika, got on the bus just after 9:00 AM, both bubbling with excitement.

"If you're going to stay in his apartment, Irina, are you going to sleep with him?" Alika asked, knowing her sister vowed to never have another man use her like that again.

"No, I'm not. You know I'm not that easy."

"But what if he tries to take advantage of you, Irina?"

"I know him. I know he's not that kind of man."

"You've known him two days, Irina. How good do you know anybody in two days?" Alika asked seriously.

Irina thought a moment and replied, "If I call you and complain about having a bad stomach ache, you'll know I'm in trouble and you'll need to come get me. But I know that won't happen."

"Misha keeps bugging me about what's going on," Alika said.

"You promised to keep this a secret!"

"I have, Irina. But the family knows something is up. Been a while since they've seen you this happy, in spite of your trying to act normal."

John took a taxi and walked into the Belanov office on Monday morning at 9:40 AM to a cheerful greeting from Natalyia and Sergei once he got off the phone. Both of their desks were flooded with paperwork and he noticed several envelopes and stamps, as the two appeared to be working on a mass mailing of some sort. He stated that Sergei's services would be needed for lunch again and shared the agenda regarding Irina's sister, which tickled the two hosts to no end as John also acknowledged that things must be going well for the two.

Natalyia declared rather boastfully, "I told you this girl was perfect for you, John Masters."

John smiled in resignation, still intrigued that this woman so mysteriously resembled others he had bumped into before. "Is this common? I mean, meeting a sister like this?"

Natalyia and Sergei shared a glance, and the assistant raised an eye in the process. "Wouldn't say it happens all the time, but are you concerned about it?" Sergei asked.

"Oh no, no. Quite to the contrary, I take it as a good sign. I suppose if the roles were reversed, I would want her to meet my son fairly soon."

"Well, John, she has no children, so?" Natalyia added enthusiastically.

The woman always seems to have the right...something. "How often does this happen in your business? Where a guy comes in here, a strange man like me, and hits it off right away with one of your... clients?"

"Frequently," Natalyia replied. "Sometimes a man has to meet quite a few girls to have success. Counting Anna, you are one out of three. Not bad, don't you think?"

I guess so. *One out of four if you count Nadia in Odessa last spring. Heck, I was zero for twenty back home.* "Is this the way most of your success stories happen? I mean, a guy like me just shows up, you arrange a lunch or other meeting, and then it's off to the races?"

Natalyia and Sergei were both stymied as the agency assistant asked, "Off to the races?"

Oh, I forgot they wouldn't understand our slang expressions. "How do I say,... love at first sight?"

"Once a man travels all the way here from Europe or North America, especially North America, they are usually serious and we often succeed in finding them a Ukrainian wife," Natalyia answered, offering no specific statistics. "Of course, sometimes a man shows up and is not attractive to our girls. You are not such a man."

"I'll take that as a compliment," John replied, smiling.

"You should," Natalyia quickly replied, also smiling.

The three spent the remaining time as he questioned them on the general process, exploring whether they knew something he didn't, as he had done extensive research prior to traveling to Ukraine months ago. John was intrigued by their business model, his curiosity peaked by the fees he was charged for Sergei's interpreter services, quite reasonable he thought compared to what he had paid in Odessa earlier.

I've been here for over an hour, he thought as he looked at his watch, *and they seem to have nothing to do but chit-chat with me. And all those letters. That's how they generate revenue, translating and mailing letters. They send the email letters initially and then get paid for the translation and forwarding. I wonder if I ever got a real letter from Anna or if she ever personally responded? No, Sergei was too sincere about contacting her, I think. And Irina? I got that email letter from her a few months back and she claims she never sent me one. Such irony that I never replied... And here I am... All these email letters... Like casting a lure for a big bass... It worked, it got me over here... And I can't complain about the result so far.*

John and Sergei left the office and drove to the Pushka, John's favorite restaurant now, and arrived a few minutes early. When a waitress approached and seated the two, John asked her if Andrei was working today, wanting to quiz the bilingual young man if he thought he knew Irina. Strangely, their waitress, whose name was Liana, claimed to have no knowledge of any employee of the restaurant by that name.

"Unless he just started yesterday," she stated in her native language, prompting Sergei to translate.

Irina and Alika appeared a few minutes later and joined the two guys at a center table. Without waiting for pleasantries, John stood and briefly embraced Irina, and then turned toward Alika and offered his hand as a form of introduction. "So happy to meet you, Alika."

"I happy meet, John," she answered in her very limited English, now seeing why her sister would be attracted to this man who appeared quite warm and outgoing.

Curiously, John thought, the two sisters appeared to be about the same age but looked nothing alike.

The waitress brought out water glasses and menus for each in the party and then focused her attention briefly on John, who caught her dialog through Sergei. "By the way, sir. I checked the schedule in the office and we have no waiter here named Andrei."

John caught Irina in a somewhat surprised state, her grasping the server's comment right away as John listened to Sergei's translation. *Very strange,* he thought. *Oh well, not important.*

The four ordered lunch, a tasty variation of soups and crepe-style sandwiches while Alika began a series of questions as if initiating a job interview, all of which were translated through Sergei. "How do you feel about having children?" she began, cutting quickly to the chase, as if to reiterate the importance of the issue Irina had posed the first day.

Now John was a bit amused as if reminded of the interrogation by the "KGB woman" at the airport. *No, Irina's sister is too petite to be that mean,* and he thus gave the same response. "As I said on Saturday, I have been there, done that, don't need to do it again. But I have no problem with it, and how would I stop it, anyway?"

The girls shared a chuckle following Sergei's interpretation, and Irina generally kept quiet as Alika pressed on. "How I know my sister would be safe in America? We see on news these killings. We hear every man in America have gun."

Sergei qualified her question and John thought carefully, curious that these foreigners would consider the United States as being a dangerous place.

"America is a huge country, kind of like the former Soviet Union. Yes, there are dangerous places there, places I never frequent, but the town I live in is very safe and generally a very good place to raise a family. I would never consider living anywhere that I considered dangerous."

Satisfied with his reply, Alika pressed on. "Irina would need to travel back to Ukraine to visit family. Would you be good with her doing that?"

John noticed Irina strongly tuned in on his response, something not brought up before but obviously very important to her.

"I would support that. I know family is very important to her." *You want a woman with strong family values, so don't be surprised by this,* he thought.

The two sisters exchanged some dialog briefly, and Alika asked, "Does your family know how young my sister is? What do they think about you marrying her?"

John listened intently as Sergei carefully translated. *Marrying her? Strange hearing that word thrown out here at such an early stage. But then, I guess that is the purpose of this whole exercise.* "Frankly, they don't know much about Irina, yet. But I know my family will support anything that makes me happy. What about your folks? This has to be big news, right?"

Sergei looked confused a moment and asked, "John, folks?"

"Oh yes, their parents."

Sergei chuckled briefly and relayed his question to Irina and Alika. John could tell by their expressions that neither had shared the information about him to the "folks" yet. He wondered if he would get to meet them before he departed.

Reaching the midway point of his stay, John was confident things were going well but had mostly resigned himself to the fact that another trip was going to be needed to nurture this *courtship,* if not more than one. This was a plan he had not counted on as John was unsure about when he could even return, as taking this much time away from the business was costly, not to mention the overall cost of these trips themselves.

His spirits were lifted, however, when his lunch interview was nearing its end and Irina declared that she had called in sick and would spend the remainder of

John's holiday with him, if he wished. This wasn't expected and John took it as a complete sign of progress, though recalling the experience months before with Nadia in Odessa, wasn't fully clear about what it meant. *Are we going to sleep together? I hope this girl doesn't think that's a condition but maybe these women over here think sex is mandatory to get a foreigner like me to propose.* John thought momentarily about the one woman who posted sexually explicit photographs of herself in Belanov's catalog. *And even if not, she is certainly bold, wanting to stay with me after us only knowing each other a few days. Hmm... Oh well, one step at a time.*

John excused Sergei for the day and accompanied Irina in escorting Alika back to the bus stop. The two sisters chatted openly about the lunch meeting and about John generally, aware the American wouldn't understand a word they shared back and forth anyway.

"I like him, Irina," Alika indicated. "I think you make good choice. Maybe you can have Momma and Papa meet John before he leaves."

"Don't you say a word yet, Alika. Papa will have a fit. You know this...You promised."

"I won't say anything. But Momma knows something is up... And Misha, too."

"I'll figure out something and we'll talk later," Irina replied as she gave her sister a goodbye hug.

Arkady Petrov's day was anything but smooth as he realized who actually ran the place and when Irina was out, his routine was turned upside down. After answering what he deemed the millionth phone call of the day, he was interrupted by a most unwanted guest in none other than Colonel Pavel Kuznetsov.

The business had gotten a full shot in the arm when the contract with the Oblast had been signed. The bureaucratic bottleneck had miraculously disappeared during Kuznetsov's suspension, which occurred as a result of the incident weeks earlier the night of the unpleasant dinner engagement between the colonel and his office manager. His return to command, however, had made fulfilling the terms of the contract, which involved month-to-month billing, a nightmare as the colonel kept coming up with all kinds of "technical issues" that required a constant overload of the company's resources.

The company owner had no choice but to bend to the SSU commandant's will as an interruption of payments by the Oblast could put him out of business. "Good afternoon, Comrade Colonel. What can I do for you?"

Kuznetsov looked around, displeased that he and Petrov were the only two in the office. "We are still having problems with the security cameras, Arkady. I believe the hardware is faulty and needs to be replaced."

Petrov had sent technicians around to the various Oblast facilities numerous times, all reporting no issues found and had repeatedly reloaded software, needless but in an effort to placate the overbearing colonel. He knew these "issues" had much to do with that ill-advised dinner meeting with Kuznetsov and the attractive young Irina Balabanova, a meeting Petrov himself had a hand in orchestrating. The colonel had a reputation as one who did not take rejection from women well and would take retribution on his company as a result or until,... the thought unpleasant to contemplate.

"We are monitoring the system daily, Comrade Colonel. We have an important security patch update due in from Taipei any day, which should clear up most of this."

"That is most reassuring, Arkady. I would hate for the purchasing director to hold back payments over this. Perhaps you could have your office manager contact me to set up a meeting and discuss a plan to present these so-called solutions to the director. She is quite competent in such matters," the colonel stated with an obvious air of contempt.

Petrov struggled to hold back lashing out at Kuznetsov, knowing full well the security camera system he installed for the Oblast worked flawlessly. This was all about Colonel Kuznetsov still lusting for Irina, a young woman who vehemently detested the man. The nerve of such an egomaniac after what happened in Kharkov.

"Irina will be out for a while with an illness, Colonel. I will be happy to accompany you and see the director, myself."

"I am sorry to hear about that, Arkady. She looked like such a sight of health. Is she in the hospital?"

"No, not yet anyway. I will send your regards," the security company owner answered, hoping that would end this conversation.

"That would be most appreciated. Irina, she lives with a young man who also works here, does she not?" Kuznetsov asked.

Petrov knew the colonel was fully aware of the apartment complex where Irina Balabanova lived and he also knew the young man she lived with very well, as he had served under the colonel as a corporal. Petrov also knew Kuznetsov would have the means to easily find Irina's whereabouts, a thought that gave him nausea. "She rents a room out to Dimitri Gusev, but they are only roommates, nothing more."

"She is a fine young woman and needs a good man to take care of her," Kuznetsov stated, yet again.

Yes Colonel, she does, but she needs a husband, not a married man like you who just abuses these young women and then discards them... or in some cases... "Right now, I just want her to get well and back to work. Will there be anything else, Comrade Colonel?"

⋙⋙ ⋘⋘

John and Irina walked back to the apartment, and after settling in, the two sat on the couch and he fired up his laptop, reopening his new favorite language-swapping program. She looked on pleasantly and watched him type in a paragraph, taking time to digest the translation. As was usually the case, lengthy sentences often made little sense with the different sentence structures, and it took a bit of keyboard pecking back and forth between the two to positively understand each other.

They finally gathered that another trip to the market was needed, as John wanted tonight's dinner to be something special. The two headed out in unison and by now were getting more comfortable in their communications, although still much with sign and body language. Now having shopped here for three days, John pushed a grocery cart while prompting Irina to just fill it up with whatever they needed.

Knowing by now what kind of money the average citizen in Ukraine earned, John was struck by how pricy some of the food and drink items were and wondered how most of the local population afforded to shop, period.

The newly acquainted couple got back to the apartment and immediately shared some mutual laughter as John proceeded to place what he perceived to be small ice cream cups into the refrigerator. Irina grabbed one of the small round cups and held it up, attempting to ask him why on earth would he believe these needed refrigeration.

Upon closer inspection, John saw his "ice cream" cups were actually small candles and amused at himself, he now wondered why his new girl had bought so many, thus his first exposure to Irina's love for candles.

All the groceries in place now, Irina began to search the cupboards for cooking essentials and fired up the stove in preparation for dinner. Eager to please her new man, she prepared a very tasty "Russian" ravioli, local cuisine John didn't know existed.

John spent some time in the parlor on his laptop, catching up on some business emails and checking the news. As the apartment only had one bedroom with a double bed, other guests would have to sleep on this couch, one tired with age and not all that comfortable to sit on, much less sleep on. This will give some indication on how she feels about this subject, John thought, studying mentally on how this may play out as he was still uncertain about how Irina would react to the sleeping arrangements.

He got up and entered the small kitchen, approaching Irina from behind and gently putting his hands on her shoulders.

She froze just for a moment and spoke with her limited English. "You are tender."

The two embraced in what would be an emotional milestone, warm in other's arms as though they had known for years they belonged to each other.

The two parted as they shared a mutual smile, each knowing they had only a few days left together.

Following dinner, John got on the laptop and wrote Irina a message regarding the bedding facilities, specifically how there was only one bedroom and one bed in the place. She immediately replied that she would sleep on the couch. *I guess my intimate appeal has its limits,* John thought with a bruised ego. Being all the gentleman, John then insisted that he would sleep on the couch, followed by some ample dispute from Irina, who seemed to consider herself as some sort of interloper. In the end, John would have none of it, although he dreaded sleeping on the "lumpy" couch with his long history of insomnia.

With all open issues about the sleeping arrangements out of the way, the two enjoyed some after-dinner wine and delicacies such as shrimp and some tasty mushrooms stuffed with cheese, an Irina original it seemed, while watching an old Russian comedy on John's laptop, which of course had English subtitles.

Irina lay in bed, thinking about John and the meaning of these few days as though this was some fable that she would awaken out of, suddenly realizing it was just a dream. Her thoughts drifted to the waiter at Pushka, Alexei. How familiar he appeared, this stranger who always appears at just the right time. I wonder where he'll show up next... *It's almost as though someone had hired this guy to watch over me.*

Finally falling off just after eleven, Irina slept soundly while John tossed and turned, terribly uncomfortable as he struggled on the well-worn couch. Awakening at 4:00 AM, he spent a couple of pre-dawn hours reading his new Vince Flynn novel, a habit he had when his insomnia became overwhelming, and eventually fell back asleep at just past six. Irina entered the parlor an hour later, amused and even pleased that John was still sound asleep on the couch, as if he'd slept like a baby on it all night,

John was awakened a few minutes later to the aroma of instant coffee coming from the kitchen. By habit, he would always jump in the shower first thing in the morning to freshen himself up, and was very pleased when he entered the kitchen, as Irina stood there sporting his favorite racing theme tee shirt.

She proceeded to serve some homemade crepes with honey that John found quite tasty, although he had to grin and bear it on the instant coffee. The two sat together at the small kitchen table and comfortably got through breakfast without his laptop, by now getting by with a few words each had learned back and forth, and some more creative sign language.

Following her shower and his shave, John and Irina sat down together again in front of his computer screen as he wished to express his desire to visit a local establishment for some "real" coffee, and then perhaps she would take him on a tour of the town. Irina proceeded to search online for such a café close by, signaling to John that she didn't frequent those kind of shops often. *Probably only for the retired,* he thought, as he gathered Irina didn't work banker's hours, as did few others in this former Soviet republic.

The weather was cold this Tuesday morning and the two took off on foot, John not wanting to appear as being too "soft" in calling a cab but all the time lamenting at his not packing along a heavy winter jacket or thermal underwear.

To the contrary, Irina came prepared and dressed the part, looking quite chic in her warm white overcoat and ethnic style ushanka hat. Some eight blocks away, they entered a quaint appearing Café Barista, and each ordered a coffee with Irina relating John's choice of adding cream and artificial sweetener. Doing a quick mental calculation of the price per cup in US dollars, John thought these people were fairly proud of their coffee. *I suppose since they don't tip over here...*

The true shock hit when the waitress brought out their serving on a tray and Irina could tell John wasn't especially pleased. The coffee was rich, a brew favored in Eastern Europe he would learn, and served in very ornate cups and saucers, but content and style wasn't the rub as each cup couldn't have been over three ounces, very much to John's chagrin. *What am I supposed to do with this?*

Irina, as well as the rest of the café staff and local clientele, was quite amused by this foreign guy who purchased and consumed six cups of coffee. John had to force a grin when he signed the credit card receipt. *And I thought Starbucks coffee was too high.*

Full of caffeine and now fully alert, the two departed the café and headed toward the main downtown area where they perused the various shops and businesses. For his part, John wasn't much of a shopper but knew Irina probably would be, as were most females, and just being in her company while taking in the local architecture turned out to be most relaxing. The two took many photos, knowing they would need ample proof of having been together should a visa application be pursued.

Back in the apartment, John and Irina had a pleasant dinner of borscht, a soup blend that John would come to learn was as much a part of Russian culture as were the czars. Finished dining, Irina began to clean up while John took a bit of time to conduct some business online.

The two sat down in the parlor, Irina very curious about the place where John lived and the local geography around it. Opening his laptop browser, he pulled up the home screen of his native city of Cape Girardeau and panned the online map to illustrate the town being located on the great Mississippi River just north of where another great river, the Ohio, intersected. She viewed with interest as he displayed some of the more famous landmarks close by, such as the Gateway Arch in St. Louis and the Beale Street entertainment district in Memphis.

Like most Eastern Europeans, Irina was intrigued with America and John was most informative, having lived and worked in many of the fifty states. They shared much about the various sects in each of their own native lands, John relating how Americans in the old south had such a different accent than those in places like New York or Boston while Irina explained the difference between ethnic Russians, of which she was a part, and native Ukrainians, who were more closely connected to the Poles, Czechs, and Hungarians. This gave John a better understanding regarding the burgeoning civil war in the region, where most Ukrainian citizens in the eastern part of the country were ethnic Russians and some felt more aligned with the government in Moscow than their own in Kiev.

Irina offered to have John sleep in the bedroom while she took the couch the second evening, but as he endeavored to be the consummate gentleman declined, *although it was tempting*, he thought as he eyed the tired sofa.

The following morning, now a full week since John left home, the two had a pleasant breakfast which Irina fully prepared and John decided to just weather the instant coffee, still somewhat reeling from the liquid gold they served in small cups the day before.

A light snow was now falling to add to the crisp cold air in Kharkov, and the two strolled down the street to a local park where they engaged each other in a hearty snowball fight, predicating that Irina insist they go shopping to buy John something to warm himself better than his light denim jacket. Recalling a men's clothing store they passed by the day before, they entered the establishment and Irina picked out a wool muffler and some gloves for John and prepared to pay for them when John vehemently refused, displaying an etiquette of gentility that she found most appealing, and he later purchased her some fine perfume.

They also happened by a corner toy store and John opted to purchase a large stuffed panda bear for Sergei's young son, something that Irina saw as most heart-warming and seldom witnessed from the local population, mainly due to the lack of extra income.

By now, the newly acquainted couple were sensing they were getting close, but also knew they only had one more day together to make plans for the next phase in their relationship. John decided a symbolic celebration was in order, so he had Irina call the Belanov Agency to invite both Natalyia and Sergei out for dinner that evening at, of course, the Pushka.

By now, John and Irina were becoming very familiar with the waiters and waitresses at the restaurant as the two arrived just before the Belanov staff, namely Natalyia and her lone employee, Sergei, a young man ecstatic when presented with the stuffed toy he knew his two-year-old son would just love.

Toasts were abundant. as Natalyia appeared to see John and Irina as a great accomplishment, particularly since her establishment had such an intricate part in it. John took the opportunity to rehash the tale of his lost emails, while Natalyia seemed much less intrigued than Sergei, almost as though she had prior knowledge of it. Irina was feeling much better toward the agency in general now as clearly reflected in her mood and she proposed a final toast to "Yahoo". Sergei started to bring up the topic regarding the kilogram typo error when a sharp kick in his left shin was felt under the table, his boss giving him an unfavorable look as to imply he should hush.

The evening dinner was complete with an abundance of food, drinks, and laughter as the Pushka staff were all pleased at having guests who seemed nonchalant regarding the final tally of their check, not the least of which would be an anticipated generous tip from the American, a bonus they had now become well accustomed to.

John and Irina returned to the apartment late for the final night together as John would leave before dawn on Friday morning and Irina planned to return home late on Thursday. Once in the foyer, the two discarded their heavy winter wraps and suddenly, almost as though both were in complete harmony, John and Irina knew the time was right and fell into each other's arms, their lips warm together in a lasting embrace.

Pulling away following the magic moment and smiling, Irina headed for the kitchen and produced a bottle of sparkling white wine, which the two shared in the parlor as she lit up half a dozen small candles.

As close as the two had gotten the past few days, Irina was still unsure and somewhat uneasy about the plan after tomorrow and for his part, John needed some more assurance about how she felt about him before he could even get his arms around a plan, although now certain there would be one.

He chose to stoke the fire a bit and pulled up on his notebook computer their favorite webpage again, the online translation program, and typed in a message,

"This couch is becoming really uncomfortable. Perhaps we could both sleep in the bed tonight?"

Irina studied the translation in her native Russkie, and quickly typed in a reply that was translated back,

"I'll think about it."

There he goes, again, she thought while observing John shutting the bathroom door and hearing the sound of his turning on a faucet. That man does like his showers. Awaiting her time in the bathroom, she typed in a message on the laptop to be translated, one that he couldn't miss.

John exited the shower and while drying off, contemplating how critical this night's ending would be. If she says no and relegates me to the couch again, should I take that as a put-off? If she says yes, does that mean it's open season? How come I feel I have to get this exactly right? He thought it over and over and then made a decision, wanting to cover all bets as he swallowed the little blue pill.

She met him exiting the bathroom door and they crunched briefly together in the doorway, deciding on a brief kiss and smile as a parting. Irina shut the door behind her as John wandered back into the parlor where her reply to his earlier request was waiting right there on the screen of his laptop.

"We can sleep together, but we're not going to have sex."

John swallowed hard as he looked toward the bathroom door, suddenly feeling at a loss for confidence while also knowing how that little expensive pharmaceutical would affect him. *Oh, oh. Big mistake... Big!*

Irina returned from the bathroom in thirty minutes, by now wondering if he thought she bathed enough, and saw John sitting on the couch, staring blankly at his computer. Sporting a comfortable bathrobe that was among the limited apartment amenities, she sat down beside him, wanting to strike the right tone, and spoke in her limited English, "Now you not happy."

John produced an emotional smile. *I'm not happy, all right. But not for the reason you think.* "It's okay."

Moments later, the two lay in bed, side by side together in strangely unchartered waters. John stared at the ceiling for a brief period before Irina rolled toward him and they embraced, spoken words unnecessary as the two fell asleep in each other's arms.

⫸⫷

John awoke at the crack of dawn on Thursday morning with a severe sore throat and feeling the onset of a very, very bad cold or something coming on. Irina made a tacit attempt to ease his pain by serving up some very hot tea and honey, but all to little avail. The apartment was cold and the windows drafty as she more or less dragged him back to the bed and piled on every blanket and anything else she could find of substance to comfort him.

Fearing the worst, she wrapped herself for the frigid weather and took off out the door for the nearest drug store in order to procure some medicine while John began a severe whooping cough. As the Minister of Health in Ukraine is less restrictive regarding pharmaceuticals, Irina was able to purchase some strong antibiotics without a doctor's prescription, as well as a myriad of standard over-the-counter cold remedies.

Back by mid-morning, Irina gave John a one-of-each serving of medications that put him to sleep in short order. Using her idle time, she called and updated Alika on what was happening, knowing that sometime by the end of this day she and John would have to talk about what would happen next.

"Irina, maybe you should ask that Sergei arrive and help you two have a conversation before he leaves," Alika suggested.

"That crossed my mind, but John is too sick now. I worry about him even traveling back to Kiev," Irina answered, keeping her voice low while forgetting briefly that John wouldn't know what they were saying, anyway.

"You will not let this man get away! Maybe we should have Momma and Papa come up there this evening."

"Are you crazy?" Irina nearly yelled into her phone. "I hope to God you haven't said anything to them, Alika. There are still too many things that could go wrong. Promise me!"

"They think you're just in Kharkov visiting friends for a few days... Actually, that is what I told them, but they know something's up," Alika replied. "When *are* you going to tell them, Irina?"

Irina paused, unable to respond. *I have been visiting friends.*

"Are you still there?"

"Yes, I'm still here. I'll worry about that when the time comes... I have to go," Irina replied and ended the call.

John woke up mid-afternoon, feeling somewhat better and shocked at what effect the "Russian" medicine had on him. Irina stirred in the kitchen as he entered and she approached with a brief light embrace before standing back a step and placing her right palm on John's forehead. Making a statement in Russian, he was pretty sure she was saying he didn't feel like he had a fever.

Irina cooked up some more borscht for him, as hot as she felt he could stand it, which he took in heartily. Following their late lunch, the two spent the bulk of the afternoon engaged in petty small talk, charming but both knowing their holiday together was about to expire. The day approaching dusk, John saw Irina starting to pack up in preparation to depart and decided some initiative on his part was prudent.

Motioning for her to come sit down beside him on the old couch, he took to his laptop and using the translation program typed in a message:

"Irina, you know this is not a typical courtship that either of us have ever experienced. I am leaving early tomorrow morning and returning to America, halfway around the world. I will not be back next weekend to take you out on another date. You do know this?"

She read the translation, taking a few moments to decipher the reality and looked at him with her sad brown eyes and typed in a reply:

"Yes."

John thought carefully about what would come next, and slowly punched in the next litany to be translated. The translation did not come across exactly how he worded it, although the question did hit home.

122

"Well, do you want to come to America and be my wife or not?"

Irina was jolted as she stared at the screen, rereading the translation to make certain she understood this correctly. John sat nervously awaiting her reply, one that would be monumental in his life of a half-century, one way or the other. He noticed her typing in a response fairly quickly, trying to decide whether her haste was good news or bad.

"It is big decision. I have to think about it."

John thought for a second and immediately replied.

"No problem. You have got about ten minutes."

Irina looked seriously at the screen while holding back the urge to laugh, while John sat nervously, wondering what he would do if she said "no". She finally responded.

"Let's do it!"

John and Irina embraced in a warm kiss, both knowing something monumental had just occurred. The two of them now knew they had a plan and just had to carry it through. The enormity of the moment still setting in, they both knew things could still go amiss, but the hope and dreams they both shared gave each an emotional high and John's cold symptoms had suddenly sunk to mere insignificance.

They shared the remaining time together briefly covering steps in the process, which included the submission of much documentation, John's check to the US State Department, and finally the tedious process of waiting. Her bag in tow, the newly engaged couple stood together in the foyer by the front entrance, preparing for an emotional good-bye. Both embraced for a moment and then stood apart, momentarily at a loss for words when Irina broke the silence, speaking in her best limited English.

Looking up at John with her big brown eyes, misty with the sadness of their departing but breaking through with a strong semblance of joy, she exclaimed, "I don't know what to say... I love you."

Irina walked out the door and John could hear the creaking stairway of the old apartment as she thundered down them, followed by the sounds of the large front security door opening and closing. John then went quickly to the bedroom window, struggled to open it, and looked out from the second story which overlooked the wintery street below, watching her trudge through the falling snow. "I love you, Irina!" He yelled out.

She turned to look up, smiled and waved. *I love you, too!*

CHAPTER EIGHT

Roommate Betrayal

The flight across the Atlantic seemed to go smoothly and relatively quick compared to most return flights as John relaxed, the pleasant memories of his holiday with Irina still fresh in his mind, easing the stress of all his return flights and connections, which couldn't have gone any more abysmal.

The "KGB woman" at the Kharkov Airport, indeed the same babushka who confronted him before, gave John a hard time because his luggage weighed a few more kilograms than before, predicating a stern debate and rerun of her rummaging through his belongings, nearly causing him to miss his flight.

The shuttle back to Kiev was similar and perhaps the same plane as the one he'd flown into Kharkov the previous week, but at least the weather was clear, which made the short stint on the loud twin-engine prop plane more sustainable. The bureaucratic procedure to board in Kiev took well over an hour to add to the three-hour fight on a UIA Airbus, time that John hardly noticed.

The tough part came at Schiphol International, which had nearly completely shut down because of foul weather. Indeed John's incoming was fortunate just to land, stranding literally thousands of layover passengers at one of Europe's busiest airports. John was forced to stand in a line for nine hours to rebook his flight and then spend a night in a very claustrophobic local Amsterdam hotel room that he felt was smaller than his own bedroom closet.

Last but not least, Northwest lost his main luggage bag, which they managed to deliver by express courier the day after he finally landed in St. Louis, relegating he and his parents to an extra hour at Lambert International's baggage claim department prior to the final two-hour commute home.

Despite it all, John was upbeat and optimistic. He suspected in the back of his mind that Irina would worry or even doubt their engagement would come to fruition, somewhat due to the seemingly cynical outlook of many who he encountered in her native country. *There had to have been some divine intervention to orchestrate this.*

Recalling a famous line in the Patton film, "This latest incident could not have been the result of an accident... It must be an act of God!"... *I will stay the course, I will do everything I've promised, so help me God.*

Such thoughts served as a backdrop on the two-hour drive south as he had to fill his mother and father in on all the details. The two seniors, both in their seventies, had felt much anxiety as Johnny had kept them updated the past week through the very limited information contained in John's few emails. They had known John for fifty years, of course, and upon learning he had romanced a girl twenty-plus years younger, their natural skepticism crept in, although with little surprise, as their eldest son had spent most of his adult life stepping out of the box.

Once back in town, they pulled into John's driveway and the three entered through the garage where Johnny awaited, his cousin Ryan also there for the weekend. John's mother then heard the first positive benefit of her son's new disposition as she and his dad prepared to leave.

"I'm going to church with you all tomorrow."

Irina entered her apartment at just past 7:00 PM to a curious and anxious Dimitri, holding a rather fat-looking gray cat, complete with a large red ribbon wrapped around its neck. "Irina, I have a present for you," he spoke sheepishly, as he approached and handed her the fluffy kitty.

She forced a smile, embarrassed at yet another of her roommate's futile efforts at courtship. "What is this for, Dimitri? It's not my birthday or anything."

He looked at her as a timid child, struggling for the right choice of words as he noticed her carrying in a travel bag. "I missed you, Irina. Have you been all right?" Dimitri wanted to know where she had been but lacked the confidence for such a bold question.

"I have been wonderful! Just wonderful," she replied, wanting to back him down without disclosing too much information. She then let the cat fall to the floor, walking past him and toward her room.

Dimitri awkwardly followed behind her, standing at her door. "I've been worried about you, Irina. I even told Colonel Kuznetsov—"

"Kuznetsov!? When do you ever talk to Colonel Kuznetsov?... Why would you talk to an SSU man about me!?" Irina demanded.

Dimitri seemed to shrink down to the floorboard. "He was by the office yesterday, and he asked about you."

Irina's blood ran cold. She no longer wanted her name and Kuznetsov's used in the same sentence, ever. "What did you tell him, Dimitri?"

"I told him you were sick," he answered.

"What else, Dimitri?" Irina screamed.

"Oh, nothing. That was it."

Kuznetsov would never take that as a final answer. He is former KGB. He makes his living pressuring people to extract information. It is no telling what this buffoon told him. "I don't believe you. Would you please just stay out of my personal business?!"

She thought back to the day she left, regretting not waiting for her roommate and coworker to leave that morning, knowing he was too foolish to be trusted with even a pittance of confidence. She then angrily slammed the door in his face, any and all goodwill generated with the cat now forgotten.

⋙⋘

The day was particularly dreary in Chuguev as the snow and freezing rain that had fallen overnight had stymied traffic, made worse by a slight warming early Monday morning which produced a mix of continued snow and rain. In spite of that, Irina seemed to be particularly cheerful as noticed by the rest of the staff, all the more welcoming as most of the administrative functions in the company had come to a standstill while she was out sick the entire past week.

"Irina, I hope you're feeling better," Petrov asked, strongly suspecting her absence the previous week had much more to do with the purveyor of the flowers delivered the previous week than any actual illness.

"Yes, I'm doing much better, sir. Thank you."

"You know your desk is full now. Very little was done last week on all the pending contracts," he added expectantly.

"No problem. I'll catch up right away."

Petrov nodded, satisfied with her reply and could not help from noticing her change of mood. *Irina has a man in her life again.* The slightly built man lingered in the outer office, appearing obviously uncomfortable in front of his subordinate. After a while, he asked the young secretary to come into his office for a word. She rose from behind her desk to comply, nervous as her boss's mannerisms seemed quite irregular.

"Please sit down, Irina."

She sat down, fearing he had found out somehow that she was not really sick last week, although the practice of taking periodic sick time off was hardly unusual for employees there and she had rarely done so, nevertheless.

"I have some news you will not find welcome. Pavel Kuznetsov was here last week. He has had his rank of colonel reinstated and he is back in charge of the Oblast SSU office."

"But I don't understand. We finalized the contracts with Major Cherko weeks ago. Has something gone wrong?" Irina asked.

Petrov stood and walked over to the large window which looked out over the office lobby. "Irina, he demanded to see your personnel file, as well as Dimitri Gusev's, and then left with the two of them."

In the days of the old USSR and the KGB, confiscating one's personnel file by a high-ranking security officer would spell big trouble for any individual or those close to them. In modern-day Ukraine, most such horror stories were mostly legend, although the purpose of Kuznetsov wanting her file couldn't be anything good. Irina had nothing derogatory on her police record and couldn't imagine why this colonel would still be interested in anything about her, or Dimitri.

That night at the restaurant... He made such a fool of himself... But that was hardly my fault, Irina thought. "Was there anything in those files that I should worry about?"

"Not that I know of, Irina," her boss answered, thinking of what typical documents were in the files of his employees. With little or no warning, he would not have chanced getting caught doctoring with a file as the SSU colonel walked in. He also knew that following the incident at the restaurant in Kharkov, Kuznetsov was very embarrassed and bitter toward his company, and probably Irina personally, a fact Petrov avoided to discuss due to his own guilty part in exposing her to such.

When Captain Grigoriy Cherko was promoted to major and temporarily took Kuznetsov's position, he quickly finalized the business with his firm that Kuznetsov had been redundantly dragging out. Following a short period of being suspended, Kuznetsov was reinstated and Cherko transferred, with Petrov strongly suspecting the mafia in Donetsk had something to do with it.

Even though the More Security Supply phone system was not in place at the time, the vengeful colonel still strongly suspected Petrov's people were somehow behind the "ghost" terrorist attack on the Oblast base and coordinated bogus call that night to General Morozov in Kiev.

Knowing the SSU colonel could be a nightmare to deal with for anyone who got on his bad side, he looked seriously toward Irina and directed, "Let's just make sure we monitor everything regarding our contracts with any SSU

facilities, very carefully. Let's not give Kuznetsov anything to use against us."
He will fabricate enough evidence himself without our help.

Irina left his office and returned to her workload, a mixed mood of thinking about John while also worried about this Colonel Kuznetsov in possession of her personnel file. She would go by her parents' house after work for dinner. Papa's old boss at the petrol factory knew some big bosses in Kharkov. He would ask him to help find out what was going on with his daughter's file.

⟫⟩ ⟨⟪

Within a couple weeks, John received the required documentation from Irina, copies of her birth certificate, Ukrainian passport, and police certificate, which he combined with his own American documents to apply for her K-1 fiancée visa.

The two planned to limit their communication to mostly email to avoid the extreme expense of international cell phone roaming charges, the quality of connections being very poor. Even then, a week often passed between communiques as residential internet service in Chuguev hardly existed at the time, and thus, Irina's sending and receiving emails were limited to her visits to a local internet café. Adding to their cumbersome system of dialog was the necessity of their still using translation programs.

During the first week of January, John received a notice of receipt from the US Citizenship and Immigration Service regarding his application as petitioner, a check-off step in the process. He scanned the letter and sent a copy in an email to Irina, knowing she would be elated just to see something happening.

A few days later, Irina retrieved her anticipated emails from John, generally three or four days' worth, and upon reviewing the official-looking document from the US State Department, she experienced a heartwarming moment. *This may be more than a fable now. This is truly going to happen!*

Overcome with emotion, she couldn't resist calling John on the phone, committed to keep the conversation brief at nearly four dollars per minute.

After dialing the numerous numbers to get an international connection, Irina jumped for joy when John answered. "My honey! I miss you!"

"I miss you too, Irina! Did you get my email with the immigration document?"

"Yes, yes. What does it say to us?" Irina replied anxiously.

"It is simply a receipt stating the government has our application and is working on it. It's a first step," John answered, speaking slowly while knowing she would still only comprehend a few words. He chose not to elaborate on the fact that the whole process would be expected to take another six or seven months to complete.

"I will get off now to save money. I love you."

"I love you too. Keep checking emails. Bye."

The two disconnected, and Irina took the opportunity online to begin checking out some local sources to learn English, believing some ample study time with some popular software programs would serve her best, as there seemed to be no one affordable in Chuguev who taught such lessons and now wishing she had taken the English language class in college.

Irina's new bout of optimism fueled her mood, as she had more on her mind now than ever in her life, at least that she could recall.

I believe you are for real, John Masters... I still must inform my parents... And that evil Kuznetsov!

The office was small and in bad need of an upgrade. The paint on the walls was dingy and cracking in places, the stucco-covered ceiling heavily stained from the many years of roof leakage, and the old metal desk, left over from the days of Brezhnev, was rusting out in places. The past images of Gorbachev and all other reflections of the old Soviet Union were long gone.

Marko Palenko had been at the refinery all of his adult life, his rise to management made possible years before by virtue of his becoming a Communist Party member, a status that would often overlook other necessary qualifications.

Nearing retirement age, he had slowed down in recent years as the world price of petrol, along with the new capitalism instilled in Ukraine, had taken some pressure off the job.

He was all too happy to receive a former maintenance mechanic this cold February morning, a favorite back when Palenko was a foreman before his visitor was forced into retirement with disabling health issues.

"Mikhail Viktor Balabanov! So good to see you, my old friend. How long has it been? Eight, ten years?"

"It has been nearly twelve, Marko. You look well," Mikhail replied, genuinely happy to see his former boss.

"So, how is your health, Mikhail? You look healthy as a bear! I should put you back to work," Palenko added jokingly.

"Doing as well as can be expected," Mikhail answered.

"And the family?"

"They are good, Marko. I have a new son-in-law living under my roof now, Anna's husband Misha," Mikhail replied proudly. "Recently served in our army."

"I would have thought your eldest daughter, Irina, would have married by now. Such a pretty girl."

"No, not yet. She has many suitors but cannot settle on any of them. Had American boyfriend recently whom we thought would marry and move her to America, but he left without her almost a year ago," Mikhail answered, shaking his head. "Marko, I need some advice and perhaps help from you. It concerns Irina."

"Oh, how can I help, old friend? I have a regiment of young men here who would jump at the chance to marry a beauty like your Irina. But this younger generation, so full of themselves and disowning the proud past or our great motherland. I cannot think of one whom I would wish on your daughter."

"Marko, Irina may be in some sort of trouble."

Palenko could sense all the good humor of the visit was absent now. His former maintenance mechanic was a troubled man. "Please Mikhail, sit down and tell me about this."

"A Colonel Kuznetsov from the SSU Oblast office showed up where she works a few days ago and confiscated her personnel file."

"Kuznetsov, huh? A very dangerous man, and holdover from the old Party KGB," Palenko stated, ignoring the fact that he was an old Party holdover himself. "What has Irina done, Mikhail?"

"Nothing criminal, I can assure you of that. It seems that Kuznetsov and Irina were having dinner in Kharkov—"

Palenko loudly interrupted. "Your daughter having dinner with Colonel Pavel Kuznetsov!?"

"It is not as it sounds, Marko. From what I understand, it was a business dinner meeting," Mikhail answered defensively.

"And?"

"My daughter told me the colonel was quite intoxicated and tried to take advantage of her."

"You say he tried?"

"Yes, Marko. He got interrupted by an important phone call at the restaurant that immediately called him away. She doesn't believe anything worrisome is contained in that file," an obviously worried Mikhail claimed. "Is there any way you could look into this for us?"

Palenko got up out of his old office chair and began to pace around a bit, his hands clasped together behind his back. "The worry is not what was in the file, Mikhail. It is what may be in the file after the SSU has it for a period. I had one dealing with Colonel Kuznetsov a few years back, Mikhail. Must have been after you left. A yard worker was arrested for stealing, I believe it was. Kuznetsov was quite rough on the young man whose girlfriend had somehow shunned the colonel while attending college in Kharkov. I will tell you this, Mikhail. Colonel Kuznetsov has a reputation as an evil man and abuser of younger women. I even hear stories from time to time of his connection to the mafia in Donetsk, particularly related to human trafficking. Only rumors, mind you."

Mikhail was shaken. He had heard Kuznetsov was a bad state police official but had not heard this before. "Can you find out anything for us, Marko? I know you know some political bosses."

"I will see what I can do, Mikhail. I will contact you when I have news. In the meantime, have Irina,...in fact your entire family,...stay clear of this Colonel Kuznetsov at all costs.

⤜⤛⤚⤙ ⤝⤞

Dimitri sat nervously in the metal chair, the small room surrounded with walls of dull gray as if they existed in an ongoing tedium with no other company of hanging pictures, paintings, or even official bulletins. There were few furnishings other than two more of the cold metal chairs and a small metal table in front of him. He had been detained for questioning while onsite at the SSU facility, updating their new camera system.

Nearly thirty minutes later, the single entry door opened and in walked Colonel Pavel Kuznetsov, standing proudly in his impeccable SSU uniform that featured all his various badges and ribbons, denoting a stellar career in state security.

Saying nothing, he sat down at the small table opposite Dimitri and opened his briefcase, extracting a pair of vanilla files which he lay flat in front of him. Kuznetsov opened one, which Dimitri could readily see as containing his own police photograph, and studied through the various contained documents while remaining silent, a common tactic used to unnerve the "suspect".

Following several minutes, which seemed to Dimitri like hours, the SSU colonel spoke. "Dimitri Borisovich Gusev, born June 13, 1980, in Gori, Georgia... Ah! The childhood home of Josef Stalin. Tell me, Dimitri Borisovich, what do you think about Comrade Stalin?"

The young man sat nervously intimidated by such a surprise question, knowing any answer would be welcomed or offensive, depending on present company. Deep down, he held a personal resentment for the former Soviet strongman and the whole USSR, a contempt fueled by his own family legend of his great grandfather being gunned down by his own comrades, branded a traitor with literally hundreds of others for attempting to retreat back across the Volga River in the face of murderous German machine gun fire during the battle for Stalingrad, in December, 1942.

"I believe Josef Stalin was an important historical figure," he replied.

The colonel grunted. "Important historical figure, huh? You should have become a politician, Dimitri Borisovich... How is it that you migrated from Gori, Georgia to Chuguev?"

"I was transferred here while serving in the army. I just stayed," Dimitri answered truthfully.

"Do you consider yourself to be an ethnic Russian?"

Dimitri again stiffened as he pondered another loaded question. Guessing the colonel, whom everyone knew was a former KGB officer, would likely be sympathetic to Russian causes, he nodded affirmatively.

"I see you were involved in the installation of our security communications and video monitoring system for the Southeastern Oblast SSU facility. Correct?"

"Yes Sir. I was part of that team," Dimitri replied, curious about where this was going.

"And now you are tasked to service that system on an ongoing basis," the colonel said in the form of a statement, not a question. "Do you ever have need to remove any system data from the SSU premises?"

Dimitri stirred uncomfortably, assuming he was here as a result of some sort of missing data but not recalling if he ever had need to bring any such data, stored electronically, to the office. "Not that I can recall, no."

"You reside at 16 Kozheduba Street in Chuguev, correct?"

"Yes, that is correct, sir," Dimitri replied.

"And you live there with another More Security Supply company employee, I see," Kuznetsov stated as he stared firmly at the young Dimitri.

"Yes Sir."

"Irina Viktorivna Balabanova. Oh yes, the office manager at More Security Supply, correct?"

"That is correct," Dimitri answered, suspiciously knowing this colonel knew well who his roommate was and indeed had more than a passing interest in her, curious that Kuznetsov seemed to have forgotten their discussing Irina at the office while she was absent.

"Are you and Miss Balabanova lovers, Dimitri Gusev?"

What a question. Where is this heading? Dimitri worried as beads of sweat began to form on his forehead. "No Sir. We are just roommates. In fact, she owns the apartment."

The colonel then placed the other file on top of the Dimitri Gusev file and proceeded to open it. "Do you not find Irina Balabanova attractive?"

The young man was now becoming quite nervous as well as somewhat embarrassed. Not certain why this line of questioning was necessary, he replied cautiously. "Irina is a beautiful girl."

"And?" Kuznetsov added.

"She and I are only roommates and friends, Sir."

The colonel plowed forward, sensing this young man had strong aspirations for his lovely roommate, something that could be useful. "And what of your other relationships with the opposite sex?"

"I have none right now," Dimitri answered lowly.

"Does Irina Balabanova have a man in her life?"

Why is this stuff important? Dimitri thought, irritated at the questioning but knowing the risks of not answering. "I am not aware of any right now. She had an American boyfriend who lived there before I moved in, but he left and returned to America months ago."

Kuznetsov looked up abruptly. "An American?"

"Yes Sir."

"What can you tell me about this man?"

"I don't know much about him, Comrade Colonel. I only know he was some sort of teacher or trade representative or something. His name was Daryle. I don't recall her ever mentioning his last name."

"Dimitri, this Balabanova woman has much knowledge and access to data related to the state security systems for the entire Oblast. Do you know the risks to our great nation should this information be compromised?"

The young man hesitated briefly, trying to formulate the correct answer. "Of course, Colonel."

"The contract for those security systems was pushed through last year during my absence. There were no proper security checks performed by the incompetent Major Cherko, an act of negligence that begs to be a crisis in the making. It is my job to provide security clearances for you and all the other More Security company personnel. I would hate to see a fine young Ukrainian woman like Irina Balabanova be criminally compromised by some liaison with an American imperialist. I want to know everything about Miss Balabanova, Dimitri. I want to know the details about anyone she communicates with, especially foreigners. And you will help me."

"Me, Sir?"

"You will check her mail, her cell phone, her computer, everything... I want to know of any possible security information being transferred into the wrong hands through that apartment... And, it would be most unfortunate for you to be implicated, Dimitri... Do you understand?"

Dimitri felt his throat get dry... *I understand perfectly.*

The first week of March John received an email from Irina including the word "URGENT", requesting three hundred dollars to go to the hospital. *Why would you need three hundred dollars? I thought they had free healthcare over there(?)*

He replied that he would call her. *This is very strange? It's been four months and she has hardly requested anything.*

He dialed the phone and waited for the call to go through, his mind thinking momentarily about his next cell phone bill. The call was cutoff before connecting, a common enough occurrence and thus he would try again a couple hours later.

With little wait, his phone rang right back and seeing the numbers pop up on his flip phone screen, John knew it was Irina.

"My honey, I miss you so much," Irina said in the accented voice he so missed.

"Miss you too, Irina. I got your email requesting three hundred dollars for the hospital? What is wrong with you?"

"If the money is problem, forget about it," she replied with an edge to her voice that expressed disappointment.

"Irina, I don't care about the three hundred bucks! I want to know what is wrong with you."

"I have infection,...in my reproductive parts. It has gotten very painful."

John wanted to legitimately know the purpose of the three hundred dollars as he thought Ukraine had a socialized medicine system and any and all doctor, clinic, and hospital costs were taken care of, but knowing her still very limited English would prohibit an adequate conversation about it. *I'll learn about this later,* he thought.

"I'm going to setup a separate bank account for you and send you visa debit card," John claimed, knowing that would take at least a week and feeling tired of the whole exercise of wiring money.

"Meanwhile, I'll run to Walmart and wire you the money on Western Union. You may go and retrieve the cash first thing in the morning," He added, knowing the hour over there was very late.

The two disconnected and John would later learn Ukraine indeed had a two-tier healthcare system. Citizens requiring medical attention could contact a local clinic or hospital but wait times were typically four to six weeks. However, an offer of sliding a doctor three or four hundred dollars in cash would secure an appointment that very afternoon.

⟫⟫ ⟪⟪

Two weeks later, John received a "Notice of Action" letter from the USCIS stating the petition had been approved and forwarded to the National Visa Center, or "NVC", for processing, a step that had happened much sooner than expected. As such, John and Irina agreed that she would move to resign from her job at the security company to concentrate full-time on learning the English language, a skill which had improved gradually since their memorable "laptop proposal" back in November. John agreed to provide her with replacement income, a negligible amount in US dollars.

⟶⟫⟩ ⟨⟨⟨⟵

Irina spent long hours in her apartment studying English, upbeat as she waited anxiously for the next steps in the K-1 visa process, a scheduled medical exam, and appointment for an interview at the US Embassy in Kiev. She sat on the front room sofa and heard some familiar footsteps in the hallway and the entry door open as Dimitri had gotten in.

"Irina, I heard you gave Arkady notice today you are leaving," he said inquisitively.

"Yes, I have," she replied, not looking up from her studies nor wanting to disclose additional information to Dimitri, a guy who long ago had lost her trust.

"But what are you going to do?" He asked.

"Not certain, yet....I need to make a call." Irina picked up her phone and called Alika, needing an excuse to interrupt this "inquisition".

Dimitri stood in the hallway dejected and faced reality,...that Irina may likely be talking on the phone for hours.

⟶⟫⟩ ⟨⟨⟨⟵

Irina spent the first of her final two weeks in the office, routine but with a single exception. Colonel Kuznetsov stopped by to return the two personnel files while acting neutral but friendly, which was totally out of character for him, especially in the aftermath of the earlier restaurant incident. She listened intently as he and Petrov conversed behind closed doors, not picking up on anything as their conversation seemed unexpectedly cordial and casual. Upon leaving, the colonel approached her desk, her anxiety limited by virtue of her boss having followed Kuznetsov into her outer office and looked on as the SSU officer spoke.

"I hear you are leaving Arkady's company, Irina. Where are you going?"

She quickly tensed up, not knowing what Arkady may have told him. "I am just taking off for a while. I want to take some foreign language classes and see what opportunities are out there." Irina replied, having trouble maintaining eye contact with the evil Kuznetsov, a sign in his mind that she was hiding something.

"You may be aware that I am conducting an update to all More Security Supply Company's security clearances. I may have need to stay in contact with you for a period, regarding such matters," Kuznetsov stated, attempting to appear friendly but a bit intimidating, the latter trait coming naturally for him. "I will require your contact information."

Irina begrudgingly wrote down her apartment address, cell phone number, and email address, all of which she strongly believed he already had possession of. She was also naïvely unaware the colonel had knowledge of her recent request for a copy of her police certification.

"Thank you, Irina...Arkady...Paka, *Good bye.*"

>>>> <<<<

Wanting to leave on good terms, Irina offered to stay on a few more days if Petrov desired, to help train her replacement. The boss declined but expressed gratitude for the gesture and an appreciation for her five years of service. The issue of the SSU examining her and Dimitri's personnel files still lingered but the two had chosen not to discuss it.

"It is none of my business, Irina, but who is the man in your life now?" Petrov asked, noting like the rest of his staff her being very coy in talking about it. He had also noticed his office manager being somewhat carefree the past few weeks and with quitting her job, he figured she must have male support somewhere. He feared that support was coming from Colonel Kuznetsov, a fact that would surprise him but not to discount the cunning SSU colonel.

"What makes you think I am involved with someone?" Irina replied, thinking she had been most secretive regarding John, particularly around the office.

"Irina, I have known you for five years now. I have seen you up and I have seen you down. You are really up lately. I hate to ask, but are you involved with Pavel Kuznetsov?"

"Pavel Kuznetsov?... Oh no! Why would you even suspect such a thing?"

"I don't know. Just haven't seen or heard of any other man around, and I know it is not Dimitri," Petrov stated.

Irina couldn't help but chuckle a bit. "No, it is not Dimitri, Arkady."

"Ah! So there is a man in your life. Tell me, is it the American who you were involved with last year?"

Irina hesitated, not sure if her soon-to-be former boss was genuinely concerned or just being nosy, and thus she gave a very guarded reply. "Well, maybe."

"Irina, I hope that works out for you and wish you all the happiness."

"Thank you, Arkady. Very much," Irina replied, believing herself somewhat clever. *Well, my answer to your question was truthful, Arkady...You just have your Americans mixed up.*

CHAPTER NINE

Engagement Under Siege

J ohn pulled into his driveway just past 6:00 PM Friday after what seemed like a very long week. He had been all over the southern Illinois part of his territory, installed three contracts, and looked forward to a weekend of rest and relaxation, a thought interrupted by the sight of the bronze-colored Toyota Camry with Illinois license plates that was parked in his driveway.

He opened the garage and made his way to the back door, a man who wasn't by nature inclined to invite himself anywhere and didn't appreciate it likewise. He was certain she didn't possess a key to his place, so Johnny must have let her in. He entered the kitchen to the smell of chili cooking on the stove and heard the metal door of the dryer opening in the washroom, as well as Johnny's pop music coming from his room. John stiffened for a period as he thought of how he was going to handle this.

"Well, well, well. It's my favorite cowboy," the woman stated, as she approached to greet a man she had not seen in twelve months.

"You should have called before driving all the way down here, Becky," John replied, his expression very telling this reunion of former romantics was not to be what she had hoped for.

"What's wrong, John? Don't tell me you haven't missed me." Becky Stewart, a divorcee from Marion, Illinois, was one of several of John's short-term relationships he had prior to his overseas endeavors. She had always been serious about John and hoped she could convince him to eventually see her in the same light.

"Becky, you're not hearing me. You should have called. I have plans for this weekend."

"Oh, so you have another woman in your life now?" she asked expectantly.

John detested her using the term "another", which implied she herself was still in his life. "The fact is I'm engaged to be married."

"Engaged?" Becky exclaimed. "Who is the lucky woman? Someone I know?"

"Hardly, Becky. She is from the Ukraine."

"Ukraine! Isn't that part of Russia or something?"

"Used to be part of the Soviet Union, but now it's an independent country."

"John, don't tell me you met this woman online," Becky stated as a form of ridicule.

"Becky, I met you online."

She stirred around for a bit, trying to contain her disappointment. She had been working out for the past three months and lost twenty pounds, feeling she looked better than she had in years. "Don't tell me. She's fifteen years younger than you."

"She's at least that," he responded with a short answer, agitated and of the belief he owed no explanation, particularly to an uninvited guest.

"The place looks like it needs a woman's touch, cowboy. I'm washing your linens and all of your and Johnny's clothes," Becky added. "You know all those foreign women just con a man into paying their way over here. How do you know this isn't a setup, John?"

He stood silent for a moment, recalling all the reasons Becky Stewart was his former, and not current, girlfriend. "You really should have called before driving down here. I know you want to spend the night and spend the day here tomorrow, meet the family at church on Sunday, and then everyone will think we're an item again," John stated firmly. "I'm not going to do that to you, Becky."

"I see," she replied and went to the bedroom, gathered up her few belongings, and prepared to head to the front door. "I hope this works out for you, John," she stated rather insincerely as she departed.

Johnny came out of his room, seeing his dad looking out the front window as Stewart backed her car out of the driveway and drove off. "Dad, did I miss something?"

"Son, did she just pull up and knock on the door?"

"Sort of. I was out in the garage when she drove up. She acted like you knew she was coming."

"You do know I'm engaged now, Son, right?"

⤜⤜⤜ ⤛⤛⤛

Mikhail and his wife, Nadine, had not updated with the times and replaced their traditional landline telephone with cell phones, as their late evening meal was interrupted by the ringtone. Alika got up from the table and ran into the parlor to answer, quickly returning.

"Papa, it is Marko Palenko."

Mikhail moved briskly to the phone, pleased that his old boss was getting back to him so soon. "Oh, Marko! Privet!"

"Privet, Mikhail. I have some news for you."

"Very good, Marko. Tell me."

"The SSU office is running a security clearance investigation on the company Irina works for. This is standard procedure for a supplier to undergo something of this nature, but there is something very troubling about it. It is being handled by Colonel Kuznetsov personally, very unusual for something this routine, and it gets worse. The only two individuals who seem to be under investigation are your daughter and one other employee there, a man named Dimitri Gusev."

Mikhail took a deep breath. "Dimitri?"

"Do you know this man?"

"Yes, Marko. He rents a room in Irina's apartment."

"That does not sound good, Mikhail. Kuznetsov has something on one of them, or maybe both. What is Irina's involvement with Gusev?"

"Nothing. Irina seems to have no interest in him, other than his helping pay for the apartment expense."

"There is one other thing, something that may be important. Apparently, Kuznetsov has learned that Irina has recently acquired an updated copy of her police certificate. That is worrisome, Mikhail. Colonel Kuznetsov may believe she is preparing to leave the country. He will still recall the incident you told me about and is known to be extremely vindictive. The man does not take rejection from women well. I just learned he was involved with a young girl from Donetsk last summer who accompanied him to the Crimea for a meeting. It was rumored they got into an ugly dispute down there and the girl disappeared. The young woman has not been seen or heard from since. Be discreet about what I just told you, Mikhail. My source at the SSU office placed herself at great risk by looking into this for me. I gathered from her that Colonel Kuznetsov is both feared and disliked there."

Mikhail digested this unwelcome information and now became extremely worried. "Thank you, Marko. You know how much I appreciate this."

"Sure, Mikhail. I'll let you know if I find out anything else. Stop by late some afternoon. We can have a drink and talk about old times... Paka."

⤜⤜⤜　⤛⤛⤛

He sat in the colonel's large office, which was much more comfortable than the interrogation room he had found himself in the last time. It appeared his standing with the colonel had improved, at least somewhat.

"I found some documents and addressed envelopes in her closet. His name is Daryle Adams. I made some copies," Dimitri explained as he looked around sheepishly before handing the paperwork to the colonel.

Kuznetsov began to examine them as he continued to listen. "What else do you have?"

"I managed to look through her phone briefly while she was bathing. There were some calls in and out to what I think are numbers internationally, to America. There are also emails regarding money transfers and she has a new debit visa card from Bank of America now."

"Did you make note of those numbers and email addresses?" Kuznetsov asked seriously.

"No, Colonel. I didn't think of that," Dimitri answered, believing his status in the eyes of the overbearing SSU officer had just somewhat diminished.

Kuznetsov didn't let up. "What else can you tell me about her?"

"Not much, Comrade Colonel. She doesn't say much to me and now just mostly sits around studying her English."

English, huh? She wants to become an American! Kuznetsov thought with a suppressed anger. As much as the colonel resented a woman who rejected his own manly overtures, his deep-rooted belief and personal loyalty toward the old Soviet system made him extra vindictive with women involved with any man from the West. To have a young, attractive Russian girl forsake a man like him for an American was the ultimate stab in the back.

"I want those dialed phone numbers, Dimitri," Kuznetsov demanded. "And I want that account number on her new bank card, also!"

⤐⤐⤐ ⤎⤎⤎

She heard her phone buzz and seeing it was her parents' number calling, she picked up.

"Irina, I want you to come by for dinner this evening. Papa wants to talk to you about something," Nadine stated, sounding as if she was under duress.

"Momma, what is it?"

"It's about the investigation at your work."

Former work. "Momma, is it bad?"

"Your father wants to tell you about it himself, Irina."

So he can yell at me, no doubt. "I will come."

Irina drove to the small cottage, slightly less crowded since she had moved out. She entered and was greeted by her mother, a woman now appearing extremely worrisome, an expression Irina had not seen on her since her father had his second stroke. Mikhail looked up and nodded as he spoke on the phone.

"He is talking to Marko Palenko, his old boss. This is the second time he has called," Nadine said in a near whisper.

After a few more minutes, Mikhail hung up the phone and approached the dinner table solemnly. "So, Irina, you are planning to leave for America? I thought that young Daryle had left you a year ago!"

He thinks I am still involved with Daryle? Where did this come from? "This is not true, Papa!"

"I would have thought you would at least informed us of something like this, daughter!"

"Papa, I am telling you! I am not leaving to live with Daryle! Where did you get that idea?"

"You asked me to find out what was behind the SSU confiscating your file at work. Marko Palenko has friends in Kharkov and looked into this. This Colonel Kuznetsov has some sort of investigation on you and Dimitri,...and only you two. He believes it has something to do with what happened between you and Kuznetsov at that restaurant last year."

"I know he took our files for a while, but they were returned. I also heard the colonel was not happy about that incident at the restaurant, but he did not act angry the other day when he stopped by the office," Irina replied defensively. "What does that have to do with Daryle?"

"Marko just learned today that Kuznetsov now knows that you recently requested and were given a copy of your police certificate and were involved in several communications and money exchanges with an American over the past several weeks. Was it Daryle who sent you that extra money for the hospital last month?"

Irina was shocked. *How did Kuznetsov get all this information? Calls on my phone?... Sure, but that money from John's bank accounts? And how did Papa's old boss learn so much about this?* "No, Papa. Daryle has not sent me any money."

"You must come clean with us, Irina! Your mother and I would not like your moving to America but if that is what you wish to do, you are an adult woman."

Irina hesitated as she gathered her thoughts. She was not prepared to tell her parents about John, yet. Something could still go wrong and why cause such consternation. *But the family temperature is already extremely high, and if not now, when?* "It is not Daryle... I have met another American."

The entire dinner table became dead silent for a few seconds. "What!? Who is this new American? Why have we not met him?" Mikhail demanded excitedly.

Irina and Alika shared a look as in preparation for something rash, expressions not lost on the rest of the table.

"His name is John Masters. He lives in a place called Missouri, in the center of America," Irina stated, trying to prepare herself for the rest of the story.

"And where is this John Masters? How come we have not met this young man?" Mikhail countered.

Young man? Ouch! "I met him in Kharkov while he was here on business," she replied sheepishly. "We spent some time together."

"Irina, why didn't you tell us?" Nadine asked, wanting to assume some of the questioning in order to calm the family patriarch down.

"I didn't want to upset you," Irina answered. "He has applied for me to get a visa to travel to America. It takes so much time for the process, and it may not get approved anyway. I thought I would wait until it was official and then tell you."

"You had better stop this *process,* girl. Colonel Kuznetsov is targeting you and it has something to do with state security and some legal document you signed when you first started work at the security company. He is also pushing the possibility that your American is somehow connected with an intelligence agency and may be using you to get classified information on the SSU," Mikhail strongly stated.

Intelligence agency? Classified information? Absurd. "Papa, you say you learned this from Marko Palenko. How does he know so much about this?"

"You asked me to get help, so I asked him. He has friends in the government up there and it seems one of them has a daughter who works under Kuznetsov, and the girl despises this colonel. She apparently sees everything he is involved in and knows him very well. She believes her evil boss will attempt to use his power to pressure you to become his mistress, as he believes you have shunned him for an American. That information does not leave this room," Mikhail replied, looking eye to eye with everyone at the table and making certain that last part was clearly understood.

"That sounds crazy, Papa. I have just recently seen Colonel Kuznetsov briefly when I was still at the security company. Arkady was right there, and he didn't appear angry or act strange toward me," Irina replied defensively.

"According to the staffer inside, he has your file open with your picture and a note with your cell phone number recently stapled to it," Mikhail added, hoping there wasn't more to this story and deciding some vodka was in order. "I'm going out to check on the dog."

Mikhail and Misha shuffled out the door while Nadine and her daughters gathered in the kitchen. "I'm afraid for your father, Irina. You know him. He will drive to Kharkov and confront this SSU colonel and get himself in big trouble, maybe even get shot or taken to prison. You must stop this business with this American before something bad happens. If you only saw this foreigner while here on business, how can that be love?"

Irina didn't answer and only had her own thoughts. *I don't know how, Momma. I just know it is.*

⟫⟩ ⟨⟨

A week passed when Alika stopped by the apartment for a brief early afternoon visit. Irina looked terrible, having not slept well in days, her eyes indicating she had been sobbing continuously. The apartment was a total mess with unmade beds, dirty dishes piling up in the kitchen, and unwashed clothing sown everywhere. *This is all totally out of character for her*, Alika thought.

"John keeps calling me, Alika... And sending me emails... What should I do?"

"What do you want to do?"

"I don't know! That's why I'm asking you... I want to go to America and marry him. But I don't want to hurt Momma and Papa... And Momma is probably right about Papa. He will confront that fanatic Colonel Kuznetsov. You know he will always run to protect us," Irina declared, tearing up again.

"You were never one to keep your life simple," Alika replied, not believing her sister would take such an observation seriously at the present.

"Who said I need my life to be simple?" Irina replied, mostly to herself.

The two chatted while Alika helped straighten up the apartment somewhat. "What about your job? You will need to earn some money sooner or later. Or is John still supporting you?"

"I haven't even checked the account he set up for me lately, Alika. I keep hoping this is just all a bad dream and I'll wake up one morning and everything will be fine... But I should know better."

"I should be going, Irina. Maybe you should stay at the house a few days. I hate to see you in such a state."

"No, I'll be fine, Alika," *I can't handle too many more questions from Papa right now.* "I just don't know what to do about John."

"You miss him, don't you?"

"Yes, terribly."

⋙ ⋘

John walked out toward his car following a challenging interaction with one of his clients. The business was rather soft as of late and his mental energy being off was not helping. It had now been nearly two weeks since John had heard from or received any emails from Irina and he was beginning to panic. Since last seeing her in late November, they had never gone more than five or six days without communicating and it was generally every two to three. The family kept asking about her and he kept responding that everything was fine, answers that became more and more uncomfortable by the day.

He made a habit of checking her bank account he had set up daily. *She still had a little money in it and had not requested any additional transfers lately. If she wanted to just con me for money, she certainly wasn't very greedy. No, that's not it. Something is wrong.*

He made a mental note to call the Belanov Agency first thing in the morning, which would be midafternoon there, and ask if they could check on her.

But if they can't help, then what?

Irina listened intently to her voicemails again, the last from Natalyia Belanov asking if she was alright and that John was trying to contact her. She began to cry again. She wanted desperately to talk to him, to just hear his voice again. *What would I tell him, that I want to cancel our engagement after he spent all that time and money? That problems at home have stopped me?*

She gathered what courage she could muster and began to dial the numbers to make an international call, followed by prompts to enter her credit card number, and then prompted to dial the country code, area code, and number of the party to call... She listened as she counted two rings. Then she hung up and began to cry again.

Driving in traffic, John heard his flip phone ring, rushed to grasp and open it, and then it stopped before he could answer. The caller ID popped up as UNKNOWN. He was almost certain it was Irina, or at least hoping it was. He dialed her number in return and heard it ring the four times before going to voicemail again.

Irina saw the call come immediately back in. She could not bring herself to answer it yet as her eyes began to well up again.

Kuznetsov summoned Dimitri to his office again, officially under the guise of checking on their security system. The colonel had his staff run a check on the phone numbers communicated through Irina Balabanova's cell phone and found she had repeatedly dialed out to the United States, a number for a phone registered to an LLC with a 314 area code, a limited liability corporation with a billing address which turned out to be a small shipping store. This told him little about who specifically this American was. *Probably a front shell company.*

"She has not made any international calls lately that I can see, Colonel, unless she's using another phone somewhere else," Dimitri stated.

"You have actually physically examined her phone?" Kuznetsov asked, having the ability to monitor the phone records by now, but just wanting this informant to keep all eyes open.

"I did while she slept last night. She left it on a charger in the kitchen, uncommon for her but she has not been herself lately."

"Has not been herself? Explain."

"She just lays around the apartment and sleeps a lot. Totally out of character for her," Dimitri replied.

"I see," the colonel replied. "How about official documents? Did you uncover anything in her possession that resembled anything classified?"

Dimitri stalled, trying to appear cooperative. "No, I didn't see anything like that."

This young loser has little more to offer me, Kuznetsov observed. "But she does have knowledge of how your support technology accesses our security systems, correct?"

"I do not believe so, Colonel. Irina was never involved in that part of the company," believing he had a limit on giving Kuznetsov what he wanted to hear.

"Never involved in that part of the company, Dimitri? Are you suggesting a staffer in Petrov's security support company, a person that I have observed as being totally alone in that office, could not possibly access that information?"

Gusev felt as though he was being pressured and put in a box, one that he desperately wanted out of. "I could not say it would be impossible, but—"

"That will be sufficient for now, Dimitri." the colonel stated, cutting him off.

"Comrade Colonel, I was informed that my personnel file at More Security has been returned and nothing new or derogatory has been added or changed. Can I assume that I have nothing more to worry about?"

"Are you worried, Dimitri Gusev?"

"No sir, not worried," the young man from Gori, Georgia answered, appearing anything but. *Just being here as a snitch for you is a worry in itself.*

"That will be all for now, Dimitri." The colonel said. "You will wait in the retention room while my staff prepares a written sworn statement that you will sign."

The young security system tech walked out of Kuznetsov's office as the colonel jotted down some handwritten notes and took one last look into Irina Balabanova's new file, one that he had duplicated prior to returning the original containing a newly "updated" document.

It appears Irina Balabanova has had a disconnect with her American boyfriend. But I must add some insurance... Just in case.

The colonel completed a previously prepared correspondence, proofread it, and then sealed copies in two officially marked envelopes. He then buzzed his assistant who entered his office a short moment later.

"Calina, see that these get marked URGENT and CONFIDENTIAL and make certain both go out today. And also prepare a sworn affidavit for Dimitri Gusev to sign," he instructed coldly as he handed his staff assistant a sheet containing his hand-written notes.

The young staffer looked at the two envelopes and note paper briefly and replied, "Yes, Colonel." The young woman, now in her third year on Kuznetsov's staff, knew the drill all too well.

❧❧❧ ❦❦❦

John struggled in his business to focus as he could not stop thinking and worrying about Irina. He could not mentally get his arms around her not calling or taking his calls. *If she wanted to end our relationship, at least extend me the courtesy of telling me... No, that's not enough. She must look me in the eye and tell me this... And there is only one way that can happen.*

That evening, Johnny got home and noticed his father's travel bag on the kitchen table, open and half filled with clothing and some small travel-sized toiletries. He ventured down the hallway where he heard him in the master bedroom.

"Dad? Are you leaving for somewhere?"

John looked up, seeing his teenage son standing in the doorway. "Yes, I am leaving for Ukraine tomorrow morning."

"Really? So she got her visa and is coming here finally?" Johnny asked excitedly.

John thought about the implications of what his boy and the rest of family thought, that this was the final trip required to bring his new bride-to-be back here. *What happens if I fly over there and get the door slammed in my face? What happens if I get over there and cannot even see her?... This is a fool's errand, ole boy... Best just let it go.*

"No Johnny. The process isn't complete, yet. Something has gone wrong and I have lost communication with her."

"Lost communication? What does that mean, Dad?"

John looked at his son, a boy matured by sheer necessity beyond his years. "I haven't talked to her or even shared email messages for nearly three weeks now."

"That don't sound good, Dad."

"I know it don't, Son." John paused his packing while mentally struggling to face reality.

He hadn't even shopped online for airline tickets, yet. Just to walk up to the ticket counter at Lambert and purchase on the spot would be disastrous and probably cost him at least three grand. *I better slow down and think this through. Perhaps sleep on it... Who am I fooling? I don't sleep well during the best of times.*

The next morning, father and son shared a quick breakfast of instant grits as Johnny got ready to head out and catch the school bus. John had shopped online and found round-trip tickets for just under fourteen hundred dollars, even though the connections through Chicago and London required over eight hours layover.

"I thought you decided not to go, Dad."

"I know, Son. That would be the smart play, wouldn't it? I could get all the way over there and strike out."

"Or even get robbed or killed," Johnny added smartly.

"That could happen right here... And I've never lived my life being choked by caution, you know that."

Knowing it to be fruitless to try and talk his father out of it, Johnny lightened up a bit. "Who knows, you may come back with another one of those foreign babes."

"Hmm, no...that's not going to happen," John responded slowly as in deep thought. "I left Mom a message that you would be staying over with them a few days."

"What should I tell them, Dad? They'll want to know what's going on."

John thought about his reply, figuring he would just call the folks on his way to the airport. "Just tell them it's something I have to do."

⋙ ⋘

Irina returned from some brief shopping, still distraught emotionally and struggling to pull herself together. The guilt she felt inside at not calling or messaging John had her stomach tied up in knots. In the back of her mind, she retained a glimmer of hope that something good would happen and this nightmare regarding Colonel Kuznetsov would go away and allow her dream to return. But as each day went by, that glimmer faded and soon she would have to get back to work somewhere and support herself. She had called Arkady Petrov at her old company and was told he would gladly hire her back, but a replacement had already taken over.

As many times as she tried, she could just not bring herself to call John and break off their engagement. She wasn't sure she wanted to and suffered in the thought that he may have just gotten disgusted by now and moved on himself.

155

John doesn't deserve this. He has been my true man since that first day we met. He has followed through with everything he promised. We were only together a few days... But he loves me!... And may God help me. I love him, too.

Her emotional strength, which had been stressed gradually over the past three weeks, now collapsed. She then broke down again and cried.

CHAPTER TEN

Dear John

John took a shuttle flight that ran daily from the Cape Girardeau Regional Airport to Lambert International. Upon exiting the small aircraft, he entered the terminal and made his way toward his gate in preparation for his departure to Chicago. A former boss in Atlanta once told him he should never make important decisions when you're emotional, advice he always valued but couldn't apply this day. Once settled and waiting to board, he dialed up his parents' phone, and his mother answered on three rings.

"Mom, I'm in St. Louis, getting ready to fly out to Kiev."

"My, this is sudden. So, when is her interview?"

"I don't know,...yet," John replied and gave his mother the long litany of events, or lack thereof, that had occurred over the past three weeks.

"You know this doesn't sound too good... And there's no sense in us trying to talk you out of going back over there," his mother stated, knowing her oldest son all too well.

John paused before answering. "Johnny knows to come to your place after school, Mom. I'll call when I get there. Love you all."

"Love you too, John. We'll be praying for you."

After yet another long and sleepless night, Irina entered the kitchen in dire need of some coffee. She picked up her phone to check for missed calls and messages, noticing the battery being nearly dead. *This is strange, I know I plugged this in to charge it overnight. It had to have been unplugged... Dimitri!*

There was now little mystery as to where Kuznetsov had received such detailed information over time about her calls and she assumed Dimitri had also snooped around the apartment for any other incriminating information he could find. The damage had now been done and the only remaining question was how she would get rid of him.

Setting the issue with her tenant's betrayal aside, Irina decided to send John an email message, one that she hoped wouldn't break his heart as much as it was breaking hers.

Dear John, I am sorry you have not heard from me. Because of issues within my family and a police investigation on me, I cannot emigrate to America in the foreseeable future. I hope you will forgive me. You will always have a place in my heart.

Love, your Irina

PS: Feel free to transfer the money still in my account and cancel it. I will try and pay you back the rest someday.

She sat and proofread the message, preparing to hit SEND when she heard a knock on the door. *Who could this be at this time of morning? Momma and Papa or Alika would have called before coming over here... And they never knocked before entering anyway.*

Irina opened the front door and standing before her in the hallway was a young woman, perhaps her own age and one distant in memory, wearing an official-looking female uniform and the SSU badge displayed prominently on the collar. Irina saw a red flag of concern flash before her, which immediately instilled an extreme sense of dread. "Yes?"

The young woman struggled to recognize the lovely Irina Viktorivna Balabanova, as the woman facing her looked terrible, one who appeared to have not slept, washed, or applied an ounce of make-up in days. She thus held up a copy of her photograph for credence, while also handing over a prepared handwritten memo and signaling with an index finger to her lips to be silent. Irina read the scribbled note, looking up at her with a confused blank expression, and then the SSU agent leaned forward to whisper in Irina's ear.

"I am Calina Zhvikova, from the State Security of Ukraine, Kharkov Oblast office. Your apartment may have listening devices. I suggest we talk outside, perhaps around in back of the building."

Extremely wary about the nature of this visit, Irina also knew she had best cooperate with this female officer. She nodded and hurried to don some clothing while the official woman waited, and stepped out into the corridor, closing the door behind.

The two walked quietly down the hall together and toward the stairway, descending to the first floor, out the rear building exit, and into the small courtyard when Zhvikova asked, "May I address you as Irina?"

"Yes, of course," Irina replied, her pulse rate starting to subside, if just a bit, as if realizing this woman may be a friend and not a foe, although still suspecting the probability of the evil Colonel Pavel Kuznetsov somehow being behind this.

The woman looked around for bystanders, already knowing there were no security cameras overlooking the rear of this particular apartment complex. She guided Irina toward a park bench in the far corner, away from the building and under a large shade tree where the two sat down together.

"I work in the SSU office. My superior is Colonel Pavel Kuznetsov, a man whom I believe you are quite familiar."

Irina's facial expression turned from being serious to genuinely fearful.

"You need not be afraid of me, Irina. I know by the colonel's actions that he has eyes on you and that you have rejected him in the past. He is also a man who hates Americans and gets enraged when an ethnic Russian woman, especially one young and beautiful as yourself, leaves this country for a man in the West. He has been watching you for some time now and is also getting much information from the man you live with, Dimitri Gusev."

"I know Dimitri has been spying on me," Irina said in a sign of resignation.

"What you do not know is he was called into Colonel Kuznetsov's office yesterday. I know not the total of what they discussed behind closed doors, but within minutes of Gusev leaving his office, the colonel handed me a memo and ordered me to type up a sworn affidavit that he pressured Gusev to sign, stating that you had accessed the More Security Supply company codes for entry into the SSU security system. He also handed me two sealed envelopes, one addressed to the US Embassy FBI Liaison Office in Kiev, and the second to SSU National Headquarters, Emigration Security Division, also in Kiev. I do not believe this was coincidental."

"It matters not now," Irina replied in resignation. "I am halting my relationship with the American I have met. I haven't even spoken to him for weeks now. And believe me, I worked at More Security Supply for five years and was nothing but a receptionist and accountant. I had nothing to do with the technical side."

"Regarding your relations with an American, that is your personal business. But I will tell you that Colonel Kuznetsov is a wicked man and one who does not accept failure when it comes from women. He will use the Gusev statement to keep an investigation open on you indefinitely. I know that you attempted to reacquire your old position with Arkady Petrov. He would have brought you back and even given you a generous raise in pay, but the colonel stopped it cold. He was suspended by the SSU Commandant in Kiev last fall for weeks and he somehow blames you. Trust me, you have not seen or heard the last of him."

Irina listened carefully to this government policewoman, one quite attractive in her own right. "Calina? Did you not state that as your name? You were the staff agent at the SSU who disclosed this information to Marko Palenko, my father's old boss at the petrol refinery, were you not?"

"Yes, that is true."

"You place yourself in great peril," Irina added, curious why she would do such a thing.

"I am not worried about Marko, Irina. He and my father are old friends. But I caution you, do not share what I have told you too openly. Colonel Kuznetsov will suspect where it came from," Calina replied. "If you need to contact me, here is a number. But do not call me on your home phone, Irina. I have not seen the order as of yet, but the colonel may have it bugged, the same with your cell phone. We cannot listen or record calls on cell phones yet but are able to identify the phone numbers in and out of calls made."

As the SSU staffer stood and prepared to leave, Irina grabbed her arm gently and asked, "Calina, why are you telling me all this? You do not even know me."

The young woman briefly looked around nervously and sat back down. "I do know you, Irina Viktorivna Balabanova. I see you every time I look in the mirror. I was in love with Pavel some time ago and then learned he was a married man. I prepared to leave him but found out I was pregnant. He promised to divorce his wife and that we would have a life together, get married, and raise a family. But he backed out, telling me it would damage his career if he left his current wife and children. I was afraid and had an abortion. The operation was difficult and left me unable to conceive any more children," the woman explained, her eyes starting to well up with an obvious painful sadness.

"Pavel Kuznetsov is an evil man who knows nothing of love but only sees young women as trophies to be won and paraded around with. He would not hesitate to do the same to any other, and right now, Irina, he has his sights on you."

Irina listened intently, herself saddened by this Calina's story, and realizing no matter how tragic her own life's saga had been, there would always be someone who had it worse. "Calina, it is not my business, but how do you still work there, around that,...that monster?"

"My parents know nothing of my abortion and Pavel Kuznetsov would care less in telling them. He holds that over me. And I have to work to support myself."

The two young women embraced each other warmly while both came to tears.

"We did almost meet before, Calina," Irina stated emotionally. "It was at a company Christmas party two years ago. You were with Colonel Kuznetsov there. I am sorry."

"Yes, I remember," Calina responded solemnly. "Please do not have pity on me, Irina. If I didn't work at the Oblast security office, I would not be able to help women like you. That is my reward."

"I don't know how to thank you, Calina. I hope you find happiness in your life, somewhere."

"No man wants to marry a woman who cannot have children, Irina," Calina replied, as she rose and strolled toward the side of the building and out to the street.

Irina sat motionless as she watched the brave young woman walk away. *I have an idea!* She got up from the bench quickly and ran swiftly to catch up with the SSU girl, speeding around the corner of the building, just as Calina entered the awaiting car and closed the door.

An official vehicle from the SSU? Oh my god, Calina! Kuznetsov will know you have been here!

Her terrified look changed quickly to an optimistic bewilderment as she watched the black Mercedes pull away from the curb and make a sharp U-turn before heading back in the other direction and passing right in front of her. Not easily recognized through the bulletproof and tinted window, the driver rolled it down and appeared to give Irina a friendly wave,...a slightly built man for one serving in the SSU,...*and wearing a goatee!*

"There will be a man who would love you someday, Calina!" Irina yelled out, oblivious to any listening neighbors or bystanders.

She stood by the curb as she watched the black sedan motor off into the distance, a sadness overcoming her as she felt the irony of getting such support from this unlikely of sources, "I even know a man like that," Irina spoke silently to herself, becoming misty-eyed again.

⋙ ⋘

Tired from the layover in Chicago, John settled in for the long trans-Atlantic flight to London, attempting to settle back in the cramped coach section and get a bit of catch-up sleep following the standard fare airline dinner. He would arrive at Heathrow at 7:00 AM local time and would be thankful for the lengthy layover, as getting routed to connecting flights at the large and aged airport was very challenging, especially for infrequent international travelers.

Per habit, John sought out an internet access source at the main terminal to check his emails, prudent in handling agenda items in his business and hopeful that something from Irina would be there, a wish not forthcoming.

John boarded and got seated on the connecting Ukrainian International flight, having a tentative plan in place on what was going to happen in the next couple days, as he felt the need to do something and face this crisis head-on, and avoiding any thoughts of possible failure.

Had he received some sort of communication while still in London, either by email or voicemail, that Irina was cancelling their engagement, he had resigned himself to cut his losses, halt travel on the spot, and return home, even as difficult as that would be. As there was nothing, the UIA Boeing 737 flew eastward over Europe while he still held out hope that a live visit could resolve whatever had come up.

Landing again at Boryspil International in Kiev, John completed the now routine formality of passing through Ukrainian Customs and Immigration and then approached the domestic flight ticket counter where, lo and behold, the same two female agents awaited, smiling at him as though it was only yesterday. *There is that supervisor! Like I haven't seen her before.*

As if John had a reservation, the supervisor waved him over to an unoccupied terminal, smiling at him as she logged in and powered up the idle system.

"I feel like I know you from somewhere, Nastya," John stated, reading her nametag.

She looked up, again smiling. "Do you fly in Ukraine regularly, Mr. Masters?" she asked as she glanced at his passport and credit card.

"Well no, but?"

"I am afraid the last shuttle flight to Kharkov has been cancelled. The aircraft has some sort of mechanical problems," Nastya stated, still smiling.

Mechanical problems? Didn't ground that museum piece before!... "Okay, well when does the next... Wait a minute. How did you know I was planning to fly to Kharkov from here?"

Not changing an expression, she replied, "I see you in the system. Your last ticket was purchased for travel to Kharkov. That was back in—"

"Yes, yes, that's okay. I know when it was." *Your system also shows I bought a ticket to Odessa once and wanted a second ticket... Oh well.*

"May I suggest a car rental. The agencies are right down the hall, and it may be difficult for you to rent a car in Kharkov, and actually more expensive."

A car rental? Not very good sales people, these agents. "Very well, I'll head to the car rental counters. Will you be the agent there, too?"

"Excuse me, Sir? I do not understand."

"Never mind," John replied, smiling off-handedly as he gathered his passport and credit card before walking away.

Not resisting a final glance, he turned around. *I know that face...*

Already preparing to assist the next flyer, the ticket agent supervisor looked up toward John...*and smiled.*

Irina hadn't slept a wink as she now had the burden of this seemingly never-ending SSU investigation to add to the emotional trauma regarding John. Still feeling tremendously guilty over cutting off communications with him, she decided to proceed in sending him the message she had written out early the day before. Thinking herself strong enough to finally send it, she began to feel awfully weak afterward and began to tear up, yet again.

She picked up the gray cat, one that Dimitri had given her earlier. The pet was fat and ugly as cats go, but she had gradually gotten attached to it, enjoying the sound of the purring as she stroked its fur.

You're supposed to have nine lives... I wonder how many I get?

Suddenly she heard a knock at the door. Not a subtle, polite knock, but three hard knocks seconds apart. Opening the door, she faced the last person she ever wished to see, Colonel Pavel Kuznetsov. Displaying perfectly white dentures that only served to accent a devious smile, he began, "Irina Viktorivna Balabanova, how pleasant to see you again."

Attempting to hide her contempt, more out of fear than respect, she replied, "Colonel, how may I help you?"

The arrogant SSU official walked in and past her without an invite, looking around as he stood in the foyer. "Dimitri is not home, yet?" he asked, as if a formality.

"No," Irina replied. She suspected Kuznetsov knew exactly where her tenant was.

"How old is this building?" The colonel asked, looking around as if to imply her apartment was subpar. He continued to stroll from room to room, much to Irina's exasperation.

"I believe it was built in the 1960s. What can I do for you, Colonel?"

"I spoke to Arkady Petrov just the other day. He informed me that you wanted your old job back," the colonel commented with a feigned expression of concern. "But he had already hired someone. A great pity, Irina. You were very good in your position there."

What an arrogant ass! You know very well why I cannot get my old job back! "I knew the business."

"It must be very difficult for a young single woman to support herself, no?"

"I will find a way," she answered, now extremely uncomfortable and wishing the sinister Kuznetsov would leave.

"You are quite versed in security affairs, a talent we could use in the SSU Oblast office, Irina."

"The Oblast has my application, from years ago," she replied, trying to say anything to conclude the conversation and unpleasant incursion by this pompous official.

"Should you decide to move to Kharkov and work for me, I could arrange a modern apartment for you, paid for by the agency, of course," Kuznetsov offered, believing such an offer could not be refused, considering the young woman's current financial predicament.

"I will think about it, Colonel," she repeated, almost shocked this wicked man could behave so casually after their earlier restaurant encounter, even if it was months ago.

"How much does Dimitri pay you in rent every month, Irina?"

"He pays me six hundred hryvnias per month," she replied, continuously irritated at dealing with questions she was quite certain this SSU man knew the answers to.

"Six hundred hryvnias... That is about a week's pay for you, correct?"

"Yes, Colonel. It was."

"It was...it was," Kuznetsov repeated as he continued to snoop around the apartment, very much to her displeasure. "You know, Dimitri may very well be suspended from his position at Petrov's company, pending the results of the investigation on his security clearance. In fact, you yourself may have difficulty finding employment for the same reason...Hard times we live in nowadays, very hard times, Irina. But you know a man in my position—"

"I wish you to leave, Colonel!"

"You wish me to leave?... You wish me to leave?! Let me tell you something, Irina Viktorivna Balabanova! You will never leave this nation with your American lover! I have made certain of that! I know you! I know you better than you know yourself. You will give me what I want. Women always do!"

"Get out! Get out or I'll scream!"

Irina, now terrified and backed into the kitchen, struggled as Kuznetsov placed his left hand around her neck while tearing at the top of her blouse with the right. Fearing the worst, she spied her collection of cooking knives out of the corner of her eye, arranged on a hanger below the cupboard. She was a split second from grabbing one when yet another sudden hard knock was heard at her front door. The two froze just for a few seconds when the hard knock continued.

"Open up! This is an emergency! Open or we will have to break in!"

The voice was loud and authoritative. Kuznetsov released her as she ran for the door, opening it as fast as she could turn locks and knobs. Two uniformed men walked in, carrying a myriad of tools and small tanks. Seeing the young woman in a state of distress, the older of the two inquired, "Is everything all right here, Miss?"

Kuznetsov stepped in front of her and stood erect. "What is your business here?!" he demanded, staring back at Irina sternly as if to command that she remain silent.

"Sorry for the interruption. We are from the gas company and there has been a serious and very dangerous gas leak detected somewhere in this building. We have been ordered to have all occupants assemble outside in the courtyard until we isolate and repair the problem."

The still angry and excited colonel shot past the three of them and out the door, moving rapidly while shoving people out of his way who were exiting their own apartments, eventually stomping his way out of the building to his awaiting staff car and then drove off.

Irina marched down with the other apartment owners and tenants to the courtyard, extremely thankful for the timing and trying to recall if they had ever had such a drill in the building before. Thirty minutes later, the two servicemen in gas company uniforms walked out, announcing to the crowd it was safe to return to their apartments.

Irina overheard one tenant ask if they had found the problem and the youngest and largest of the two replied, "Yes, just some loose pipe connections in the basement."

Still in process of lowering her heartbeat, she engaged in some small talk with the two, along with a few of her neighbors, as they gathered their tools and supplies preparing to leave. She asked the older one just how long he had worked for the gas company.

"Just long enough, I believe," he answered, smiling, before downing a huge gulp of cold water, kindly given to each of them by an elderly tenant. He then made an amusing display of using the lower part of his shirt to wipe the dripping water off his beard, a *goatee*.

John left the airport in his rental vehicle, a Renault Logan sedan, not clear on the overall rate he would pay for a few days but certain it would be too much if he had to extend the time on it. No sooner than he pulled out and onto the E40 Expressway, he noticed the fuel tank was down to less than a quarter tank, so he motored into a gas station just off the four-lane highway to fill up. The weather was warm but rainy, so he chose to check under the hood where he found a near empty windshield washer tank. Walking inside, he purchased a gallon of the cleaner and topped off the small reservoir, which held just less than half of it, thus he sat the remaining half-full plastic jug on the back seat.

Left over from the former Soviet days were traffic checkpoints, something many foreigners were not accustomed to. Aside from speeding and responding to accidents, Ukrainian police would be posted every 150 kilometers, less than one hundred miles, to halt motorists and check everything from car registrations to passports (Ukrainians had to carry internal passports) to narcotics to open onboard liquor.

John's first encounter occurred approximately a third of the way toward Kharkov and went smoothly. The officer checked his documents, reached in the car and sniffed around a bit, and happily waved John on his merry way.

The second stop was unnerving. That officer followed the same routine but asked John to step out of the vehicle, and began to go through all of the contents, including his travel belongings. John's lack of the local language didn't meet with any reprieve as the officer began barking numerous questions that John couldn't comprehend. When the policeman got on his radio and began to chatter to someone, John thought he was in big trouble. The two stood side by side, leaning up against the front left fender of the Renault for what seemed like an eternity, when a second police vehicle drove up and parked right behind them, as John wished he had more hryvnias in his pocket right then. Another officer got out and the two talked for a just a few minutes prior to the second officer, who spoke a bit of English, approached John.

"You have vodka? Liquor?"

Making certain he understood clearly, John made some signs of a man drinking, then pointed to himself, and said, "No."

The officer then began to check in the car again and pulled out the half-full jug of washer fluid. He took the cap off and took a whiff of the strong-smelling chemical, quickly grunted to himself, then promptly re-secured it, and placed it back on the rear seat.

The two officers made a point of then chatting away from John, an act he thought of as folly because he would little understand what they were talking about anyway. The second officer then chose to revisit John's documents, strolled back to hand them back over, and stood away from the car to wave the "tourist" onward as John's heartbeat started to finally subside a bit.

He slowly pulled away, thinking he would hesitate to use the wiper washers again.

He must have smelled it on the outside... Who said this renting a car was a good idea?

⇢⇢⇢ ⇠⇠⇠

John had come better prepared this trip, at least partially, as he had picked up a prepaid phone at the airport in Kiev and proceeded to call over to the Belanov Agency. They agreed that Sergei would arrange for an apartment as before and that he meet John early the following morning, planning on a day as a hired interpreter. It was well past midnight when John got into Kharkov and arrived at the reserved apartment in the same building as before.

Treating with the same security guy at the check-in kiosk, John was remembered and happily handed the key to his apartment, this time on the third floor. The place was laid out identical to the previous apartment with an entry foyer, closet and bathroom off the hallway, a parlor, a kitchen, and a bedroom. The rental was parked out on the street and locked, well it had insurance plus John had paid extra for the deductible.

He unpacked his bags and went to the kitchen, wondering if the plug-in devices here would have the same electrical problems and decided not to chance it. Strolling to the parlor, the old sofa was of different colored material but eerily the same and very uncomfortable to sleep on, he was certain. In the back of

John's mind, he would consider it a godsend if Irina would have need to stay here and the old couch would come into play as a point of conversation again.

The place was bringing back memories as John opened his laptop, connected to the apartment's internet, and logged in to his email, seeing he had a response from Irina for the first time in over three weeks. Reading its content, John felt crushed.

Issues with her family? Police investigation? Irina?

After spending what seemed like hours wearing out the tired old carpet, John went to the bedroom and laid down, hoping to get a bit of sleep, thinking and hoping tomorrow would be a better day. Sleep was hopeless as his mind raced a hundred miles per hour.

Will I be able to find her? If so, what if things go badly? What could I do, anyway? I'm no lawyer, and even if I was, what good would that do me here?

John looked at his prepaid phone, hoping it would ring and Irina would be calling him, but then reminding himself how foolish the thought as she wouldn't know the disposable phone's number anyway. He thought numerous times about calling her but the sheer idea of getting shut down over the phone had him spooked. *No, I'm going to face this music head-on, and then let the cards fall where they may.*

Irina had just left the family home for her apartment after spending most of the afternoon. She announced to them that she had broken off her relationship with the American and now her mother worried less about Mikhail going on a rampage against Pavel Kuznetsov. Irina had decided against telling them about the altercation with the colonel at the apartment earlier, knowing that would just feed the fire.

Nadine was now concerned about her oldest daughter and wished the girl had just stayed over for dinner and perhaps even a few days. She knew the cottage was a bit crowded since Alika was married and Misha had moved in, not to mention both Nadine and Alika knowing that Irina tired of her brother-in-law's subtle but ongoing hints about hooking her up with his pal, Kolya.

The family had all seen the pain Irina went through a year ago when Daryle had left her, knew of all the sad loneliness through all those months until the weeks just before Christmas. Something had happened. She had met another guy, another American, and then saw that sparkle again in Irina's beautiful big brown eyes.

But why did she hide it from us? Nadine pondered. *Was it just the pain from her past? Or was it something else?*

⟫⟫⟩ ⟨⟨⟨⟪

Irina entered the apartment just past seven, hearing a stir in the kitchen and knowing Dimitri must already be in for the evening.

"Irina, is that you?"

"Yes, it's me." *Who else would it be?*

"I have some borscht on the stove. You are more than welcome to have some with me," Dimitri asked loudly, assuming she was in her bedroom with the door closed. "Have you found another job, yet?"

Irina suddenly appeared in the kitchen doorway showing little effort to hide her disdain. "No, and I need to make sure you pay your rent on time next week."

"How have you been, Irina?... I mean you seem kind of down these past few weeks."

"Why don't you tell me, since you have been spying on me?!"

"Irina, I know you are upset with the job thing. But don't get paranoid on me," Dimitri responded nervously.

"You are dumber than you look, Dimitri. It was you that snooped through my phone the other day. You should have at least been smart enough to plug it back in. My calls! My emails!... Colonel Kuznetsov was here! He is the reason I cannot get a job and guess what else. Did you know he may have you suspended from your job? He'll do that because then you will not be able to pay me rent!

You think being a rat and backstabbing me would play favor with a man like him? You are such a fool, Dimitri!"

He stood stunned in the kitchen momentarily and unable to speak. Now in panic mode, Dimitri replied, "Irina, think this through. I heard from over at the SSU office that Colonel Kuznetsov plans to get rid of his main staff assistant to make room and hire you, and at double what Arkady was paying. If you take that job, we'll both be in the clear."

Irina could not believe her ears. "Dimitri, you disgust me! You are nothing but Colonel Kuznetsov's lap boy! By the first of the month, I want you out of here. You hear me? I want you gone and never want to see your sorry butt here again—ever!"

CHAPTER ELEVEN

Reverse of Fortune

J ohn finally fell off to sleep around 3:00 AM and exhausted, didn't wake up until he heard the buzz on his temporary phone at just past nine. It was Sergei calling.

"Good morning," John creaked in a voice that informed Sergei he wasn't fully awake yet.

"John, good morning. Listen, I'm afraid I cannot go with you today. Natalyia has gone to Kiev for a few days and I have to be in the office. Would you like to come in and we can try to call Irina from here, or perhaps set you up with someone else. We have had many new clients sign on with us since you were here last."

"No Sergei, Irina is my girl and come hell or high water, I am taking her to America and we're getting married. I know you probably think I'm a fool for thinking that way, but it's really something I want to do. Let me think about this and I'll call you back."

The two disconnected and John sat up in bed, dejected that his plan had gone south and desperately wondered to himself what he should do. Stretched out on the bed, he stared up at the ceiling. He was still extremely tired from all the traveling and lack of sleep, to add to that of being mentally exhausted. He finally got up, thinking about chancing the plugin water kettle to make some instant coffee, but remembering he hadn't brought any and knowing the cupboard was no doubt bare of coffee and everything else. As such, he decided to take a walk down memory lane and headed for McDonald's.

After downing three cups of coffee, recalling they were small, John walked back the few blocks to the apartment, thinking he would just have to kill a day and re-institute his plan for tomorrow.

Wait a minute... Sergei said his boss would be gone to Kiev for a few days. What if she's not back tomorrow?... Or the next day? I'll be stuck here doing nothing, maybe all week! I could just take off in my rental car and head down to Chuguev myself. But with my not speaking Russian or Ukrainian, what if I need to stop for help anywhere? What if Irina's not home and I have to talk to her folks? What if nobody is home?

John was conflicted with himself all the way back to the apartment. Never one for sitting around and waiting, he decided to throw caution to the wind and head out, figuring the smart play would be to first stop by the Belanov office, get some advice, and then head southeast for Chuguev.

Sergei greeted John with a hearty handshake and the two engaged in some brief small talk. He couldn't help but notice John's attire, an expensive dark blue suit, pressed collared shirt and tie, and polished dark leather shoes.

"I must say you look very sharp this morning, John."

"I hope to meet my future bride and her family today. One must keep up appearances," he replied and sat down opposite Sergei's desk to fill him in on the details of the ongoing saga.

"This is very unusual, John. The last time we saw Irina was the last time we saw you, when we all had dinner at the Pushka. Sometimes our clients have problems with K-1 visas or other issues with their fiancés, but they generally contact us to let us know or even seek help, and in some cases repost their advertisements with us. We have heard nothing from Irina. Nothing, John."

"Well, Sergei, her email stated she had some sort of family issues and something about a police investigation. How would I find out about that?"

"A police investigation? Irina? That is hard to believe," Sergei answered, genuinely shocked. "I suppose we could call the local police, but I doubt if they would tell us anything over the phone. Even if we went down there, I doubt if they would disclose any information to us unless she has been arrested."

"I searched online for anything police, investigation, and her name, but saw nothing. Of course, much of the search results came up with websites in Russian or Ukrainian language only, and I couldn't tell you the difference in the two if my life depended on it."

"Let me see what I can find." Sergei added, and typed in a few words on his Russian and Ukrainian search engines..."Nothing, John."

"I think I'm going to just drive down to Chuguev and see what happens. Probably be dangerous, wouldn't it, Sergei?"

"I'm not certain. How about I type out some basic information you can use. It would be better than nothing."

Sergei worked up and printed out a simple memo page in three languages for John that read:

I am an American man who only speaks English. Looking for Irina Balabanova
For more information, contact my agent, Sergei Volkov, at +380-68-715-9234

Sergei also printed out a detailed street map of Chuguev, highlighting the streets to take from Kharkov in finding her address and John had him print out two additional copies before proceeding to head out the door.

"Say Sergei, is there some kind of military base near here? I passed several armored vehicles and a couple of tanks on the way here."

"There are many army exercises happening right now. We have many Russian separatists here and all along the eastern border areas. They want us to be part of Russia."

"Is it safe around here?" John asked seriously.

"Oh yes, the Russian President rants but he won't bother us. We have a treaty with the United States which guarantees our protection."

"A treaty, huh? I wasn't aware of that."

"Yes, it was signed in Budapest just over ten years ago," Sergei declared. "It was also signed by the leaders of Russia and the UK."

Ten years ago, huh? Best sleep with one eye open, Sergei.

⤜⤜⤜ ⤛⤛⤛

The small garage would house two vehicles, but usually one as much space was taken up with the various tools and other equipment. There were four vehicles waiting to be repaired and Mikhail had left to visit an area salvage yard to buy parts for two of them, parts he would have to remove from salvaged vehicles himself.

Misha had moved in and worked for his father-in-law shortly after marrying Alika a little over a year earlier. He worked steadily, preparing to pull the engine out of the old Lada. His wife Alika, now pregnant with their first child, had gone with his mother-in-law, Nadine, into town with his sister-in-law, Irina, to do some shopping. He worried about her likened state as she was having intermittent bouts of morning sickness.

He heard their dog bark heartily and slowly rolled himself on the "creeper" out from under the car to check on the distraction. Other than the mail carrier, they rarely had company during the day with exception of their own auto repair customers, and all of them knew about the dog and to call first as the shop was located at the rear of the property.

Misha chained the animal to a post beside the shop and made his way toward the front gate, unlatching it to greet the visitor and tensed up when he saw the late model four-door sedan parked out on the street in front of the house, and a sharply dressed tall and fit man get out of the car and approach.

John offered his hand but Misha, having greasy hands from the shop, declined and the two greeted each other simply by saying, "Privet."

John thought Misha may be a hired hand, not knowing Irina's sister or her husband lived there or ever knowing or recalling the brother-in-law's name. Cutting to the chase, John showed Misha the note Sergei had printed out for him and was disappointed the young man had little reaction excepting a confused grin.

"Irina Balabanova?" John stated, pointing around as if to signal and question her whereabouts.

Misha was now leery of this man, one he took for some sort of government agent, and just shook his head repeatedly, John interpreting that as either he didn't know any Irina Balabanova or was simply telling him she was not around.

Frustrated, John got out a blank postcard with their address written out on the back, held it up for Misha to see, and with crude sign language attempted to qualify if this was indeed the correct residence for that address. In response, Misha did nod his head affirmatively, which was some progress at least. He then signaled to John by repeatedly holding up his watch that he needed to get back to work, implying that his "visitor" leave so he could close and secure the gate.

A frustrated John left Misha the note from Sergei and returned to his car, choosing to wait, at least for a while, to see if Irina or anyone else showed up. Local residents and others seemed to randomly appear on the street and make a point to pass by him in his parked vehicle, staring curiously as if he was a stranger from another planet. Upon reflection, most of the vehicles in the local vicinity were quite dated compared to his Renault and unlike Odessa or even Kharkov, where formal business suits and ties were prevalent, his attire must have appeared a bit over the top.

After sitting there for three-plus hours, John had enough and decided to head out, wishing he had brought some of his business cards as it may have been a good idea to leave one.

Misha had stuffed the crumpled note with Sergei's name and number in his greasy shirt pocket, along with a couple of wrenches as he returned to the shop. Once he rolled back under the car, he reached into the pocket for one of the tools and the note fell to the floor into a pool of spilled transmission fluid. By the time he realized it, the wheels of his creeper had rolled over the piece of paper a few times, grinding the note into the soaked concrete. *If it's that important, he will be back,* he thought as he continued work while thinking about Alika.

John drove slowly through Chuguev, backtracking as if following breadcrumbs to make his way back to the highway. Once exiting Irina's immediate neighborhood, the citizenry in the town had an unpleasant attitude about themselves, almost as if depression was rampant. It somewhat reminded him of driving through the poorer side of town in a major US city, the difference being the locals hanging out on the main boulevards here paid him little attention and in a strange sort of way, were not at all threatening.

Maybe I'll be back tomorrow... Or maybe I'll wait until Sergei can come back with me, assuming that won't take too many more days waiting... I hope I still have a business to return to or don't go broke trying to get back to it!

John made it back to his apartment with little fanfare, with even the one police checkpoint passed as routine, made easier by virtue of John choosing to keep the windshield washer fluid jug in the trunk. Having little in the way of an appetite, he stopped at a local convenience market and picked up a few canned soups and a liter of milk, shaking off a pause as there was no expiration date stamped on it.

After checking his email and digesting the continued disappointment of having no additional messages from Irina, John pondered briefly about going out, maybe have dinner at Pushkas, but he was tired and chose to make an early evening of it. Swallowing two Ambien pills, he soon crashed.

Irina saw her phone was dead and plugged it in to charge while she soaked in the bathtub for nearly an hour, as it seemed to relax her a small amount. Drying off and donning her bathrobe, she powered the phone back up and saw there were three missed calls, dialing her parents' number back immediately.

"Irina! We've been calling! Where have you been?"

"Calm down, Momma. I was just taking a bath... What?"

"Papa is so upset. He says a police investigator came by looking for you today!"

Oh my god!... Kuznetsov! I cannot believe he is tracking me down at their place now! "What did he want, Momma? Why did he stop in there? He knows where I live."

"Hold on, I'll get Papa."

Irina waited patiently while her mother ran to get her father on the phone. She was both shocked and angry that Colonel Kuznetsov would now be bothering her parents.

"Irina, what is happening? Now the government police are looking for you here!" Mikhail exclaimed, obviously very much alarmed.

"Papa, what did he say?"

"I don't know all of it. I was gone. Misha talked to him, and he left right away to take Alika to the doctor."

Morning sickness, Irina thought. Her sister being pregnant with her first child, she had been up and down continuously for a week or better. Irina had dropped her and their mother off earlier, knowing Alika was getting sick, but didn't bother to stay and had driven away before Misha even knew they had gotten back from shopping.

"Papa, I don't know what to do. Call me back when Misha and Alika get home," she directed and then hung up.

Irina stirred around the apartment a nervous wreck while waiting for the callback, now feeling totally helpless. Desperate to do something, anything, she dug a piece of scratch paper out of her purse and started to dial when she caught herself. *Oh my god! Calina told me specifically not to use my own phone to call.*

Following another thirty minutes of waiting and pacing the floor, she stepped out into the hallway and knocked on the next door neighbor's door, an elderly woman who had occupied the apartment long before Irina was born.

"Privet, Mrs. Cherenkova. I wonder if I may ask to use your phone a few minutes. My cell phone has problems and I think it is broken. The call is local," she added to assure the frail babushka.

"Oh, let me show you. My telephone is right in here," Mrs. Cherenkova responded as she led Irina by the hand and into her parlor where the phone was tethered to a wall outlet.

Irina called the number, prepared to keep her voice low as Mrs. Cherenkova stood attentively behind her. Greeted immediately with voicemail, she left a message, "Calina, this is Irina Balabanova. Please call me back at 380-68-387-7812, after six o'clock."

Hanging up the phone, Irina immediately thanked the old woman and prepared to leave, wishing to drive across town to the parents' place right away.

"Is everything all right, child?" The longtime neighbor asked sincerely, having known Irina's family here from the time she was a toddler. "I'm not being nosey, but I have heard some loud disputes coming from your apartment lately."

"Thanks for your concern, Mrs. Cherenkova. I just have much happening right now." Irina replied. *That is an understatement.... And of course, you are being nosey!*

⟫⟫⟫ ⟪⟪⟪

Irina arrived at the family cottage thirty minutes later, wanting to hopefully calm her parents down and be there if and when Calina Zhvikova returned her call. Her mother met her in the small foyer and her father sat solemnly at the dinner table. The overall mood was anything but good.

"Daughter, you must have serious things going on. Now you have the SSU and even a foreign police detective investigating you!" Mikhail was obviously completely upset.

Foreign police detective? Irina looked to her mother for some moral support but Nadine was patently uncomfortable, now sitting down at the table and at a loss for words.

"Papa, what did the investigator say?" Irina asked desperately. "How do you know he was foreign?"

"I know few details. Misha was excited when I got in," he replied.

"Alika was very sick and they were in a hurry to get her to the doctor," Nadine added.

Irina now felt as someone who was in deep trouble, reflecting on how her simple effort in placing an ad at a marriage agency had turned her into a criminal. She now disclosed the details of most of her earlier conversation with Calina Zhvikova, her blow up with Dimitri, and the visit the day before she received from Colonel Kuznetsov, leaving out the part about him assaulting her in the kitchen, as knowing that would completely set her father off.

"You may have to consider the colonel's offer to work at the SSU," Mikhail stated.

Irina had a blank look as Nadine interjected, "No way, Papa Balabanov! How could you even suggest such a thing like this?"

"She may face going to jail, Nadine!" Mikhail yelled and then got up from the table "I'm going to step outside and check on the dog."

The two women began to clear the dinner table, finding it difficult to have a conversation after Mikhail had returned from the outside. He departed to the parlor after a bit, and Irina and her mother soon heard the TV bellowing, a habit he long possessed when attempting to suppress anxiety.

"You may have to accept Kuznetsov's job offer, Irina. You would be working as an office administrator, not a prostitute," Nadine suggested.

"I am not certain there would be much difference, Momma."

"Papa just doesn't want you in trouble, that is all."

"I know, Momma. I know," Irina replied, conscious that her parents were still in the dark on part of the saga. *You and Papa don't know Colonel Kuznetsov the way I do... How much worse can things happen in my life?*

Forty minutes later, the women heard the phone ring in the parlor just one time and assumed Mikhail had answered it. He soon shouted toward the kitchen, stating the incoming call was for Irina, and she quickly ran to the parlor to take it.

"This is Irina."

"Privet Irina. This is Calina Zhvikova."

"Oh, thank you so much for calling me back, Calina. Are you at a place where we can talk?"

"Certainly, Irina."

"I had a very unpleasant visit from Colonel Kuznetsov. And then I unloaded on Dimitri," Irina replied, continuing by filling her newly found "kindred spirit" in on the details. "If Kuznetsov would fire someone on his staff to make room for me, would that be you, Calina?"

"Of course, Irina. I am the only one at SSU assigned exclusively to the colonel. The other two staffers are shared between him and four other officers."

"Calina, did Dimitri sign some sort of statement that I illegally accessed SSU data while I worked for Arkady Petrov?"

"Yes, Irina, a sworn affidavit. But Dimitri knew when he signed it they were likely not his exact words."

"He said that?"

"No, but I am the one who was tasked with typing up the document. It came from the colonel's handwritten notes, notes which had lines crossed through and other comments written to replace them and add to the testimony. This is not the first time I have been tasked to do this. I am so sorry."

Irina could tell there was immense remorse coming from the other end of the call. "Calina, do you have an apartment paid for by the SSU?"

"Not anymore, Irina. That was the arrangement for a little longer than a year. I was told it was all because of budget cuts which I knew was a lie. But by then, I was happy to just pay my rent and live free of him, at least somewhat," Calina relayed in a saddened voice, as if ashamed.

"I would not consider a job there under those conditions and definitely not with knowing I would take the position away from you," Irina stated truthfully.

"You should not in your life want my job, Irina. And not because of any consideration toward me. I would deserve it... It was another sad girl who lost her job because of me three long years ago," Calina confessed, as much to herself as to the woman whom her former lover had targeted to take her place.

Irina listened as tears formed, so happy to hear Calina's admission and yet so sad for her. "Calina, do you think the SSU, I mean Colonel Kuznetsov, would involve Interpol or the American FBI to investigate me?"

"Interpol? American FBI? Where did you get that idea? The colonel despises those people, as they feel toward him."

Irina then proceeded to inform her about the visit to her parent's home earlier in the day from,...a visitor.

"I have no idea who that could be, Irina. But I can assure you, they had no connection to Colonel Kuznetsov's office. I would know."

Irina took in her reply, now fully mystified regarding the totality of the day's events. "Thank you for calling me back, Calina. In fact, thank you for everything. Perhaps if this all blows over, we could meet sometime, over a cup of coffee or something."

The line went silent for a few moments. "I wish you well, Irina Balabanova."

Irina heard the phone disconnect and sat alone in the parlor, completely silent for several minutes before returning to the kitchen to join her parents at the family dining table. They could tell their oldest daughter was quite emotional and prepared to ask about it when they heard the foyer door break open as Misha and Alika had returned from the doctor.

The two expecting parents joined them around the table and some initial conversation ensued regarding Alika's doctor visit while soon the pregnant daughter quickly headed for the bedroom.

"She is fine," Misha stated. "The doctor says it is just typical morning sickness."

The small talk having died down, Mikhail began to question Misha about the mysterious visitor who stopped by earlier.

"I do not know. He was not from here as he didn't speak our language. We could not communicate so I just told him I was busy." Misha elected not to mention the note left, which he lost. "I was worried about Alika."

"What did he say exactly, Misha?" Mikhail asked.

"I could not understand most of it, but he did call out Irina's name, her full name,...twice, I think."

"Why do you believe he was a police investigator?" Irina asked anxiously.

"Tell them what he looked like, Misha," Alika interrupted, having just returned to the table.

The family paused briefly as they helped seat Alika, all having a shared concern for her condition.

Misha had an expression as though thinking. "Hmm, he was kind of tall, at least taller than us, and had a fancy suit and tie on." He then paused, pondering what he should add.

"Just tell them what you told me, Misha, word for word," Alika insisted.

"He was maybe forty to forty-five years old, medium weight, and had blond hair. I remember, he had a mustache that was a little darker, more brown color," Misha stated.

"Oh my god!" Irina cried out loud as she looked at her sister for affirmation.

Alika was without words as she sat frozen, staring at Irina misty-eyed while slowly nodding her head up and down.

"What's going on?" Mikhail asked as he and Nadine stiffened in their seats, anxious to be enlightened.

Somehow I knew it... I knew he would come, Irina said to herself. Now totally in tears, she was unable to speak and as such, Alika spoke up on her behalf. "It was John,... John Masters from America."

"Irina's boyfriend? But Misha said this man was forty-five years old!" Mikhail said, nearly yelling.

Irina and Alika shared a mixed look of tears and laughter as they soon embraced, their mother and father both appearing bewildered and wondering what their girls knew that they didn't know, and when they would be a part of it.

Irina, now badly in need of an emotional recharge, knew the moment was at hand. "Momma, Papa... I need to tell you about John. I met him at a marriage agency in Kharkov."

"I thought you said he was here on business," Mikhail responded quickly in retort. "Marriage Agency? What is that, anyway?"

"It was *personal* business, but that is not important right now." *Best get ready for this, Irina!.* "He's the same age as you, Papa."

"What?! The same age as me? Are you out of your mind?"

Nadine, nearly as shocked with the news as Mikhail, chose to intervene and take a more diplomatic tact,...before the family patriarch had another stroke. "Irina, why did you not bring this John Masters here to meet us?"

"I am sorry about that, Momma," Irina replied while looking at both her and her father. "I knew you would be upset,...about John's age, so I wanted to wait until I knew I would really get a visa to go to America. I have learned the SSU, namely Colonel Kuznetsov, has stopped the process, anyway."

"Of course it has upset us about his age!" Mikhail replied angrily, not able to contain himself.

"He does not look fifty, Papa," Alika interjected, believing she had need to play advocate for her embattled sister, while at the same time disclosing the fact that she got to meet Irina's new beau, while the folks did not. "Even Misha guessed him at being in his early forties," she added as she looked toward her husband for support, who would respond with a slight shrug of his shoulders.

"That still does not excuse your not having us meet this man! What daughter, did you believe I was going to shoot him?" Mikhail asked in an off-humor way, believing the group needed to lighten up a bit.

Irina bit down on her lower lip. *Here comes another one, Irina!* "John was only here for one week."

"A week! When was this?" Mikhail asked, now raising many more questions. *All right, Irina...here goes!* "It was before Christmas."

"Before Christmas! It is almost May now! So you met this American for a week, you have not seen him in five months, and you plan to run off to America and get married!?" Mikhail became all the more animated. "Nadine, say something!"

Irina sat there getting a dress down, having the mixed emotions of joy at finally letting the cat out of the bag, while also the worry hanging over her regarding the SSU investigation. She did have a huge sense of relief in learning this mysterious foreign police detective was none other than John, himself, and now the elation crept in at the prospect of seeing him again. *But to tell him what, that her own country's security police had destroyed their plans?*

Nadine had quietly taken a break from the heated conversation and returned shortly thereafter with a handful of envelopes, the daily mail.

"Maybe this has something to do with it," Nadine stated in a lowered tone, handing Irina an official-looking envelope addressed to her from the United States Department of State in Kiev.

The whole table became silent as Irina began to slowly open the post, a fear creeping up the back of her neck that it had something to do with Kuznetsov. Finally opening the envelope and unfolding the enclosed document, the family could see the change in her expression as she read it. It was a notification to set an appointment for her visa interview and to schedule her medical examination in concert.

Is this what I think it is? Irina sat back, took a breath, and just laid the letter down on the table for the rest of her family to see. With all the turmoil the past several weeks regarding Kuznetsov and the SSU, she had nearly forgotten the one thing she and John had been waiting for all this time—this letter!

Mikhail picked up the letter, which had both the English and Ukrainian languages. "This is confusing. I thought the SSU had put a stop to this?"

Irina took the letter back and studied it some more, thinking she must have missed something. Whatever Kuznetsov had done, or threatened to do, it must not have worked. *Oh my god! I need to see John!* "Misha, did John leave a number or address where he is staying, or anything?"

Misha thought a moment, knowing he should have called Irina on her cell phone. "No, nothing. Once we both figured out we didn't speak the same language, he took off. Sorry." He avoided any mention of the discarded note the stranger had left.

"What are you going to do?" Alika asked on behalf of everyone.

"I need to send him an email," Irina responded. "If he was just here today, he must be staying somewhere... He is probably in Kharkov. But where?"... *Belanov!*

Having no internet, Irina left her parents and drove home where she could email a message to John. *What will I say to him? I put him in the dark for more than three weeks and then broke it off with an email. Will he forgive me? What if he refuses to even meet me?... No, he flew all the way back over here. He will.*

Entering the apartment, Irina spied Dimitri lounging on the couch, both going out of their way to avoid eye contact. Irina logged in to her computer with the new password she had changed as part of her newly acquired disdain for her tenant. She began to type out a message to John but paused. *No, I want to handle this in person.*

She called the Belanov Agency but it went straight to voicemail. She then dialed the cell phone she had stored for Sergei, hoping he still worked there.

"Irina! So good to hear from you," he replied enthusiastically.

"Sergei! I am so happy to connect with you. Have you seen or heard from John?"

"Yes, Irina. He is here. Did you not see him earlier in Chuguev? He drove down there."

"I know, Sergei. So much is happening and I missed him. How is his mood? Is he mad at me?" Irina asked, anxiously.

"I do not think *mad* is the right word, Irina. I would say worried would be more accurate," Sergei replied.

"Oh Sergei, I am sure that poor man has been through hell because of me."

"Well, you should know, Irina, that John had an opportunity to meet other girls and he passed. He traveled all the way back here just to find you, again."

Irina listened, assuming now that either Sergei or his boss, Natalyia, offered or even suggested that John meet other of their clients. She suppressed a sudden anger at the perceived betrayal on their part but thought better of saying anything. *I would deserve it, but my man, my real man held on to me.*

The two disconnected a few minutes later with her now knowing John's location and her requesting that Sergei keep their conversation in confidence, as she wanted to surprise him. Irina lay back on her bed, now overcome with a tremendous feeling of fulfillment. John was here in Ukraine, a man who traveled all the way back here, even after she had "poured cold water" all over him. She had received the visa letter from the American embassy! She was to be married in America! She also felt a huge sense of relief for her family now having full knowledge of it all, even though her father had gone into his predictable rage over it. Irina knew ultimately that her family was behind her and only wanted her true happiness.

Someone must be watching over me!... Life is so wonderful!

Irina was mentally wired and up late, awaiting a call as she half expected and hoped John would show up again at the parents' home and no longer concerned about it, as his mere existence, nationality, and age were no longer a secret. If he were to show up, the family had been prompted to get her first on the phone and then to just make him feel welcome as best as they could, considering the language barrier, until she could drive over there.

Having gotten to sleep late, she woke up late and surprised at confronting Dimitri in the kitchen, who sat at the small dining table having coffee. He remained void of eye contact.

"Why are you not at work?" Irina asked with an obvious edge in her voice.

"Should be of no surprise to you. Petrov suspended me," Dimitri answered sternly.

"You were suspended because Colonel Kuznetsov wanted to hurt me, knowing I would need your rent money all the more because of my being out of work. But you made a deal with the devil and now you're facing the consequences," Irina replied forcefully.

Dimitri felt very small now, knowing for certain she was correct, but the jealous and vengeful part of him still wanted to lash out at her. "You will give Kuznetsov what he wants, Irina. Then we will both benefit and I will catch up on the rent."

She should have been hesitant to announce anything to him, but Irina couldn't hold back. "I'm leaving for America to get married in a few days and the family will sell this place. What are you going to do for Kuznetsov then?" she replied contemptuously, before storming out of the kitchen to occupy the bathroom in preparation to leaving.

CHAPTER TWELVE

The Streaker

John slept late as he decided to no longer head out into the hinterland of Ukraine alone without an interpreter, having worked out a plan to meet with Sergei after work and the two would then drive down to Chuguev together. John noted that Sergei seemed overly cooperative, even though the two failed to discuss how late they would be and what time Sergei could expect to return home to his family.

With little to do until 5:00 PM, John chose to go out and do a bit of shopping, perhaps get a bite to eat. While out and about on the streets of Kharkov, he noticed an ever increasing military presence, something he hadn't seen to such a degree back in November. He would come to learn the threat of civil war in the eastern part of Ukraine was imminent, another worry to add to his already ample list.

After checking his email and verifying his various banking and credit card balances, John decided to call home. Getting the voicemail, he left a detailed message updating the family on his exploits, or lack thereof. As mid-afternoon approached, John struggled to retain confidence. He had traveled all the way back to Kharkov, so far on his fourth day since leaving home, and had done nothing but lost ground. His only communication with Irina had been a "Dear John" email, he had driven to her home as addressed on all the immigration paperwork, and had still not gotten an audience with her. He felt sure she must have known by now he was in Chuguev the day before, and yet not a peep. Surely, she would at least have called the Belanov office, but Sergei would have informed him. If his second incursion to Irina's hometown failed, John would face a difficult decision on whether to extend his stay, ill-prepared to keep funding Sergei's fee while apparently being stuck and just shooting in the dark.

He waited on edge for the young interpreter to arrive when a knock on the door sounded a half hour early. He opened the door and there she was, having been nearly six months. The two both faced each other for an emotional moment, at a brief impasse as to who should speak first or what those words would be.

"Irina? Please, come in," John began as he stepped out of the way and allowed the young woman, one he came halfway around the world for, to enter.

She took two steps past him, stopped, and then turned around as the two embraced and she squeezed John as though she never wanted to let go.

"Irina, why? Why are you here?" he asked her. "I mean, I'm glad you're here but... Explain, what is going on."

She led him into the parlor where the two sat down. "My honey, I am so sorry. I missed you so much... I just did not know."

She grabbed his neck and the two kissed passionately before John stopped abruptly and asked. "What do you mean? Did not know what?"

"I did not know my visa interview was approved. When did you learn of this?"

"Irina, I don't know what you are talking about." The two spoke very slow and deliberate English but John was quite surprised and pleased at how much better she had grasped his language since they had last seen each other.

"My visa interview, my medical appointment. I have the letter right here in my purse!" She informed him as she managed to dig the folded envelope out for his review.

John took the envelope from her and proceeded to open and read the official letter enclosed. "This came way before I expected. I thought we would not see this until July or August. This is great news! Have you already scheduled these appointments?"

"No, my honey. I just got this late yesterday," Irina declared. It just registered with her that John had flown all the way back just to find her while knowing nothing about her visa notice.

John thought a moment and asked, "So, did you know I was at your place yesterday?"

"That is my parents' home. But I was there late yesterday and got this," she replied.

"Irina, why did you not contact me?" John asked, not registering that she didn't have his phone number.

"I called Sergei but I asked him not to say anything. I wanted to surprise you. Will you forgive me?"

"But what about that email? Police investigation, Irina?"

"Oh, my honey, it has been taken care of. I hear you have car. I want you to drive me to Chuguev, tonight. You need to meet my parents. Oh, and take whatever you need. We will stay there tonight."

"Stay there?" John replied, showing some skepticism. "Do they even know about it?"

"Oh yes, and they are quite excited," Irina responded anxiously.

"You need to tell me why you sent me that email, Irina," John stated seriously.

"My honey, can I tell you about it on the way?"

⋙⋙ ⋘⋘

The Balabanove family cottage was dated by Western standards, but John could tell Irina's mother took pride and made the necessary effort to assure their home had a warm feel to it. The family had resided in the small two-bedroom apartment Irina now occupied for many years before Mikhail was rewarded by acquiring this place set on the banks of a small river in 1991, a partial result of the turbulent times when Ukraine established independence and pricing for real estate was very low. Thus, John's future in-laws owned two properties, something rare for working people in Ukraine at that time.

John and Irina drove up and once introductions were made, Mikhail and Nadine immediately became more comfortable and nothing doing, their future would be son-in-law would be staying for a huge celebratory dinner.

Having sized each other up, John and Mikhail both realized their being from the same generation and very much into their cars, not to mention both having been born in the same year, they probably would have been close friends in their youth, absent the reality of the Cold War and the anti-American, anti-Soviet propaganda that was part of it.

Most local residences in Ukraine were generations behind what John was accustomed to and he noticed the house had no bathroom. There was an outhouse in the far corner of the backyard opposite the garage, which served as the auto repair shop, and Mikhail had built a separate shed attached to the garage that included its own wood stove and rather antique-looking bathtub, although having no water supply plumbing to it. As such, hot baths had to be prepared for by first heating the shed and then heating a supply of water to fill the tub, reminding John of something he had seen in an old western movie.

Irina knew an issue was brewing and thus informed her parents, "There's something you need to know about John. He takes a bath or shower every day."

While Nadine appeared slightly embarrassed and searched for the right words, Mikhail immediately took charge and stated, "No problem. We will accommodate John's desire to be clean, but we'll do so after dinner."

The family spirits were upbeat as Irina, her sister, and mother put out a huge feast that included nearly every ethnically Russian dish imaginable, much of which came right out of Nadine's garden. From John's perspective, much of this family's culture and its customs heartily reminded him of visiting his grandparents as a child, with some of his family lineage dating back to southern Germany and Bohemia.

While enjoying most of the spread, John had little appetite for the various beet dishes or cold chopped meat served in a clear gelatin, but out of respect and politeness, he took in a bit of everything and far more than he was accustomed to in one meal. Another of the ethnic Russian traditions were the many toasts at the beginning and end of every festive dinner, and that involved lots of vodka.

John was not a big consumer of alcohol generally, but indulged, again out of respect and politeness. Adding to the onslaught, following dinner Mikhail spoke to Misha, words of course John could not comprehend.

"Misha, come on. We will show this America how to drink like a real man."

The two went outside to chain up their dog to the fence near the outhouse, an animal that would not hesitate to attack John as a stranger, then invited the future family member outside where the three endeavored to consume even larger amounts of vodka, an act John quickly picked up on as a custom not to overindulge in front of the ladies.

Following dinner and well past sundown, John suggested to Irina they return to his apartment in Kharkov, much of which in consideration toward the cottage's limited sleeping arrangements, having only two bedrooms as he would be sleeping on the sofa in the parlor while Irina slept on the floor, but also as he wanted a shower before bed and didn't want to, in any way, put Irina's family out on his behalf.

Mikhail would have none of it, insisting that his future son-in-law stay with them and abruptly proceeded to go outside and prepare a tub of hot water for him. Now realizing he may be insulting Irina's family by even a suggestion of their leaving, John had Irina gather for him a bath towel, thinking the hot bath may do him some good following such a large feed, not to mention the many drinks he had just consumed, all of which was making his stomach begin to feel quite queasy.

Irina and her father escorted John out back and to the prepared hot tub, leaving him in the closed shed after a brief "orientation". John looked around the small room which was lit only by a couple of candles. *Part of Irina's love affair with those,* he thought. It was relatively cool for late April, but Mikhail had not bothered nor did John suggest anything about firing up the wood stove. He started to gather that Irina and her whole family, being originally from the far northern reaches of Russia, were somewhat cold-natured and as such, he didn't wish to embarrass himself or burden them by constantly requesting any more special treatment.

He stripped off his clothing and placed them on the small table set up in the corner of the room and reached in with his hand to test the water temperature. *Perfect!... Hot, just the way I like it.* John just started to breach the tall side of the tub and get in when it hit him.

"Oh my god!" John bent over and clutched his abdomen as the most severe stomach cramps in recent memory stuck home. All that food! All that vodka! John then sat on the concrete floor, crunched over with his arms wrapped tightly around his midsection, hoping the pressure would pass... It only got worse.

Trying to think fast, it came as a severe reminder, and much to his dismay, that the only thing resembling a toilet was all the way across the lawn in the outhouse. Considerations of getting fully dressed were quickly discarded. *I'll never make it! No, I cannot... Somebody will see me!... No choice!*

Totally stark naked, John shot out of the shed door, and still bent over and clutching his brutally cramped stomach, he ran headlong with as much speed as he could possibly muster for the outhouse, all the while hoping against hope no one would suddenly appear, when yet another calamity struck... The dog!

Just as he was about to put his hand on the outhouse door, the yelping hound came at him and the mere fortune of having the chained leash reach its stretched limit saved John from having the vicious canine take a chunk of flesh right out of his rear end.

Having entered and secured the wooden outhouse door, John quickly sat down, relieved in finally conducting Mother Nature's business, and feeling so much better in more ways than one.

Thank you, Lord! Thank you, thank you, thank you.

Having heard the dog so riled up, Mikhail stepped out on the back porch, flipped on a flood light, and looked around, seeing nothing exciting and quickly retreated back inside prior to abruptly hearing the barking again.

The immediate crisis over, John prepared to streak back across the yard to the shed. Knowing now that if he just ran out and made a quick motion to the right before racing back toward the shed, the angry barking hound couldn't catch him, his only remaining challenge being that of reaching the shed again without being seen. Taking a deep breath and still naked as a jaybird, John took off full speed, no longer slowed physically by the major inconvenience of having an abdomen under full pressure.

Mikhail stepped out on the back porch after again hearing the loud barking and flipped on the flood light, just as John was closing the shed door. He looked a second time, thinking, *Did I just see what I thought I saw?* Shaking his head, he said to no one in particular, "No...surely not."

The next morning, John was treated to a hearty breakfast while Irina began to pack, so happy that he had chosen to travel lite himself. They would be toting two large suitcases, both the older style luggage common before the evolution of pullout handles and rollers became popular. Understanding that Irina would be leaving on an extended trip—as in the rest of her life—he stood by patiently as she made her goodbyes to Momma and Papa, who planned to see them off in Kiev days later. The two then departed for Kharkov as he needed to gather up his stuff before another five-plus hour excursion to Kiev.

⤜⟫⟫ ⟨⟨⟨⤛

Dimitri was in a panic now, stunned by this latest development and knowing full well Irina was right. He had no doubt made a deal with the devil, a deal that was turning out to be grossly one-sided. After pacing madly for over two hours, he picked up the phone.

"Colonel, I have given you everything you want, but Irina is going to America and now I'm out of work. What do you want from me?"

This peon thinks I'm his guardian now, Kuznetsov thought, who was himself surprised at this news. "You are wasting my time, Gusev! She will not be going anywhere. I have seen to that."

"She has an interview at the American Embassy in Kiev in three days," Dimitri stated in desperation, thinking he had to give Kuznetsov something he hopefully did not know.

196

"And how do you know this?" Kuznetsov asked attentively.

"She told me this morning, and while she was in the bathroom preparing to leave, I went through her purse in her bedroom and found a letter from the American Embassy."

How is this possible? Kuznetsov wondered. "Where is she now?"

"I suspect she is on her way to Kiev, Colonel," Gusev replied.

"Do you have anything else? Any hotel reservations, apartment rentals, flight ticket info?"

"No, none of that."

"Then this conversation is concluded," Kuznetsov stated flatly.

"But Colonel, what about my job?"

"What about your job? You signed a sworn statement that you saw Irina Balabanova extract the codes to access the SSU security system."

"I said I believe she would have possible access to the codes. But you know, Colonel"...

"No! You know that I have in my possession your signed sworn statement that you saw her access those codes and did not report it at the time. That makes you an accessory to the crime, young man. I suggest you just stay low and keep quiet until called upon, Am I clear?"

Dimitri hesitated. Not recalling having signed any such thing but, upon reflection, knew he did not read the document word for word before signing, either.

"Am I clear, Dimitri Gusev?!" Kuznetsov repeated angrily.

"Yes, Colonel."

⤜⤛ ⤚⤚

Kuznetsov came out of his office and instructed Calina to duplicate the entire files on Irina Balabanova and Dimitri Gusev and prepare completed copies for him. She went to work on them right away, not knowing what the purpose would be. She was then directed to arrange a staff car and driver for the colonel, as well as lodging in Kiev for at least five days.

She completed the tasks in short order and assumed she would be expected to accompany him, wondering if she would be allowed to go home to gather some changes of clothing and travel items first.

Kuznetsov exited his office, locking the door behind, and approached his secretary's desk. "Calina, I will be in Kiev for a few days and there is no time to brief the rest of the staff. You must stay here at Oblast Headquarters to manage the current agenda. You know how to contact me."

She watched him as he headed out of the office, briefcase full of documents in hand, knowing his business in Kiev affected Irina Balabanova and Dimitri Gusev, somehow, and probably in a very bad way. Calina was also somewhat struck by his not having her travel with him, knowing that had rarely happened, although she was not unhappy about it. The many nights of playing stand-in mistress for the malevolent colonel had long since lost its misguided appeal. She knew her tenure with Pavel Kuznetsov, both personally and professionally, would soon expire, if her not being replaced by Irina Balabanova, then someone else sooner or later.

This wickedness has to end, Calina thought seriously.

❄❄❄ ❄❄❄

John and Irina left early the next day for Kiev as her required medical examination was set for the following morning, two days prior to her scheduled visa interview at the US Embassy. He enjoyed sharing the unforetold details of his streaking through his future in-laws' backyard, a tale Irina caught little of but joined in her new beau's laughter, nevertheless.

Irina had found a nightly apartment rental near downtown Kiev, a place right up the street from the famous Independence Square and within easy walking distance of the American Embassy. The two felt right at home as they enjoyed dinner at a TGI Fridays, one of many American imported restaurants they found close by.

Even though she personally lacked confidence in it, John appreciated the immense progress Irina had made learning English since they had last been together six months earlier. The laptop computer and language translation program they had solely relied on back then was rarely needed now.

Irina passed her physical exam with flying colors, the clinic providing her with the completed certification she needed for the next step, the K-1 visa interview. That evening, she and John sat down and went over all the visa application documents and sample interview questions in detail. While both were excited to get to this important step, Irina was still quite nervous as she would be the one actually questioned and John's being there was simply a formality, so far as the embassy was concerned.

Taking a day for leisure, they entered the building the following morning at 9:30 am, wanting to be a bit early as the appointment for the interview was scheduled for 10:00. The couple was directed through the building to the immigration section where Irina penned a sign-in sheet, and they sat in queue, a small waiting area with two other couples similar in status, as one of the women, who appeared to be somewhat older than Irina, was applying for a K-1 visa also. The woman's fiancé, a man also older than John, was from New York.

Forty minutes later, a lady with the department opened a door and called out, "Irina Balabanova?" Irina immediately stood and followed the diplomatic representative through the door and into a small office where the interview began, mostly routine as the officer asked Irina about her relationship with John and was asked to show some proof of their relationship, which she provided by displaying copies of their many emails back and forth over the preceding months, as well as several photographs taken together both back in November when they first met, as well as a few in the past few days since she and John had reunited. Irina's confidence built as the process was going much more smoothly than she had anticipated, that is until confronted with a sudden and unexpected obstacle.

"There is a footnote here attached to your Ukrainian passport copy. It regards a security document you signed as a condition of employment in 2000 at the More Security Supply Company..."

Irina sat silently as the embassy official summarized the document issue that could derail her application and her entire future. All the sudden a sick and empty feeling began to consume her.

⤜⟫⟩ ⟨⟨⟨⤛

John sat patiently out in the waiting room as Irina exited the office door with quite a different expression than he anticipated. He knew when she approached that something had gone wrong as his future bride-to-be struggled to keep her composure while others looked on.

"Irina, tell me. What happened?" He asked her, trying to comfort her while at the same time keeping their conversation low in the mixed company of the small waiting room.

"Let us go," she tearfully answered. "But Irina, what?"

"Please. my honey. Let us go. I will explain."

They exited the embassy and John could tell Irina was extremely upset and emotional. The two entered a nearby café and quickly settled into a corner booth where coffee was ordered.

"Irina, you must tell me about it," John stated, feigning signs of patience while knowing something had gone very badly.

Irina took a long sip of the coffee, temporarily unable to make eye contact with John as she looked out the window and onto the crowded sidewalk. A terrible nausea had crept in as she contemplated the worst. Since digesting the contents of the visa appointment notice a few days earlier, her life had seemed to take such a turn, the fable that had begun six months before was suddenly restored. Now she sat in a café booth across from the man she had fallen in love with, a man she now feared would be lost forever, and struggled to come to terms and even explain it.

How cruel the world is to women like me. All I ever wanted is a good, faithful man to love and raise a family with. I have fallen for two Americans, one who ultimately did not want me and now one whom I cannot have. Please God, tell me what I have done to deserve such unhappiness.

"John, I told you before that my problems with the police certification were taken care of. I was wrong."

John himself now dealt with nausea, bracing himself mentally for what was coming. "Go on."

"I told you about the security supply company where I worked for five years," she began. "When I started, I had to sign a confidentiality agreement that would be in effect for up to five years after leaving. It had stipulations in fine print that I would be prohibited from leaving the Oblast."

John pushed back against his seat, stunned by this latest revelation. "Irina, why did you not bring this up before?"

"I am sorry, my honey. These kinds of issues never come up. I thought...maybe just hoped, this would just fade away. You came into my life so unexpectedly, like a fable as if the answer to all my prayers. I had faith and just refused to believe anything like this could happen," Irina expressed, now fully in tears again.

John took it in and as the two now sat holding hands, he waited a few seconds for her to regain composure and asked, "Irina, tell me exactly what the embassy agent told you."

Irina took a napkin to dry her eyes before collecting her thoughts. "Everything was good on the questions. Then at the end, there was a note in my file they had about that document."

"But you got the required police certificate that showed you have no criminal record."

"I know, my honey. But this has just happened," she replied defensively.

John deeply inhaled, the disappointment and devastation building rapidly. *I'm no attorney, but this kind of thing would never stand in the USA. But here?* "So what now? Did they tell you your visa was being denied, or just what did they tell you?"

"The woman at the embassy said this would have to be referred to their legal attaché for review, and they would then contact me."

"Legal attaché?" *That means lawyers and that means nothing will happen quickly,* John was thinking. "I'm going to talk to somebody, anyone in our government who can shed some light on this."

"I worry this could somehow get you in trouble."

John was becoming drained. *This is falling apart, like it was just never meant to be. But I am not just going to leave without her and have a nice day. No, I have to give this my best shot.* "So, Irina, did they say they would call you or just send out another notice in the mail, or what?"

"She only said they would contact me. I am sorry, I was so upset at the moment, I did not ask," Irina sadly replied.

"Come on, let's pay and head back to the apartment," John stated. "I have to notify someone in authority that I'm in Kiev a few days and hopefully get some movement while I'm here," he added, knowing it was probably just wishful thinking.

As the two strolled back toward the apartment, Irina asked, "John, would you ever consider moving here, to Ukraine, so we can be together?"

John felt jolted, unprepared for such a question and feeling awful that he had to provide an answer. "No, I would never leave my country. I am sorry."

Irina was not taken aback and regretted asking. *He is an American who is very patriotic, something we do not feel here as much.*

As their apartment entrance approached, she called her sister to relay the bad news home, telling the folks to abort their plan to drive all the way to Kiev for an emotional send-off.

⋙⋙ ⋘⋘

Neither had slept well the night before, and having stayed up late, Irina opened up over coffee, sharing with John the whole saga regarding her history with Colonel Kuznetsov, expressing no doubt in her mind that he was responsible for the problems with her visa. She felt a tremendous sense of guilt now, knowing how much time and money John had invested in her.

The mood was dire as the morning faded away and the two decided to explore Kiev some, a task to hopefully distract from the unpleasant reality of their engagement plans gone amiss. John possessed a return airline ticket to depart Kiev in two days and fly home, knowing he would have difficulty remaining any longer. He had been away from his son and business for nearly a week, a few more days would be tenable but expensive, and though unspoken, neither took much stock in the idea the embassy would resolve the problem before then...or likely at all.

CHAPTER THIRTEEN

Miracle From Heaven

T he knock on the door came before ten, just as he had gotten out of bed and sat down for a cup of instant coffee. Assuming the visitor would not be there to see him, few ever did, he slowly gathered himself up and made his way toward the door. Opening up, he stood back upon seeing the uniformed officer. *What do these people want with me?*

"Dimitri Gusev, I want to talk to you."

After slight hesitation and confusion, he stood back and allowed the agent to enter, a woman he had seen recently when signing that ill-advised sworn statement. She followed him into the kitchen and the two sat down across from each other at the table, the formality of his offering her a cup of coffee not forthcoming.

"I suppose my station in life must have fallen. Colonel Kuznetsov is now sending a secretary after me and not bothering himself," the young man re-marked untactfully, while still barely dressed, unwashed, and unshaven.

"Dimitri Gusev, you are talking when you should be listening. You are in serious trouble,...and you have endeavored through your imbecility to destroy Irina Balabanova's life, also," SSU Officer Calina Zhvikova stated.

"How am I in big trouble, other than being suspended from my job? I gave the SSU what it wanted."

"You gave Pavel Kuznetsov what he wanted, Dimitri Gusev. And now, we are going to do the right thing."

"What do you mean *we*, and what is this right thing?" Gusev asked dubiously.

"Shut up and pay attention, while I explain…"

⟫ ⟪

The afternoon of shopping and sightseeing attempted to lighten a somber mood, while John purchased a few going away presents for Irina and her family, but as that Thursday evening approached, neither of them could ward off the overwhelming air of sadness and emptiness that would be felt jointly when John would soon depart, a departure likely to be for the rest of their lives.

The two elected to dine in the apartment for their last evening together and visited a local supermarket for groceries. As they walked together through the aisles of the market, Irina kept her arm in his, an act of emotion as she fought the dreaded feeling of knowing her man was going away, and likely forever.

Back in the apartment, she fought back more tears as she unpacked their packages and prepared to cook a final dinner. She heard the buzzed chime of her cell phone that was in her purse in the parlor, resigned to have the call go to voicemail. When the phone buzzed again a minute later, she decided it should be answered and ran to pick it up. *It's Alika.*

"Irina! You have a letter here, just delivered by a special courier!" Alika announced, barely able to contain herself. "It is from the US Embassy on Sikorsky Street in Kiev."

Oh my god! Irina felt a sudden uptick. "Special courier?… What does it say, Alika?"

"I did not open it."

"Alika, open it!" Irina yelled, shocked and anxious at what this could be.

John had just gotten out of the shower and was drying off when he heard the commotion, and donning the house-provided bathrobe, came in toward the kitchen as Irina had some spark in her eyes not seen since the morning before.

"It says you are to contact the Embassy Legal Attaché office at your earliest convenience to review and assess an outstanding issue regarding your K-1 visa application," Alika stated slowly and directly, also sighting the name of the official to be contacted who signed the letter.

After the two disconnected, Irina explained the letter to John and the two embraced as if in celebration of a badly needed development. "My honey, maybe they will give us the news that my visa application is denied," Irina spoke to him, unwilling to get too optimistic and get knocked down again.

"Very distinct possibility, my lovely. But hey! We've survived to fight another day!" John replied in a genuine attempt to comfort her, quickly knowing his American "old saying" would require more explanation.

⟫ ⟪

They arrived at half past midnight and Irina met them with a raucous greeting at the door, forgetting that John was a lite sleeper. Her parents had driven the near seven hours all the way from Chuguev, planning to give their oldest daughter a hearty send-off, or a sorrow-filled ride back home.

John awoke to all the excitement and greeted them, as all four gathered around the dining room table, spread at the late hour with an assortment of snacks, meets, juices, and of course, vodka. John sat down and respectfully indulged in a few hors d'oeuvres but chose to use some new Russian words he learned when Mikhail wanted to offer some toasts, which John quickly answered with "ne mnogo", meaning a little bit.

John woke up early the next morning in hopes of their getting another meeting at the embassy, but it being a Friday, he had his doubts. He called the contact number and extension listed in the letter but received a voicemail and after the third time, he thought better of leaving yet another message. If Irina failed to get an audience with them today, John would have a difficult decision to make regarding his plane tickets.

Her cell phone rang at 10:40 AM and it was the embassy. "John, this is the Embassy legal department. Here, you talk to them."

John took her phone and had a lengthy dialog begin back and forth with a staffer, after which he clicked off and stood momentarily silent while Irina and her folks sat and observed, wondering if he had good news or bad.

"She has an appointment at 9:00 AM on Tuesday," he added. This would predicate a ticket change and that will be expensive, not to mention the price of getting a ticket for her with little lead time. It was a hit he had planned to absorb anyway, assuming things would go well at the embassy. *Which was a stretch,* a thought he kept to himself.

"We could not see them today?" Irina inquired.

"Unfortunately, no. I pressed the girl on that but was told a State Department attorney would have to handle your application. I pressed for an appointment on Saturday or Monday and was told the office of the legal attaché was closed on Saturday and Tuesday morning was the first available appointment time."

After some conversation to update her parents, Irina asked, "What do you think, my honey?"

"Don't know. The girl was just a staff worker there and didn't indicate if the application would fly either way," John replied, trying to appear optimistic but under the surface was very worried. "I suppose I need to look into changing my flight arrangements."

The four of them spent the rest of the weekend enjoying Kiev, which had many interesting places to see. John was surprised but not displeased that Irina and her parents had spent little time in the city previously, despite it being their nation's capital. John and Mikhail took in the world-class World War II museum on Saturday while Irina and her mother went shopping at the new and modern mall on Independence Square.

The four went out to dinner that evening at the most expensive restaurant the Balabanove family had ever experienced, made worse over the tip John was prepared to leave. As tipping was not a part of the native culture, John's adding hryvnias to the sum total of an already pricy tab was seen as outrageous to Mikhail. A friendly "inner-family" feud ensued with Irina attempting to translate and mediate while the innocent waitress looked on, confused and wondering if she had done something wrong. In conclusion, John informed the young woman, who happened to speak English herself, that he was rewarding her with a fifteen percent tip as a compliment from America.

The four departed the restaurant with the planned in-laws having mixed emotions, believing on one hand their future son-in-law to be very generous, while on the other hand hoping he wasn't too good for his own good.

⤜⤜⤜ ⤛⤛⤛

The two entered the building twenty minutes early and followed the repeated security protocol similar to the check-in and scan utilized at airports. After a brief wait, they were escorted to an office on the second floor and greeted by a sharply dressed young attorney.

"Irina Balabanova, I assume? And John Masters? Please make yourselves comfortable. I am Michael O'Malley, Assistant Legal Counsel here. Are you ready to begin?" O'Malley asked.

"Yes, of course. Shall we call you Michael?" John replied.

"Certainly, John," the attorney responded in a tone that indicated he had known the couple were there previously. "I have reviewed the document in question and I must ask Irina a few questions."

She looked at John who grabbed her shoulder and she then nodded. She was asked to state her full legal name, date of birth, and address, replying in kind while confused as believing they already knew who she was.

"When did you begin your employment at the More Security Supply Company?"

"October 1st, 2000," Irina answered.

"And prior to that date, had you worked for the government of Ukraine, in any capacity?" O'Malley continued as he took notes.

"No, I had not."

"Had you been associated with any government entity prior to October 1st, 2000?"

Irina studied as she thought how to answer. "I attended the university in Kharkov for four years."

"Could you summarize you position at More Security Supply?" O'Malley asked.

"I was the office manager and also the company receptionist. I handled most of the paperwork for the company, including bids, contracts, account receivables, account payables, and payroll."

John observed the interview, in his mind more of a deposition, and slowly began to get pessimistic, believing this process would involve additional investigation, more letters, and more interviews, none of which he could make time for. *This will not get resolved soon and we are,...probably finished.*

O'Malley took a stapled multi-page document from the file in front of him, opened it to the final page, and placed it in front of her. "Irina, is that your signature on this document?"

"It appears so," she replied nervously.

"In your tenure at More Security Supply, did the company hire and terminate other employees?"

"Yes, in my five years there were many." Both she and John wondered where this was going.

"Did you administer the paperwork for any of the new employees?"

"As office manager, I took care of all the new hire paperwork," Irina answered honestly, trying to recall looking back if there may have been an exception and could not think of any.

"I have here a copy of the company's standard new hire security confidentiality agreement. Does this form look familiar to you?" O'Malley inquired.

Irina glanced over the form. "Yes, that is one of the new hire documents."

O'Malley retrieved the form and made some notes. "More Security Supply sells and supports security equipment such as outdoor cameras, personnel scanners, and other items related to security, correct?"

"Yes."

"And there are sophisticated software programs that require maintenance, updates, and security to protect the software itself. Is that correct?"

"Yes, the ongoing maintenance contracts. That is a big part of Arkady's business," she responded.

"When you reference Arkady, you mean Arkady Petrov, the owner of More Security Supply?" O'Malley added nonchalantly.

"Yes, that is correct," Irina replied again, squeezing John's hand as though to secure his support.

"As a part of maintaining these programs, do the technicians employed by More Security Supply have access to sensitive security data?"

"Sensitive?" Irina quickly asked. "Yes, I would say sometimes."

"How often would you personally have need to access this type of data?" O'Malley asked.

She looked bewildered as though momentarily confused by the question. "I do not understand. I had nothing to do with that."

O'Malley studied briefly, making eye contact back and forth between the couple in front of him. "So you never had need to access the so-called "codes" to get into the security system of the State Security of Ukraine?"

John gave Irina a questioning look and she responded with a look of more confusion. "No, I was not a technician."

O'Malley seemed to disguise a smile. "Arkady Petrov, a seemingly cordial gentleman, spoke highly of you in a conversation we had over the phone, yesterday. He could not explain why you, of all people, would have signed a separate and more detailed employee security confidentiality agreement than that of any other employee. Could you possibly explain that?"

Irina again shared a glance with John, shrugging her shoulders. "Separate agreement? I know nothing about that."

"Please review the document again, please, and take your time. I want to know why you would be subject to and sign off on this document."

Irina began to read over the fine print in the multi-page document, not recalling having seen it before. "This was over five years ago. There was a whole package of paperwork. I cannot honestly remember." *My file! Different from all the other employees?... My lord! Kuznetsov!*

She began to form tears and moved to hug John, now more fearful that she would never see him again when O'Malley interrupted. "Do not get upset. This is all a formality. We do have to cover all the bases."

Irina tried to regain her composure, realizing her mannerism may indicate a reflection of some sort of guilt. "Cover all the bases?"

John and O'Malley shared a grin as the attorney replied, "That is baseball lingo, Irina."

O'Malley placed another document in front of Irina. "Please read over this affidavit and sign at the bottom where indicated and date it. John, you may sign as one of the witnesses, right below where I will sign."

Irina feared signing another document, her signatures having obviously caused many problems thus far, while John also looked over the brief form. "This just states that she consented to and completed an interview at the embassy legal attaché office today. That's it?" John asked O'Malley.

"Yes, that's it. As I said earlier, I contacted your former employer, Mr. Petrov, who was quite helpful and explained that your file was taken by the SSU and returned some weeks later. He confirmed that you, as office manager, had no access or need to ever access any sensitive program security data. He also stated that as a former KGB officer, he was familiar with the document contained in your file and informed me that specific document format had not been used for many years. He was kind enough to overnight the copy still possessed in your file there. That document, an old USSR form, was only for employees who have had top secret security clearances and states that upon termination may not disclose any classified information or data related to state security. It also stipulates the undersigned may not relocate outside the resident Oblast without the expressed written approval of the Minister of Security. That would be the old KGB in Moscow."

"But Ukraine is not part of the Soviet Union anymore," John suggested.

"That is correct, sir. And the Soviet Union itself no longer exists," O'Malley claimed rhetorically. "Petrov also sent us a copy of the standard employee confidentiality agreement, which I have here for your review. It basically restricts terminated or resigned employees from working at a competitive company within the Oblast for a period of five years, a stipulation common in corporate documents used in the United States and other Western countries as well. Is there even another security equipment supply company anywhere near Kharkov, Irina?"

"No," she said, recalling from knowledge from her handling the many bids over the years. "The closest competitor is here in Kiev."

"Well, if this is the document you signed originally, it would be baseless in that regard."

Irina sat quietly, now more confused than ever and John quickly asked, "So, Michael, where does that leave us? I have a flight out of here tomorrow morning and was planning to take her with me."

"We are quite aware of that. I am just waiting for one more affidavit from another section, and we can wrap this up."

Irina again was confused and asked John, "Wrap this up?"

"Finish it," he replied and then looked up again at O'Malley. "I'm afraid to ask, but how long will that take?" *The clock is running and more time is what we don't have much of.*

"Let me make a call and see where we're at on it."

O'Malley picked up his desk phone and dialed an extension, speaking briefly for some sort of update before hanging up. "I am just waiting for one last document for the file," the embassy counselor informed looking at his watch. "You may wish to go and get some lunch."

"I appreciate your efforts, Michael, but we are really pressed for time and don't want to do anything that would push us back to the rear of the line," John replied sincerely.

"I understand your concern. We will do our best to get this done promptly."

Suddenly, the small office door opened, and a staff agent entered, a middle-aged male nearly bald with a graying goatee, who placed a document in front of the attorney who quickly picked it up for review.

"How interesting," O'Malley began, noticing Irina as having a sudden enlightened expression. "The document you examined earlier was a copy we made of the original one received yesterday, which was sent to another part of the building," he continued, declining to discuss details of what part of the building he was referring to. "Seems this particular copy, the one Mr. Petrov sent us and dated October 1st, 2000, was examined and our forensics experts state on this affidavit that this exact document could not have been printed more than six weeks ago. Coincidental timing, yes? Your file will be transferred back to Immigration, and they will contact you soon."

⋙ ⋘

John and Irina returned to the apartment where Nadine had prepared lunch for them. Irina updated the parents on the ongoing process and a mood of mixed anxiety was expressed around the entire table. It was quite evident that Kuznetsov had deliberately attempted to stop Irina from leaving the country for America, while also obvious the Americans at the State Department now knew what he had done. But neither John nor Irina and her family had much faith in government bureaucracies to move past a snail's pace and thus the prospects of her leaving with him the following day grew dimmer with every minute.

The bulk of the afternoon passed quietly, the family small talk in the apartment doing little to alleviate the all-around stress level. At just before 4:00 PM, Irina's phone rang with her wasting no time answering. Listening intently, she replied in short terms as John and her parents looked on in anticipation.

"My honey! My visa has been approved! We can pick it up tomorrow morning!"

Both John and Irina, each shocked in their own way, shared congratulatory hugs from the folks as John replied in somewhat disappointment. "But my flight leaves at 6:00 AM!" Seeing his reaction as causing some consternation and not wanting to diminish the good news, he added, "I'll have to contact KLM and make new flight arrangements right away." *And just hope my American Express will handle it.*

⤜⤜⤜ ⤛⤛⤛

John was exasperated. The apartment had a decent wireless connection but the KLM website was not cooperating in allowing him to change his flight, much less price a separate ticket for Irina. Knowing his own flight was set for 6:00 AM the following morning, a ticket he had already changed once, panic set in, as a local Ukrainian International Airlines office was located a few blocks from the embassy, but was already closed for the day.

At just past six-thirty, the family all packed up into Mikhail's car, a Chevrolet Impala, and headed back east toward Boryspil International Airport, some forty kilometers away. Having little trouble parking in the large lot in front of the facility, they all ventured into the terminal and toward the UIA ticket counter when John's tempo took on an immediate improvement, a change not lost on his fiancée.

"John, what is it?" Irina asked.

Nodding his head toward the ticket agent, he replied, "Does that woman look familiar to you, Irina?"

Irina looked through the awaiting travelers toward the counter and responded, "No... Well, maybe a little bit. Why?"

"Never mind... Just thought she looks like someone I know," he said, suddenly a bit upbeat.

A few moments later, their entourage approached the counter as the agent smiled at them and John began by showing his passport, then proceeded to request the changes he needed to make and request to purchase tickets for Irina, both on the same flights as his own, of course. He prepared for the incoming bad news, an outlandish amount airlines generally charged for last-minute changes on tickets and purchases of new tickets with no advance or flexibility on flights.

"Mr. Masters, I am afraid the next flight we could accommodate will be Thursday morning, departing at 6:00 AM, connecting through Schiphol International Airport in Amsterdam, then connecting through Atlanta Hartsfield International, and arriving at St Louis Lambert International at 1:35 PM Friday. Your total will be 782 dollars US," the agent recited fully.

John just stared at her briefly, not believing he heard it all correctly. "I am sorry, Miss. Could you kindly repeat that?"

She repeated the flight information carefully, confirming that both John and Irina would be departing early the day after tomorrow, arriving early afternoon the following day, with a total additional cost of 782 dollars. Not wanting to ask many more questions, John gave her his credit card along with Irina's passport, thrilled with the price as he fully expected it to be four or five times as much.

Wrapping up the transaction and having received their printed tickets and boarding passes, the four began to exit the ticket line and head for the terminal parking lot, John still beside himself with joy. Just before the approach to the sliding doors at the exit, John turned around to catch a glance at the very accommodating and most familiar-looking ticket agent. Already busied with the next airline traveler, she paused and looked up toward John, smiling and giving him a most assuring nod.

Irina could see John's upbeat mood and asked, "My honey, are you okay?"

"Oh yes," he answered. *Never better!*

⇻⇻⇺ ⇺⇺⇺

Having picked up her visa early the following morning, the family planned yet another robust going-away dinner and John chose a place nearby called Beef, Meat, and Wine, which was highly recommended on the Trip Advisor website. He felt they needed an uplifting bonus after all the excitement over the past several days, not to mention his impression and appreciation of Irina's folks, who seemed to never complain and were outwardly helpful in the face of adversity and the anxiety of their oldest daughter leaving for a place halfway around the world.

As the succulent dishes were served, the four had much discussion about politics and world events. John soon learned that his future father-in-law, a man a mere five months older than himself, was quite concerned over the volatile political situation in the Ukraine, especially since his family resided right square in the middle of ground zero near the eastern border with Russia.

Irina made certain her dad did not see the final dinner tab as the tip alone was half as much as his monthly pension check, and her having little appetite for yet another dispute. Commenting in her limited English that her parents would not understand, Irina expressed that her folks, and her father in particular, had little appreciation for expensive meals in formal restaurants, seeing no value in ambiance and quality of food, only considering the quantity served for the number of hryvnias spent. John assured her that his own folks, and particularly his father, shared the same sentiments, while all the while still giddy about the perceived bargain he had received at the airport.

CHAPTER FOURTEEN

Heavenly Justice

K uznetsov arrived at SSU Headquarters mid-afternoon, made to wait impatiently for a meeting in the outer office of his superior, General Morozov, treatment toward subordinates he was more accustomed to imposing upon his own people, and not appreciative at being exposed to such treatment himself.

The colonel sat fidgety and struggled to engage in small talk with his superior's secretary, a woman he found to be extremely unattractive. *Quite obviously, General Morozov has never learned to take advantage of the virtues of power, as I have.*

"This place seems to be buzzing about something, Daryna. What is happening here?" Kuznetsov asked with a legitimate curiosity.

"There is a delegation of American legislators in town to visit; some congressmen and women, a couple US senators, and State Department officials," she replied with no additional comment and paying little effort to hide her contempt for Kuznetsov, well-known within the SSU ranks as a corrupt and arrogant opportunist.

Why bend over for those evil capitalists? That will change when I move up and take control here. "I noticed a few nameplates on some doors have changed,"

Kuznetsov stated, commenting on some movement within the headquarters building since he had last visited. "*Colonel* Grigoriy Cherko? What is his "function" here now?" The colonel was not aware the previous Kharkov Oblast officer, and one with whom he shared little comradeship, had been promoted.

"Colonel Cherko is an assistant to the Minister of Internal Affairs," the general's secretary replied. "He just took over his new assignment last week."

"Internal Affairs, yeah?" *A directorate that used to be solely involved in security and now relegated to policing the police. A perfect fit for such a weak coward. It is best that I stay in Kharkov. This building has too many politicians,* the colonel pondered.

Morozov's secretary phone buzzed and she picked up, subsequently informing Kuznetsov the general would see him now. He entered Morozov's office and then saluted the aged commandant, a man grossly overweight, appearing out of shape and unhealthy, and riding out his time for retirement to a dacha on the Black Sea. The old warrior appeared grouchy as having to work past the normal hours as part of an overall effort to ready the office for visitors; foreign political visitors.

"I would like to have waited for your visit next month, Colonel," General Morozov stated, in reference to the annual planned SSU conference and review, where all the Oblast officers, including Kuznetsov, would undergo an annual evaluation, present budgets for the following year, etc. "If you have not noticed, we are all busy here preparing for an American delegation to arrive."

"We kowtow too much to these Yankees, General. We cannot place everything on hold to accommodate their presence, can we?" Kuznetsov replied, his contempt for Americans, and Westerners in general, well known.

"What is your business here, Colonel?"

"I have been investigating a serious breach of security, General," he responded, "and possible case of espionage."

Kuznetsov slid a file across Morozov's desk, which the old general quickly reviewed. "The woman has not shown up at an airport, port, or border crossing with a visa and passport?"

"No, General. I will be notified as soon as that occurs."

"We need not spend much time on this, Colonel," his superior stated looking at his watch. "Just proceed and include it in your weekly report. You are dismissed."

Kuznetsov stood and saluted, exiting the general's office while believing in his mind he himself to be much more qualified to command overall operations. On the way out, he passed the newly promoted Colonel Cherko in the hallway, a man always required in the past to salute him and clearly savored in the fact they both were of equal rank now. The former Kharkov Oblast officer's contempt for his former superior was apparent as Cherko didn't even bother to look his way, much less speak.

⇒⇒⇒ ⇐⇐⇐

The four were all awakened well before dawn as they had to pack all their belongings, check out of the apartment, and drive back to the airport, again some forty kilometers east, and following the flight departure, Irina's parents would then have another six-hour trip back home.

Traffic was light at that early hour as they headed outbound from the center of the city and a relative few commuters had their own vehicles, anyway. They arrived at the airport at 4:45 AM and following a baggage check-in involving another one-hundred-dollar charge, the four proceeded to the security checkpoint, where Irina and her family held a very emotional and tearful goodbye. Transferring to the second level, the two waited in line where they had to pass through yet another checkpoint where their tickets and travel documents were inspected and had to pass muster before continuing to their assigned gate.

They worked their way forward in a seemingly slow pace and stood before an agent at a kiosk window who inspected their items and systematically scanned their passports into a computer check system. Everything appeared to be going to plan until Irina's passport was scanned, which predicated the agent to pause and pick up a phone. "I will need you to wait a moment," the stoic young man ordered and soon two uniformed police officers appeared.

"Irina Balabanova," one officer stated as he viewed her identification. "Come with me."

"Wait! I am her fiancé!" John exclaimed.

The two officers appeared not to comprehend John's English and Irina translated. The four stood idle for a brief few minutes while one of the officers made a phone call. Completing the call, he then relayed to Irina "permission" for her man to accompany her, at least temporarily, and then proceeded to escort the couple to a small downstairs office.

⇢⋙ ⋘⇠

The man was still sleeping soundly when his cell phone buzzed and he nearly knocked it to the floor before picking up. "Colonel Kuznetsov."

He listened intently as the call he'd anticipated for days had his attention. "Was she accompanied by anyone other than the American?... No, just hold them both there until I arrive."

He was now fully awake and excited. Irina Balabanova had been detained attempting to leave the country and he would take full pleasure in arresting her. As an added bonus, he would get to look her American lover in the eye while they took his woman away in handcuffs, and perhaps even arrest him for,...*something. No, that is probably a stretch... But I will make this Yankee's life miserable... miserable to the point he will wish he had never heard of Ukraine!*

The "holding room" had no windows, and the two sat nervously in two of the three chairs at a small conference table. Irina was consumed with fear and ashamed that she had somehow gotten both her and John into serious trouble.

"Trust me, you have not seen or heard the last of him." That is what Calina told me. I pray, dear God, forgive me of my sins... But what sin have I committed here?

"My honey, I am so sorry. You should have never come back here," Irina told John tearfully.

220

He embraced her as calmly as he could. "It was my choice, my lovely... And I would do it all over again. I need to contact our embassy somehow. I guess we are not allowed to make a phone call?"

"I do not know. I have never been arrested before."

Kuznetsov rode comfortably as the official car traveled eastward toward Boryspil, his having instructed the staff driver to be in no hurry getting there. Enjoying an hour-long breakfast before leaving his hotel, he reveled in the knowledge that his "suspects" sat waiting at the airport detainment section, their nerves becoming frayed with every ongoing minute.

As his driver exited off the expressway and headed toward the airport terminal, he noticed some commotion gathering outside the entrance and a special TV van and its crew assembling. *No doubt something to do with the Yankee delegation arriving. That will not deny my mission here. On the other hand, perhaps the cameras will catch my agents escorting the handcuffed woman through the terminal, and with her sulking American lover in tow. Perfect!*

The official car pulled up to the curb before Kuznetsov got out and was confronted by a female reporter, one that sounded American. "Excuse me, sir. We understand there is an American citizen and his Ukrainian fiancée being detained here for questioning. Your comments?"

Who called these paparazzi rats? Who is this woman? "This is part of an SSU investigation, and get that thing out of my face!" the colonel barked coldly and walked past the reporter and her cameraman. "Colonel Kuznetsov, has the detained American been allowed to contact the US Embassy?" She yelled out as he and his aid entered the terminal building.

An always suspecting Kuznetsov wondered, *How did she know my name?*

The two had waited stressfully for a lengthy period as John kept looking at his watch, when the locked door finally opened and in walked two men, one of whom Irina well recognized and despite her level of fear, forced an expression of disdain.

"Irina Balabanova, it is so good to see you again. We have some unfinished business, I believe," Kuznetsov stated devilishly.

John could not hold his anger. "Who are you?"

"I am Colonel Pavel Kuznetsov, and your woman here is an old acquaintance of mine. In fact, I am such a kind old friend that I could keep her out of prison for passing classified information to a foreign agent."

"I have no, as you say, classified information!" Irina yelled.

"My State Department officials have proven you have altered her documents. I demand to be allowed a call to my embassy," John added forcefully.

"You demand nothing! This is my country, *Amerikan*. We do not accommodate criminals here the way they do in the West."

"You have nothing on us!" John exclaimed loudly.

"Be careful, my honey. This is not America." Irina spoke as she clutched her man's arm.

"We will examine your luggage very carefully for illegal documents, narcotics, and other contraband items. There is no limit to what we may uncover," Kuznetsov stated, implying rather blatantly that planted evidence would come into play. "Of course, Irina knows I am a very compassionate man and there could be a solution most favorable to you."

Both John and Irina sat, neither offering a verbal reply. Irina was becoming all the more fearful with every minute and for his part, John fought the raw sour taste of what was coming.

"Should you willfully sign a prepared statement I have right here in my briefcase, you will then accompany me back to the Oblast and I will consider accepting you into a rehabilitation program, under my supervision, of course," the sinister colonel stated, enjoying the look of anger and contempt he could read on the American's face. "Again, since I am such a compassionate man, once she signs and her rehabilitation begins, then you, *Amerikan*, will be released to return to your native country."

John could see Irina now near emotional breakdown, her tears pouring down her cheeks as she sat shaking her head.

"Do not sign it, Irina. We will fight this," John said to her, all the while staring at Kuznetsov, who sat across from them in obvious amusement.

"My honey, you have no idea what trouble this could be for you," Irina replied, her nerves now on a ragged edge. *Pavel Kuznetsov is an evil man. Calina was right. Oh please, God, help us... Please.*

The SSU colonel started to extract some paperwork from his briefcase when he was interrupted by an incoming call, one he would not hesitate to answer.

"Colonel Kuznetsov, hold a moment for General Morozov," he was instructed by a headquarters staff officer.

"Colonel, are you at Boryspil?" Morozov asked sternly.

"Yes General. I am in the middle of—"

Cutting him off in mid-sentence, the SSU commander of operations sounded angry. "Do you have an American and his fiancée in detention there at the airport?"

"Yes, General. I am about to"...

"Release them immediately!"

Kuznetsov was stunned, not believing what he was hearing. "But General. There are"...

"Now, Colonel! Release them now! Do you see what is on the live television news coverage?"

"General, I cannot concern myself with media—"

"You are not listening! Release the American and the girl now, and I want to see you in my office within the hour!"

Kuznetsov was stunned, his face turning beet red as he heard a distinct and final click. Nearly unable to contain himself, he ushered his aid out the door before giving the order for release, unable to bring himself to look Irina and her American in the eye and admit defeat.

The two original airport police officers escorted both John and Irina back upstairs to the kiosk where they were placed in front of the line and quickly cleared for departure, both in a highly state of animated shock at this latest turn of events.

"There is no hurry, Irina. We have already missed our flight and I'll have to go through the whole process of rebooking our tickets again," John stated, now concerned yet again about the costs. *But in the big scheme of things, even a few thousand for a ticket change would matter little now, would it not?* John thought.

As the two approached their assigned gate, John looked up at the airport flight status monitor, witnessing yet another dramatic change of fortune.

UIA Flight number PS9382, departing 6:00 AM,
arriving Amsterdam 8:05 AM, DELAYED

"It has been delayed! Oh my god, Irina. How lucky can we be?" John exclaimed in earnest, although in afterthought just wanting to feel that plane take off. *Our prayers have been answered.*

⤜⟫⟩ ⟨⟨⟨⤛

Kuznetsov was angrily beside himself as he rushed down the hall toward Morozov's office. Barely acknowledging Daryna's presence, he stormed in where the very contentious general sat, pointing with his finger in a gesture for Kuznetsov to sit and adjusted a hand-held remote control device to increase the sound volume on his corner ceiling-mounted TV monitor, where news coverage of an incident at Boryspil International had aired, the general replaying the recorded telecast for the sixth time.

"This is Andrea Reynolds reporting live from Boryspil International Airport in Kiev, the Ukraine, where as I speak, an American citizen and his Ukrainian fiancée are being detained on unsubstantiated charges of spying. The American, whose name has not been released, has yet been

allowed to contact the US Embassy here in Kiev and this comes at a critical time when a US Congressional delegation has arrived for consultations involving a multi-billion dollar US aid package. This potential international incident could derail"...

The General then hit the pause button, not wanting to see or hear anymore. "You damned fool! Do you see what you have done? This is a total embarrassment to this ministry and could potentially cost us billions of US dollars! I have Minister Tkachuk himself heading over here to hear how I plan to deal with this!"

"General, this is a perfectly legitimate enforcement action on our part and—"

"Save it for the Court of Inquiry, Colonel."

A shaken Kuznetsov was quickly silenced as he struggled to regain an upper hand. "A Court of Inquiry?"

"Yes, Colonel," General Morozov replied and immediately hit the inter-office intercom button on his phone. "Daryna, send him in."

Kuznetsov gathered an unfamiliar feeling of disgust and fear as Colonel Grigoriy Cherko entered and sat down beside him, now both facing Morozov. Cherko held a large envelope full of documents, which he promptly handed across the desk to the general, who began to thoroughly re-examine.

"Please summarize what is in here for Pavel's curiosity, Colonel Cherko, while I read."

Kuznetsov felt like he needed a space to crawl under. For Morozov to refer to him in the presence of another officer as "Pavel" was a sure sign his station in the SSU had taken an unfortunate turn. The fact the other officer was none other than former subordinate and now *Colonel* Grigory Cherko made it all the more unnerving.

"I have reviewed the documents, Colonel, charging Irina Balabanova with suspicion of espionage and the related alleged violation of a security confidentiality agreement," Cherko began.

"It is not suspicion or alleged!" Kuznetsov yelled as he nearly came out of his chair.

"Colonel, you will restrain yourself and let Colonel Cherko continue!" Morozov ordered while giving a nod to the two armed security officers who had accompanied Cherko and stood sentry by the door.

"These documents appear to be indeed very damaging," Cherko continued as Kuznetsov now appeared confused, wondering to what purpose these theatrics served.

"But I also have four other documents here that you will see attached, General. This item, we will refer to as Exhibit One," which Cherko held up in his hand, "is a piece of yellow notebook paper with some handwritten notes."

Gusev: "She (Irina Balabanova) had possible access to the More Security Company codes for entry into the SSU security system, but she would not have reason to..."

"Then there are some notations of alteration. The word *possible* had a line crossed through it and the words *had frequently* written above. There is also a line drawn through the last phrase: but she would not have reason to"...

"Handwritten notes, penciled lines... Is this a joke?" Kuznetsov bellowed, not able to contain himself.

"Go on, Colonel," General Morozov ordered Cherko while giving Kuznetsov a degrading look.

"Exhibit Two is an affidavit signed by Dimitri Gusev several days ago, a former co-worker and roommate of Irina Balabanova, stating:

"She (Irina Balabanova) had frequently accessed the More Security Company codes for entry into the SSU security system."

"Exhibit Three is a signed affidavit signed by the same Dimitri Gusev just yesterday that states that you, Colonel Kuznetsov, pressured him into signing the previous sworn statement, and that under duress he had not read the entire printed document in detail."

"This is an outrage!" Kuznetsov yelled. "You would take the word of a lowly peasant like Gusev over that of a distinguished SSU officer! Gusev signed that document and I have witnesses!"

Cherko listened as he sat with a steady calm, a manner that confused and began to further unnerve Kuznetsov. "Shall I continue, General?"

"Yes, Colonel," Morozov ordered after having finished reviewing the file himself. "I want Pavel to hear this."

"Exhibit Four is yet another sworn affidavit dated yesterday. It states that quote:

"I was handed some handwritten notes from Colonel Pavel Kuznetsov and ordered to type up an affidavit for Dimitri Gusev to sign. I included the changes to the wording on the document as per the notations indicated. This was a common practice in my position at the SSU Oblast office and I have saved for review other similar handwritten notes given to me for the same purpose dating back two years. I also have an original copy of an employee security confidentiality agreement dated October 1st, 2000, signed by Irina Balabanova, a document replaced in her personnel file by an alternate document, her signature a forged copy fraudulently administered by Colonel Pavel Kuznetsov."

"It is signed by Calina Zhvikova, the staff secretary for Colonel Kuznetsov," Cherko concluded.

Kuznetsov was stricken with anger and mostly fear. The betrayal, his corruption, and his many transgressions were all coming back to haunt him.

"I am sure you will wish to dispute the sworn testimony of this Calina Zhvikova, a woman who has worked under you for what, three years now?" General Morozov asked cynically. "That will be for the court to decide. Based on the seriousness of this matter and the reckless behavior you have exhibited that has embarrassed this ministry, you will be arrested and placed into custody until a Court of Inquiry may be convened... Now, this matter is concluded as I have other pressing matters."

>>>> <<<<

Now past 9:30, the emotionally drained but upbeat couple made their way to the gate where they were greeted by an airline boarding agent, standing alone anxiously as if waiting for John and Irina exclusively. After scanning their perspective boarding passes, the young bilingual woman nodded and thanked the two of them.

Just prior to entering the gangway and conscious there were no other passengers waiting behind them, John paused and asked, "Excuse me, Miss. What is the reason for this flight delay?"

"Some sort of security issue. But I can assure you it has been resolved now. Have a nice flight," she replied assuredly.

>>>> <<<<

John and Irina sat and enjoyed the complimentary late-night dinner served on the KLM flight, due to arrive in Atlanta at an hour past sunrise. With all the excitement up and down over the past few days, the normal discomfort of the coach section seats near the back of the Boeing 757 seemed of little consequence.

John was anxious to see the family again and couldn't wait for them to meet his future bride. For her part, Irina could hardly believe the fable of her life in America was finally coming true as she couldn't wait to marry the wonderful man next to her who had endured so much just to bring her to this place. *Someone up above had to be looking down on us,* she thought as she fell off to sleep.

Up ahead in the first class section sat another couple, who often worked together for the same "company" and were returning to "base" after a several-month assignment.

"I almost wish we were going to this place, Cape Girardeau, Missouri, to see them marry," the woman said as she finished her dinner.

"I suppose the boss doesn't deem it necessary," her partner, the short man stated, unshaven as he was starting to regrow something.

"This upcoming training meeting, I wonder what kind of session this is?" She asked.

"I don't know. Probably want you to work on your data entry skills," he replied grinning. "As for me, I'll probably work on something else other than troubleshooting gas leaks, giving me some more flexibility in a world moving away from fossil fuels."

"When we arrive in Atlanta, they'll ask at Immigration and Customs whether our visit pertains to business or pleasure. You've been in and out of these countries untold number of times. What should I tell them?" She asked, not as tenured as him in traveling internationally.

"Don't worry about it. You're probably the most recognizable face on earth right now, a big-time live TV news journalist. Pretty good stunt, by the way, getting all those terminal bystanders to gather around in front of the camera that early in the morning."

"That's very kind of you, but come on. What answer should I give, business or pleasure?"

He paused as he took the last gulp of tea before handing his dinner tray over to the stewardess. "Tell them business and if they ask what business you're in, just claim the same thing I always do— Divine Intervention."

Epilogue

E arly the morning of May 7th, 2006, Irina Balabanova met her new in-laws
for the first time. Upon entering their residence, she reached out and
spoke to John's father; her first words, "Can I call you Dad?"

From that moment, she had melted him down and John's two elderly parents
knew they had a new "daughter" in the family.

Irina struggled the first couple days adjusting to the culture, being in a mild
state of panic with no one around speaking her native language. With John
working all day, her new mother-in-law was ever so helpful in spending time
with her and helping Irina get to know the other local family members and
friends.

The few that knew nothing about Irina got a big awakening just two weeks
later when the two were married in a hastily arranged ceremony at the local
church the family attended, and the following day a reception party was held
at the elderly Masters' home. The highlight of the event was John explaining
to his family and friends the whole saga of how the two met, believing "divine intervention" had to have had a hand in it all. Irina looked on grinning,
knowing her new husband delighted in telling the part about his proposing
using translation software on a laptop and her accepting in kind. They were
somewhat certain their engagement could be the only one on record anywhere

on the planet consummated in such a way, especially after their meeting just a few days prior. John even commented on and off through the years that he may even write a book about it someday.

Irina's first summer spent in America was quite adventurous and included a few shocking cultural "adjustments". While the weather in the Ukraine had its four seasons and was bitterly cold in winter, the citizenry there had never experienced a tornado. Irina nearly came apart when she caught her first tornado warning on TV and became totally convinced her last days were upon her, as this terrible phenomenon of nature would surely sweep down and blow her away, She called John, who was working in St. Louis that particular day. John's one-story ranch-style home had no basement, and he thus called his mother, who proceeded to drive across town and promptly put her new immigrant daughter-in-law's mind at ease.

An amusing moment came the first time she and John went shopping at a supermarket. As the two exited the store and John pushed their cart full of grocery items out through the parking lot, a confused Irina exclaimed, "What is the matter with that girl? She doesn't even know me. How does she know I'm going to have a nice day? And why does every stranger whom I've never met ask me how I'm doing?"

The following couple of years were fruitful for the "international couple", with John's business flourishing as a result of a transfer to the Kansas City market. The Masters joined a local suburban church that had many ethnic Russian and Ukrainian members which soon became the basis for Irina's busy social engagement. Her new life in America had become truly fulfilling, a culmination coming a year later with Irina's firstborn son, Michael.

⇝⇝ ⇜⇜

Halfway around the world, the tension between Russia and the Ukraine came to a head with the Russian annexation of the Crimea in 2014. The Balabanove family cottage on the river, a property very near a budding civil war outbreak, was left for Alika and her son, as the Masters managed to help Mikhail and

Nadine emigrate to the United States, where they continued with an effort to have Alika and her son follow suit.

Pavel Kuznetsov was released from the SSU following a Court of Inquiry and relocated south to Donetsk where he found welcome employment with the mafia in the black market there. Long estranged with his wife and children, the former colonel became bitter beyond his years while serving time in prison, and upon release became involved with some violent Russian separatist groups.

Dimitri Gusev had seen his pending investigation dismissed following his offering testimony in the Kuznetsov hearing, but was never allowed employment again at More Security Supply Company. Eventually moving back to Gori, Georgia, he married a young widow and worked as a technician for an upcoming cable TV company.

Calina Zhvikova was suspended from her position at the Oblast SSU office without pay during the Court of Inquiry hearing, where she provided key testimony against Colonel Pavel Kuznetsov. Having been found culpable herself, she was released from the SSU and moved in temporarily with her parents, coming clean about her past experience with the evil colonel, including the abortion and her disposition of having no chance to have children. Her folks took the news very hard but reconciled in time and lived in relative tranquility with their daughter, although Calina subsisted in constant fear of retribution some day from her former superior officer and ill-fated lover, Kuznetsov.

Fate has a way of changing lives and a year later, Calina received a letter in the mail, a notice from the US State Department to contact the embassy in Kiev regarding her K-1 visa interview and to schedule a related medical certification exam. She was moving to Florida and planning to marry an American, a fine faith-based gentleman in the tourism industry, one she had met as result of an ad she had placed at a local company in Kharkov, the Belanov Agency.

><

John and Irina would often reflect on all the unlikely near misses and chance occurrences that led the family to its eventual destiny—the absent email server, the sudden gas and chemical leaks, the "kilogram" typo error, Irina's delayed emails, and the seeming multi-character personalities who always appeared at just the right time with all the blessed effects, all reasons among others to give thanks to heaven every day.

Hope is still alive and well in the hearts of all of us, especially with a little faith and divine intervention. During the period of this composition, Russian forces have attacked and invaded Ukraine; a war that still rages on. Many family members of the characters represented in Miracle From Ukraine have had their homes and businesses destroyed and remain in great peril. Some have fled to countries like Poland and Romania and many have found refuge in the United States. As in all wars, the very best and worst of the human condition is on display. Look for the story of their saga in *Escape From Ukraine*, a sequel to be released by Spring, 2024. Our thoughts and prayers are with all the Ukrainians as they fight on for their freedom and mere survival in the face of untold terror and adversity.

⋙ ⋘

Thank you for reading Miracle From Ukraine. If you acquired the book through Amazon or one of the other worldwide vendors, your feedback is important to me and kindly leave a review and/or visit my website at www.jamesherbertharrison.com.

About the Author

James Herbert Harrison, a native of Cape Girardeau, Missouri, has lived and worked throughout the continental United States as a businessman and industrial equipment and software sales representative. He currently resides in Olathe, Kansas with his wife Maryna and their thirteen-year-old son. James has an older son who remains in Cape Girardeau as well as two older step kids. The family are active and proud members of Lenexa Baptist Church in Lenexa, Kansas.

James' pedigree as a writer began ten years earlier with the publishing of his first novel. *Quest For Power*, a political thriller soon to be re-released as *The Programmer*. *Miracle From Ukraine*, a totally different departure in genre, was inspired by the real-life saga of James and Maryna having experienced many of the actual events in the story. James is currently working on *Escape From Ukraine*, a dramatic and contemporary sequel. For more information, visit www.jamesherbertharrison.com.